THE
THIRD MIRACLE

a novel by
Richard Vetere

SCRIBNER PAPERBACK FICTION
PUBLISHED BY SIMON & SCHUSTER
NEW YORK LONDON SYDNEY SINGAPORE

SCRIBNER PAPERBACK FICTION
Simon & Schuster, Inc.
Rockefeller Center
1230 Avenue of the Americas
New York, NY 10020

First Scribner Paperback Fiction edition 1998
Published by arrangement with Carroll & Graf Publishers, Inc.

Manufactured in the United States of America

1 3 5 7 9 10 8 6 4 2

The Library of Congress has cataloged the Scribner Paperback
Fiction edition as follows:
Vetere, Richard.
The third miracle / Richard Vetere.
p.   cm.
1. Miracles—Fiction. I. Title.
[PS3572.E85T48   1998]
813.54—dc21   98-4880
CIP

ISBN 0-743-20034-9

SIC DEUS DILEXIT MUNDUM
(FOR THOSE WHO LOVE THE WORLD)

Dedicated to the memory of
Dr. Remo Iannucci,
and to Kathryn Taylor and her precious
two and a half months

THE
THIRD MIRACLE

Prologue

"How can one pray to you unless one knows you? If one does not know you, one may pray not to you, but to something else."

—*The Confessions of Saint Augustine*

October 1985

A warm October rain fell for two weeks. Gutters overflowed with rain backed up from the corner sewers. Nearly every community in Queens had a problem with flooding. Cars parked too near a sewer had to be towed the next morning because of wet wires. Even streetlights were affected, blowing out in storms sweeping up from the south. It was hurricane season, but no hurricane appeared, each weakening as it hit New York City. Though it was autumn, the wet trees stayed green, without hint of yellow or gold. In the unusually warm evenings, a heavy mist covered the residential streets of the boroughs, softening the light from the few lampposts that did work.

Saint Stanislaus was an old brick and gray-stone three-story church in the clean, European-style neighborhood of Maspeth, Queens. The church stood in the center of the community, on the top of a hill that leveled off to the southwest, toward Brooklyn. Surrounding the church were rows of modest two-family homes with steel or wooden fences enclosing their front yards. Behind each home was a backyard where, before the rains came, clothes-lines spanned kitchen windowsills. The streets were tiny and narrow, paved nearly a century before, when Polish immigrants came to Maspeth to work in the textile factory on Cooper Avenue.

Only fifteen minutes from the enormity of Manhattan, the small community was as isolated from the cosmopolitan world of Manhattan as if it were located in Iowa. There were no subway lines running through it and the only public transportation was a private bus line that ran infrequently, and never after eleven o'clock at night. Though its residents could see Manhattan's massive skyline right across the sky from Maurice Park, which had been cut in half twenty years earlier by the newly constructed expansion of the Long Island Expressway, most of them had not been to "The City," as the locals called it, more than a dozen times in their lives.

Maria Katowski was in the fourth grade and was late for school this particular morning because her mother had forgotten that it was a special day in the parish. Helen Stephenson, who had lived and worked in the convent for the previous twelve years, was being given the tribute of a Mass in her memory. Every class from first grade to eighth was to attend. The presiding parish pastor, Father Kinnely, was saying the Mass.

Maria was late because her mother, also named Maria, didn't wake her up on time. Mrs. Katowski was an alcoholic, and many were the mornings when she couldn't get herself out of bed. Her alcoholism was something little Maria was managing to live with. Little Maria could feed herself and iron her own clothes, but she did need her mother's help with one thing: she was a sickly young girl and had the hardest time rising in the morning. Her weakness was something she tried her best to keep from her mother.

The two Marias lived alone in a small but comfortable rail-road apartment off the Long Island Expressway. The apartment was on the ground floor of a wooden two-story house which shared the block with a truck factory and a junkyard. Little

Maria slept on the couch, on which she still fit comfortably. She lay still listening to the next-door neighbor's dog bark, as it did every morning, and listened to the rain as it fell loudly outside on the metal window frame.

Maria glanced at the clock again, then managed to pull herself up to the closet where her blue and white uniform hung. She could see her mother lying fully dressed across her own bed in the next room with a half-empty bottle of vodka standing on the night table. Maria was used to seeing her mother like that ever since the morning her father walked out on them both.

Maria prayed all the time that her father would come home. Even though her parents fought and hurt each other, she wanted them together. Also, her mother didn't drink when he was around, the vodka appearing only when he was gone. She drank when she missed him. Maria understood that much. So she prayed to the Blessed Virgin, and she prayed to baby Jesus, that her father would come home. But in two years he hadn't even called. "He's gone," Maria's mother said over and over, over the drone of the television, louder with each drink until she fell asleep.

That's when Maria began to pray to Helen Stephenson. She had felt the woman's kindness when she was alive, and when she died, Maria imagined her to be up in heaven. If Helen Stephenson was up in heaven, then she could plead Maria's case to the Virgin and to baby Jesus.

Maria knew little about Helen Stephenson other than that she lived in the convent and worked for the church. She was always around the church bazaars, charities, and the small day care center.

The only other thing that Maria knew about the woman was that her mother didn't like her. Mrs. Katowski distrusted Helen Stephenson, mainly because she distrusted anyone who managed to get through life without complaining about their obvious pains.

"They call her a saint!" Mrs. Katowski would shout when talking about her. "A damn saint in this world? Yeah, right!" she shouted at her daughter. "Sure, she took the easy way after her husband died. She moved into the convent! But her daughter is old enough to go out on her own! What about me? I'm stuck with you!" She would talk about Helen Stephenson some nights until she found her way to the bed. Then she would close her eyes and fall asleep in her clothes, not remembering a thing about what she had said when she woke dry-mouthed and cranky the next morning. But whatever Maria's mother did think about her, Father Kinnely calendared a special Mass for Helen Stephenson, and Maria was late for it. So she took one last look at her mother and quietly left the house.

Maria's house was five blocks down the hill from the church. She held her books and her big black umbrella close to herself. She kept her feet together as she walked, trying to hold onto the umbrella and walk up the hill as the strong wind pushed against her. Maria's route took her to the gate of the convent. The church was at the other end of the schoolyard, so Maria walked briskly across the gray concrete.

The convent was a place of mystery for all the young schoolgirls, more so than the rectory, or the church. The convent was where the nuns lived, nuns who lived perfect lives, nuns who obeyed Christ and His Church. In fact, Christ was their groom and they all wore wedding rings as proof of their being His brides.

Wet, hungry, and anxious, Maria still could not stop herself from enjoying her shortcut past the convent. She huddled as close to the three-story red brick building as she could, hoping to dodge the rain.

She passed the room where Helen Stephenson had lived. Every kid in the school knew that room. Its window faced the school. They all knew the window because Helen Stephenson used to lean out of it during lunch recess, handing out cookies and cakes that she had baked. She had always made sure that the smallest boy or girl got the first cookie. Maria had often received a cookie from Helen Stephenson and always remembered the kind smile on the woman's face. There was nothing patronizing about the way she handed out the little desserts. There was nothing motherly, either. Maria remembered that it wasn't the woman's warmth that struck her as much as her determination that each child with a hand out received one. She also remembered how little the woman spoke and how wide a smile she had and how, at lunchtime, she'd watch the schoolyard fill with boys and girls from the first grade to the eighth, all dressed in blue and white Saint Stanislaus uniforms. She remembered the woman's eyes, how blue and deep they were. Eyes that seemed to see something else other than the blue sky overhead, the noisy schoolyard, each child with outstretched hands.

Maria stood at the window remembering, then looked up at the statue above the window. It was the statue of the Blessed Virgin. Like most of the church statues in New York City, it was made of limestone. Nearly five feet high, it stood on a small ledge, making it look even larger than it was. The white limestone had aged, fading to a dull gray. The Virgin looked down upon a small globe beneath her bare feet. Her long slender arms and tender hands pointed to the globe. Under the Virgin's feet was a snake, symbolizing Satan. The snake's head was upraised, not in defiance, but in surrender. Maria saw how the Virgin was blessing the tiny globe of humanity at her feet. A humanity drenched in rain. Maria peeked into Helen Stephenson's window again but the blinds were half drawn and the room was dark.

She then turned to the statue and prayed. But she didn't pray to the Blessed Virgin; she prayed to Helen Stephenson. And her prayer was not the usual prayer. It was a prayer for death, her own death. She prayed that she might die so that her father would hear of her death and come home to her mother again. She felt responsible for her father's leaving. And in the truest sense, she was right. Her father had married her mother only because she was pregnant, and she told him from the beginning that she would never consider an abortion.

Though Maria didn't actually know that she was an unwanted child, she sensed it. And though she knew that her parents had problems, she was too young to realize that they had nothing at all in common but a few months' lust and passion. Unfortunately, these went out of their marriage as soon as Maria was born and the same loneliness that drove her father to her mother's arms drove him to those of another woman. Her mother, stuck in a life that offered no hope, died each day as she watched her youth fade away. So her prayers for her own death made perfect sense to Maria.

Suddenly, the sky overhead exploded with a flash of lightning. Right behind, thunder roared, blasting the silent world of schoolyard and church. As Maria looked up at the torrent of rain falling from the sky, she felt a hand on her shoulder. She spun around to find only the statue, with its hands outstretched to her.

She looked into the face of the Virgin, at the two simple eyes. She could see the thin lips and the soft cheekbones with rain running down them. And that's when she saw the blood, blood that came like tears from the eyes, then out of the mouth behind the lips, then down over the chin. Blood that ran with the rainwater down the long, slender arms, onto the outstretched hands and face and raincoat of Maria Katowski.

Mesmerized, she could see how the streams of blood ran out of the sockets of the eyes and she could feel it as it fell down her own face: it was warm and sweet on her lips.

Lightning flashed across the sky again, followed by another blast of thunder. Maria stepped back from the window, dropped her books on the pavement, and put her hands to her face. Weak in her knees, she fell, for a second, against the convent, then got up, turned and ran to the church. She struggled to open the doors until a nun on the other side opened it for her.

Sister Alice paid very little attention to the young girl who came late to Mass. She was new to the parish and did not know many of the students. She taught eighth-grade math and had never seen Maria before. Yet when Maria walked past her, Sister Alice noticed something odd about the girl.

Sister Alice called quietly to one of the other nuns who stood at the last pew, trying to get her attention so they would stop the little girl who was walking down the center aisle in a daze. Sister

Alice was afraid that Maria might disturb the Mass.

But it was too late for that. Maria began to cry gutturally. The cry of terrible loss. Rows of schoolchildren, damp from their walk in the rain, turned to see the fourth grader cry in the middle of the church.

Father Kinnely, serving the Mass, also heard Maria. Though his thoughts were centered on the Mass, the agony in the girl's cry shot through him. As he turned to the pews, he could see Maria walking toward him. He looked to the nuns and stepped away from the altar.

"Child?" he said softly, as he stepped past the altar boys and into the aisle. "Child?" he said again. The nuns whispered nervously, too timid to break the silent ritual of the Mass. The boldest of them stood and walked toward Maria, but not before genuflecting as they crossed the path of the tabernacle. It was then that Maria's face and hands took on the strangest appearance. They glowed like a pumpkin with a candle inside it.

The children in the pews were stunned. Some moaned, others looked to their friends and to the nuns with confusion, searching for a sign from an adult that the chaos in the church was not out of the ordinary.

Suddenly Maria screamed. The scream sent a chill through Father Kinnely and the nuns, compelling them to step back just as Maria fell to the cold marble floor. She fell, crumpled up like a little doll in a raincoat. The glow stopped and the screaming ended and just as Father Kinnely reached for her, a shaft of light shot through the stained glass above him. He fell to his knees, hugging the tiny girl. He felt her pulse, then lifted her up and carried her to the rectory.

The news of the miracle of the tears of blood crying from the statue of the Virgin grew through the community with the same power as little Maria's scream. Every child in the church that morning went home with the story of her glowing hands. At home around the dinner table, down the park that night, in the schoolyard the next day, the talk went on. Everyone, whether they were there or not, talked about Maria.

Gino Rosa, who owned Rosa's Bakery, right across the street from the church, told everybody who came into the bakery what had happened.

"My nephew, my brother's little one, Louie, he told me that he saw the little girl fall down and cry right in the middle of church!" Gino Rosa was a big man with white hair and a large face. He leaned over the white counter as he spoke, gesturing as he did. "They say that she got cured of this lupus disease!"

Mrs. Savage, a woman in her sixties, with white hair tied back, who always seemed to be wearing a sweater no matter how cold or hot it was, listened closely. "I heard from Margaret up on the plateau that Father Kinnely got so many calls that he hung up on Mr. Peprocki last night!"

"No!" Mr. Rosa replied.

"Oh, yes, Margaret doesn't lie! She heard it from that man Jimmy at the gas station over on Eliot Avenue."

The whole neighborhood was talking about the event, wondering what it all meant when, a few mornings later, it began to rain again. That particular morning Father Kinnely was alone in the rectory, having breakfast after serving his six-thirty Mass, when it began to drizzle. It was more than just curiosity that took him out into the schoolyard, where he stood looking up expectantly at the statue of the Virgin.

He watched the rain fall against the Virgin's face. Nothing happened. Kinnely sagged with disappointment. He was a heavy-set man with the tinge of desperation drawn on his face, the product of years as a small-time pastor with no ambitions other than getting the annual bazaar to show a profit, or making sure that payments for weddings, baptisms and funerals met an unspoken yearly quota.

Standing at the edge of the school, staring up at a motionless piece of stone sticking out the building, made him feel more lost and alone than he had thought possible.

"Helen," he said, almost like a prayer. He had known Helen

Stephenson better than anyone in the parish and he didn't feel uncomfortable looking to her spirit for guidance or hope.

"Helen, my Helen," he said again in a sorrowful voice, the cry of a man who has lost his only love. And that's when it happened: a tear emerged from the Virgin's face, a tear which was distinct from the raindrops falling around it. Kinnely looked again. He inched up to the statue, tilting his head up.

Another tear emerged from the sculptured eye, and then another. Kinnely lost his breath. He leaned against the white stone wall that separated the small walkway where little Maria had hidden from the thunderstorm. The tear fell into his outstretched palm. He looked at it: red, the color of blood, warm. He raised the red tear to his mouth and tasted it. It was sweet on his tongue.

Kinnely fell to his knees. He looked up at the statue, his aging body racked with the many sleepless nights and glasses of the ritual wine he drank to forget Helen and saw a flood of red fall from the Virgin's face. Blood flowed as if a dam had opened, the floodgates filling the valley of his melancholy with the fruitful blood of redemption.

"My God, it's a miracle!" Kinnely shouted. He threw his head down and prayed—"Hail Mary full of grace blessed art thou— it's a miracle!"

Sister Alice's eighth-grade class on the second floor was busy working on a math problem when she noticed Father Kinnely on his knees in front of the statue. A woman proud of her self-control, she was excited when she heard the muffled shouts coming from Father Kinnely.

Despite the rain, Sister Alice opened her window wide, straining to see the running blood. Though she was too far away to see, she heard Father Kinnely shout:

"Come down and pray with me, Sisters! It's a miracle! Helen has granted us a miracle from God!"

On Sister Alice's side of the school building, every window opened and every nun in every classroom stood, in the rain, their faces filled with passion. One by one they rushed into the schoolyard to Father Kinnely; each looked up at the statue and saw the tears of blood flow down the Virgin's face.

Petrified, the children watched from the window. A few braver ones followed the nuns down the stairs and knelt as they did. Some prayed while others glanced around wetly, wondering if this was the second coming.

And there they were in the schoolyard, Father Kinnely, the nuns, and the children praying with love as the blood flowed freely from the silent statue. The next morning the crying Virgin was front-page news.

Local businessmen, most of them sending their children to the school, donated flowers to the statue. Soon there was a growing garden of bright red and yellow tulips and red roses. Nino Vendome, the local florist, had moved from Italy to Maspeth when he was five years old and had prayed continuously to the Virgin Mary for his safe passage. Now, he felt he had the opportunity to repay the Virgin for his safety and good fortune in America.

Nino's next-door neighbors, the Czaks, owned the local dry cleaners. Mr. Czak, a Polish American with a hooked nose, hazel eyes, and dense salt-and-pepper hair, wondered aloud about all the publicity the crying statue might bring their small community.

"In a way, all this might not be good for our neighborhood," he said to Nino Vendome.

"How can you say that?" Vendome said indignantly.

"I don't know. But something about it doesn't feel right."

"It's God talking to us! You're crazy!" Vendome said.

Czak quickly quieted down, but the thought had been spoken.

That week it rained for three days and nights, steadily enough to keep the blood flowing and the crowds gathering. When the rain stopped, despite the prayers and vigils, the tears ended as mysteriously as they had began. Father Kinnely was concerned, but wouldn't permit himself to despair. He was the first to notice that October had ended.

"The Virgin will only cry during October! That's when Helen died," he pronounced. "Let's see what happens next year!"

Father Kinnely faced the congregation from the pulpit at Mass that Sunday and told them that they should spend the year praying because, if they did, then Helen would send the Virgin back to them and the tears of blood would return.

Though Father Kinnely knew they were disappointed, he attempted to distract the collective feelings of loss. All year, whenever he was in public, he held his head high and showed confidence that the miracle would occur again.

And he was right.

The following year, a special Mass was held in front of the statue and, as Father Kinnely had promised, the Virgin's tears flowed again, inviting all to trust and hope and love despite fears and doubts.

Soon, the entire schoolyard was overwhelmed with onlookers. Tourists came from all over the city. Unfortunately, it hardly rained that month, so the Virgin had little opportunity to cry for her believers. This did not deter Kinnely at all. Instead, he called the archdiocese and asked for someone to come and investigate the miracle.

"You have to wait ten years," Cardinal Cahill said from inside his limo parked outside the schoolyard. It was the third year in a row that the Virgin had cried and the event was plastered again all over the newspapers, announced on the radio, and it even made the local TV news stations. An enormous crowd filled the schoolyard, and after Kinnely called, the cardinal decided that he would look the situation over himself. Now, he was sorry he'd come. His limo was instantly surrounded by well-wishers and every sort of fanatic who begged him to bless them and pray for their souls.

"It's a miracle from heaven!" voices shouted at the cardinal.

"God bless you!" the cardinal shouted back, straining to pull Kinnely into the limo so he could close the door on the needy crowd.

"Ten years?" Father Kinnely asked.

Cahill was wearing a maroon cap over his thick mass of black hair. He was a large man in his early forties who looked as though he would be more at home in a grand palace than the Maspeth schoolyard. "It's Church policy. If you believe this stuff here has anything to do with Helen Stephenson, and you think she should be a saint, you have to wait ten years until you can petition me."

"Then what?"

"I will read the petition and, if necessary, I will assign a postulator to investigate the alleged miracle," the cardinal told him, short of breath and patience.

With that, he motioned for his driver, a tall thin priest, to drive on.

Kinnely stepped out of the car, coming face to face with Father Paulino. "I don't understand cardinals," he said.

Though the tears stopped as Father Kinnely predicted, they started up again the following year and, once again, Cahill appeared in his limo parked outside the schoolyard, seeming more annoyed than moved.

This time he lowered his window and looked for Kinnely in the crowd. The rain was falling heavily but the masses of people in the small schoolyard were enraptured. This year, camera crews showed up from the major networks and that brought the curious from as far as New Jersey, Pennsylvania, and even Canada.

Kinnely was standing under an umbrella giving an interview to a local newscaster when he noticed Cahill's limo. He smiled widely and waved to the cardinal. Cahill saw him and his refined features glared back at Kinnely. He then raised his window and the limo slid away.

"The cardinal seems pleased with the turnout," Kinnely told the newscasters.

By the fifth consecutive year of the miracle Kinnely had learned how to promote the event. He was becoming a skilled leader in his parish and made the miracle an accepted fact. "The Virgin will cry when it rains in October," is what he would tell anyone who would listen. Kinnely was positive of this because according to the laws of the Church, Helen Stephenson had to be dead ten years before a petition could be on. Kinnely truly believed that it was the Blessed Virgin Mary who was behind the miracle of blood. He believed that the Virgin was keeping Helen alive in everyone's memory.

The next time Cahill showed up at the schoolyard, he wasn't alone. He lowered his window and waved to Kinnely to join him in the limo. Kinnely, wearing a big smile and his ceremonial vestments, jumped into the backseat. There he met another, younger priest.

"Kinnely, this is my assistant, John Beliar. He's been assigned to investigate—this," Cahill said, nodding to the statue which was way off at the other end of the schoolyard.

"Investigate?" Kinnely asked.

"Yes. He's here to look over the situation," Cahill answered.

"So soon?" Kinnely asked.

"He's just here to do a preliminary fact-finding thing. Nothing official."

"My job will be to look over events like this and see if we can't explain them in logical terms," Beliar said with a steady, soothing voice.

"Logical terms?" Kinnely asked.

"We'd like to take the mystery out of this event."

"But you won't be able to," Kinnely told him.

"And why not?" Beliar asked.

"Because it's a miracle," Father Kinnely answered.

Beliar was an odd-looking man. Soft-spoken, he had sharp blue eyes, Middle Eastern features, and a dark complexion. His father was from Baghdad and his mother was from London. He was slender, with athletic and controlled movements. There was an intelligence in his eyes that worried Kinnely. With his prepossessing confidence and his evident educational background, he looked like trouble.

"Miracles are what I investigate," Beliar said with a warm, reassuring smile. "I was wondering if you could put me up for a few days?" he asked.

Taken aback by the intrusion of a stranger who seemed to be out to ruin his five years of hard work, Kinnely reluctantly agreed to put Beliar up in a spare room in the rectory.

Kinnely then left the limo, and Cahill and Beliar drove off with the promise that Beliar would return the next day. Kinnely could see a small smile on Cahill's face as he drove off.

Beliar did show up the next day and stayed for one short week; the fifth day he was gone. He talked to a few people who knew Helen Stephenson, watched the Virgin cry in the rain, and then he left. He left without a word of good-bye to Kinnely or any of the other priests in the rectory.

By the sixth year of the miracle, unpleasant things began to occur. The water in the rectory grew foul during the month of October. Arguments and accusations broke out between local parishioners and businessmen over the exploitation of the crying Virgin. The unpleasantries turned ugly when statues in the cemetery were desecrated and several rapes were reported to the police by women who had been to the statue at one time or another to pray. Into the world of the spiritual and holy had come a presence from the other side, a shadowy one, infested with wanton acts of destruction. No culprits were caught, but everyone knew dark intentions had visited their tiny parish. One of the ugliest incidents occurred when a large penis was spray-painted on the white wall that separated the schoolyard and the rectory. No one saw who did it, it just seemed to appear there one morning. Father Kinnely noticed it first and had the walls painted over immediately.

He also kept up his hard work and, just as he expected, the statue cried tears of blood the following October and the crowd swelled. New immigrants from Russia and Poland rushed to the statue, bringing with them a mystical, foreign passion for God and religion. Those with names like Boris and Sergei, Risa and Radinka, planted themselves in the schoolyard at the first sign of rain and lived in makeshift tents. At first, Kinnely did not know what to do. So, he did nothing and the tents multiplied. For a long time the Hispanic community was showing up in droves from neighboring Ridgewood, claiming that the Virgin was there for them. Living only a few miles away, they set up tents right next to the Slavs. Puerto Ricans from the Island brought their families to pray at the statue and would drown out the others as they prayed loudly in Spanish.

Shouting matches broke out among the different ethnic groups in the schoolyard with each claiming that the Virgin was there for them *only*! Italians from Middle Village and Irish from Flushing and Germans from Maspeth all joined in to profess that God was theirs and nobody else had a right to Him.

"I have to stop this," Kinnely told the nuns and priests as he looked at the schoolyard, which was beginning to resemble a bazaar in Istanbul.

That same afternoon the arguing reached its climax during a driving rainstorm. Kinnely waved all the believers to the refuge of the church. He looked at Sister Alice and said, "God help me, but I have no idea what to say to them."

"Pray for inspiration," Sister Alice offered.

"I'll pray to Helen," Kinnely agreed.

Inside the church, he got up on the pulpit and stood under the glowing lights and faced the wet, angry, needy faces of believers. He looked up at the church's ceiling and said a quick prayer to Helen Stephenson and then he looked around the packed church, listening to the bickering as it continued in a dozen tongues. Father Paulino and Father Stacey watched Kinnely unknowingly. The nuns bowed their heads and prayed as the rain drummed on outside, on stained glass windows high above, on the ceiling.

"I thought it was the meek who would inherit the earth!" Kinnely shouted at the congregation. "Well, I don't think you people have to worry about inheriting anything because I don't see the meek anywhere in this church!"

The voices lowered.

"God gives you a miracle and what do you do? You denigrate his gift! That's what you do! You fight over whom the Virgin weeps for and you have the audacity to believe that she cries for you and you alone!" Kinnely thundered. "You set up tents and mark your own territory and bully others who have come to this parish from miles away and you think that pleases God? God is *not* pleased! God is not thrilled with this gluttony of false faith! If you genuinely believed, you would share God's grace with your brothers and sisters. *Share* it! It is no coincidence that this miracle is happening in a small schoolyard. Lourdes is a small waterfall! Why? Because God wants to see how the faithful share the good fortune of having His presence so close to them. He wants to see if we are worthy of His love. Do you understand?" Kinnely said.

The church was silent, but each face portrayed remorse. The flock had listened to Kinnely for guidance and truth. Now it would be punished for its petty actions.

"Satan is close. I hope you all know that. Satan is close because God is here. God has chosen us to witness His love and this angers the devil. He has decided to do battle at this parish and I hate to say this," Kinnely said disgustedly, "but he has gained a foothold. He is among us! We all know he is! And those tents outside this church are evidence!"

There was shocked mumbling and even moans coming from the pews. With a sudden stroke of theatrical genius, Kinnely walked off the pulpit, leaving the crowd stunned. He himself was startled by his ability to rise to the occasion.

The next morning the tents were gone, never to reappear. Kinnely saved the situation, and in the tenth consecutive year of the miracle, organized a petition for the pursuit of the Ordinary Process of Canonization for Helen Stephenson. He gathered over ten thousand signatures and sent the petition to Cahill, who was still at his post at the archdiocese. Knowing that the petition was being sent and being quite aware of the momentum behind it, Cahill knew he had to act. He read the document.

"We patiently wait for a postulator. And we know that whomever you send will be God's choice," Kinnely told Cahill over the phone. As he spoke, he looked down from his window, watching the faithful pray to the Virgin who had come to save them.

Part One

Chapter 1

October 1995

A dark-haired man in jeans, black sweatshirt and dark blue windbreaker emerged from the crowd at the pulsating corner of Union Street and Northern Boulevard. Making his way past the mixture of Korean, Chinese, and English neon signs which lit that dense corner of the world at Main Street, Flushing, in the Borough of Queens, he seemed oblivious to everything around him.

The early October breeze of twilight was cooler than normal and the man, his large brown eyes ablaze with some inner passion, seemed oblivious to it all. He had a mass of thick black hair and a handsome face that was half hidden by a thick black beard.

The Iranian, who sold hot dogs on the corner, saw the dark-haired man in the dirty windbreaker pass the corner of Union and Northern every day at the same time—between five and six. He saw the man emerge from the small SRO Hotel on Union Street, next door to the car service, and watched him walk toward Northern Boulevard as rush hour traffic flowed more east than west at that time of evening.

He also saw that the man talked to no one, acknowledged no one, and looked around for no one. He could see how the man was engrossed in his own thoughts, not even distracted by the car horns or low-flying planes on their way toward night landings at LaGuardia airport, over Flushing Bay.

Across from the hot dog man was an old armory now used to shelter the homeless. Every day at six, the man in the windbreaker waited for the flash of car lights on Northern Boulevard to stop. Then he walked across the island, across from Sears, passed the twelve-foot stone statue crowned by the large head of an eagle, dedicated to the dead of World War I, and made his way to the castlelike fortress.

Every day at six, he walked past the open steel gates, up four flights of stone steps, and entered the large doors of the shelter. Once inside, he would acknowledge the heavyset black security guard with a quick glance.

"Hey, Frank! How ya been doin'?" the smiling guard asked.

Frank Moore ignored the guard and walked down a stairway, where he found a long line of homeless men, mostly black, some disturbed, some just out of luck, waiting for the clock to strike six so they could walk up to a long metal table and get their dinner.

Another security guard, a black woman in her forties, nodded to Frank as she twirled a set of keys, balancing a dark blue security guard cap on her short but rich, thick head of hair. "We got chicken and rice," she grinned.

It must be Monday, Frank thought.

Sitting down with the roomful of men, Frank hungrily ate his meal, while watching the faces of the destitute and the lost. He saw the morose face of an elderly black man with smooth skin and gray hair, eating slowly as he stared out into the distance, facing some unknown agony. He could see the hunger in every one of the quiet faces, eating, sipping their cans of soda, all thinking quietly or talking softly to themselves.

Suddenly a white man in a dirty, baggy blue coat with a dirty blue shirt underneath it stood up. He had a ring of long white hair that circled a large bald spot at the top of his head. Tiny grains of rice clung to his chin and his light blue eyes seemed focused on some tiny object miles away.

"God is a dog!" he said to no one in particular. "God is a dog!" He then turned to Frank and glared at him. "I said God is a dog!"

"Okay, God's a dog," Frank answered.

Pleased by Frank's response, the man sat back in his chair.

After his dinner in the shelter, he walked out of the armory and down to Main Street where the Keats, an old, eight-story movie theater, stood. He walked to the large building, admiring the architecture, then continued past the old town hall and looked up Main Street, where a thousand signs flashed something to sell.

Sky black, and stars invisible, he walked in the neon glare and made his way back to the SRO Hotel on Union Street. He walked past the small desk where a thin white man in his fifties sat reading a magazine and made his way up a flight of stairs that looked as dirty as the pale green walls that bordered it.

Reaching his room, he opened the old rotting door with a key, happy that the rotten wood around the lock withstood one more day of use. Once inside, he put on the bright ceiling light and ignored the roaches that infested the once white kitchen sink. He sat in a dirty, old leather chair. Turning on the small radio, an old transistor, which sat on a small table against the wall, he listened to an inane talk show for a few minutes, then quickly changed the station to one which played opera.

Frank sat quietly, allowing the dramatic, forceful music to fill his room. The eloquent voices of sound competed with the night sounds coming from outside his window: the voices, the cars passing, and the occasional cry in the night. The only other items in the room were books and journals. There was also a pad on the desk. Frank sat at the desk and wrote, immersed in a grotesque kind of freedom.

The surface of the water was still until he stepped in, lowered his head, and pushed himself off the side of the empty pool. With strong, sharp strokes, he powered his way down the center lane, feeling the smooth, calming waters surrounding him.

With each stroke he pushed his thin but muscled frame further through the warm waters of the indoor pool. Every few feet he would lift his head to the surface to take a breath, then plunge his head back under again. His goggles protected his eyes from the sting of the chlorine and his earplugs kept him from getting ear infections. But alone in the pool, floating without the acute sense of sound and sight, he felt weightless. He felt his body glide across the darkened surface of the water, free of the clamor of the world. With each stroke he came closer to another lap and with each lap he fell deeper into the privacy of his own thoughts.

Though the pool was smaller than the Olympic-sized pools he was used to, there was still no movement or sound coming from outside its waters; no one was around except the lifeguard, immersed in a book. Through a large window at the right end of the indoor pool, strong rays of light came through the smoked glass and lightly dappled the pool, bringing to the room a look of twilight.

Having just turned thirty-five, he had been swimming most of his adult life. He used to swim four, sometimes five times a week. He didn't smoke, so the breath he needed was always there for him when he decided to swim four or five hundred yards without stopping. He needed to feel his body afloat in a world without a top and a bottom to it, without a sky above and an earth below.

Frank liked the pool. It was housed in the Y only a block away from his room. It was clean and was never very busy, especially not at six in the morning, when he usually swam. It was his main form of exercise and his only refuge.

As he swam, his thoughts drifted back to his childhood in Queens. He remembered the large pool they had in school and how he loved to stay late to swim. Back then, he didn't swim with the same passion he had discovered as he grew older, but more to float. To float alone and feel free, but most of all, to hold his breath. To hold his breath and see how long he could stay under water without coming up. He loved to do that, to sink into the silence of the pool with no one around, with no one else there but himself.

And now, as he swam, he remembered how he held his breath and wondered what it was like never to breathe again. He looked down at the bottom and thought about the tranquility his mind craved: to hold his breath, not wanting any more air in his lungs; to close out the world beyond the silence of the pool and its warm, soothing waters.

There was no loneliness for him in the pool's watery quiet. There was himself and the wide world of water. It was a world where nothing moved, nothing mattered. The bottom of the pool had no day or night, no weekend, no language, no rules. It existed as a bare place, that somehow calmed and warmed. Frank felt his heart beat more calmly in this world.

One arm over the next. Up out of water for breath, then down again. Searching for the peace lost somewhere between what he had and what now was gone. Another stroke to forget himself and who he was. Another stroke to get himself closer to the bottom.

Halfway through his swim, time and space would begin to disappear. They faded out like a slow dissolve on a movie screen. In and out, he would drift. Suddenly everything would stop. Each second of time would disappear. Space merged with emptiness and he would drift through it, alone.

On this particular morning he was fascinated by the image of a woman he had never seen before. She came to him as he pushed his way through the pool. First, he saw her face. Though it was a blur, he could make out strands of dark gray hair and watery eyes. Then came a voice that was speaking softly to him, calmly but with determination. But he couldn't make out what she was saying.

Aquatic mirages had occurred many times before while swimming. Images from his past, people from his childhood, names he thought long forgotten, all came to him in those moments when time and space melted away. But this woman who came to him he felt sure he had never seen nor spoken to before. It was as if she were right there with him as he swam. Her presence was unmistakable.

Pushing off from one side of the small pool for another lap, he glanced up at the window again. And that's when he saw her. She was standing, a silhouette at the edge of the pool, the bright light of the window glowing behind her. He could see her small, dark face watching him. He could see the outline of her body, immobile and yet strikingly alive, calling out silently for his attention.

He stopped swimming.

Standing in four feet of water, his feet felt for the bottom. He stared at the dark presence through fogged goggles which he quickly pushed up onto his forehead. He squinted. He pulled out his earplugs to help regain his senses. She was there, standing silently. All he could hear was the sound of water rippling gently.

"What do you want?" he asked, trembling.

Suddenly, the light from the window began to fade. A huge cloud was passing by the window overhead, throwing the earth below into gray shadow. He looked again. The apparition was fading with the light.

"Who are you?"

She was gone. There was no one there. It was another mirage. He looked around the pool. The lifeguard was still involved with his book. The cloud passed. Light fell back into place at the window. He may as well have been alone.

Pushing himself toward the ladder, he reached up to the top bars and pulled himself out of the water. His body felt tired yet strangely invigorated. Everything about himself felt refreshed. He grabbed his towel from a bench near the diving board and turned. He looked down at the bottom of the pool and remembered the few moments of peace. He buried his face into his towel, sat down on the bench and closed his eyes.

Nearly a week went by and Frank hardly left his room. He stopped taking meals at the armory and now bought white bread and jars of peanut butter at the grocery store. He ate this twice a day, wrote at his desk, swam, and slept for ten hours a night. He had no desire to go anywhere else anymore.

It was toward the end of this penitent week when a loud banging on the door woke Frank up. His eyes were glued shut and the pounding on the door felt like it was going on inside his head. His throat was sore and his nose felt cold. Struggling to rise, Frank could see the bright blast of late-morning sunlight exploding through his windows. He had only been asleep for a few hours.

He managed to stand and he opened the door only slightly, the few inches that the chain would allow. A heavyset round-faced man with babylike skin and small brown eyes faced him. Wearing a powder-blue suit and smelling strongly of cheap cologne, Frank knew the man to be Danny, the manager and owner of the hotel.

"Frank, you up? We gotta talk here," Danny said with a thick wise-guy accent.

Frank reluctantly opened the door, letting the large powder-blue suit with the shiny black shoes into his apartment.

Danny looked at Frank. "You look emaciated, do you know that?" he said sharply. Then, not wanting an answer, he looked around the room. "You did a nice job with the place. Now it looks like a hole-in-the-wall dump! Before it just looked like a hole-in-the-wall!"

"Danny, your humor I can handle after coffee but not before," Frank answered.

Danny turned around, sticking his large face into Frank's. "A weird thing happened to me this morning."

"I'm sorry to hear that," Frank said, finding his way to a chair and sitting.

"Some friggin' guy comes to my office in Bayside and he says he'd like to ask me some questions. I tell the guy, 'Do I look like an information booth to you?' But this guy kills with kindness so, I listen to him. He looks like a respectable guy. Decent. So, this guy tells me that he's looking for a tenant of mine. Now, I don't think this guy is a cop, and it seems that he ain't. But he shows me a photograph of the guy he is looking for, and guess what? That guy is you! I mean, the guy in the photograph was younger and without the beard but it was good old Frankie!"

Frank felt a sinking feeling. He looked to Danny, who was now dancing around the room as he told his story, showing a lot more grace than Frank would expect for a heavyset man wearing a powder-blue suit that looked like it was painted on.

"You didn't tell him I was here? Did you?"

Danny leaned down to Frank and grinned. "Look, pal, since the day you got here I've been kinda suspicious of you. I know you don't deal drugs but you don't live off welfare and you ain't checking into no hospital for no calm-you-down candies. So, what do you do, I ask myself. You pay your rent with a check from a good bank. I can't figure it, but one thing I cannot take a chance on is harboring a fugitive. See, I got a little bit of a record myself and if I hide you from, let's say, the IRS, then they are gonna come after me and I don't want those bastards checking into my background. You got that?"

"IRS?" Frank asked.

"You heard me. I bet you're one of those eccentric guys like Howard Hughes. This guy says that he found out you were here from the bank. It seems that the bank that sends me your check every month has to give your address on your income tax."

"I pay my taxes," Frank said.

"Tell that to him!"

"Who?" Frank asked.

Danny swung to the door and waved a young man into the room. This second man, looking like a choirboy with sharp blue eyes that seemed to sparkle, and wearing a cream-colored suit, walked nervously into the shabby room. Frank turned around in his chair and looked at him, then shook his head as though he had just been insulted.

The young man didn't know what to say and looked awkwardly at Frank and Danny like an uninvited guest crashing a party. Frank was half expecting him to ask for a glass of wine.

"Frank Moore?" the young man asked gingerly.

Frank could see that he was startled by Frank's appearance. In fact, Frank figured that the young man must have been shocked by the hotel itself to begin with. Frank nodded. "Well, I've done my duty." Danny smiled then leaned over to Frank, who grimaced as he did. "You runnin' from a wife and ten kids? Come on, Frankie, tell Danny!"

Frank, still not fully awake, stood and faced the young man. "Is there a problem with the bank?"

"Oh, no! I'm not from the bank."

"You're from the IRS, no?" Danny asked.

"IRS? Oh, no. I'm sorry if you got that impression. I'm with the archdiocese," the young man said, still smiling his silly smile.

"Arch who?" Danny said.

Frank ignored Danny. "So, what do you want with me?" he asked the young man.

The young man grew more nervous as he spoke. "I was told to find you. You left the retreat house sixteen months ago and if it weren't for the bank account at Chase, we wouldn't know where to find you."

"Who told you to find me?"

"Cardinal Cahill," the young man answered. "He wants to see you. Immediately. He said it was urgent."

Danny looked shocked. "You stole from a church?" he asked Frank.

Frank continued to ignore Danny and shrugged his shoulders. "I was hoping they'd forget about me," Frank said. He then walked to the closet. He glanced over his shoulder at the young man before he opened the door. "You're still in the seminary, aren't you?"

"Yes. I am," the young man said humbly. "How did you know?"

Frank opened the closet, revealing a long black cassock and

three white shirts. In each shirt pocket there was a white priest's collar. "I recognized the glowing look of piety on your face."

"I hope I never lose it, Father Moore," the young man said.

Frank took out the contents of the closet and placed them on the mattress. He then reached for a small overnight bag and saw Danny standing in the corner of the room looking startled and perplexed. "You're a priest?" Danny asked incredulously.

Frank nodded. "That's right, Danny. It wasn't the IRS after me, it was God. You did your duty just fine," Frank said sarcastically. He then filled the overnight bag and walked to the door, where the young man was waiting. He then turned and stopped. He saw a small wood and brass crucifix hanging on a nail over a crack in the wall. The words *Credo quia impossible est* were etched in a small plaque under the cross. They echoed the early Christian thinker Tertullian, who had phrased the famous paradox centuries before.

"*Credo quia impossible est*," the young man said.

"I believe because it's impossible," Frank said, translating the Latin.

"I know," the young man asked looking to Frank. "Is it yours?"

Frank looked at it, then nodded.

"Would you like to take it with you?" the young man asked.

Frank thought a moment then shook his head. "No. Leave it for the next tenant. It might be of more help to him." With that, Frank handed his bag to the young novitiate, who quickly left the room. Frank then took one more look around, nodded goodbye to a stunned Danny, and walked out.

Chapter 2

Cardinal Charles Cahill sat in the far corner of the room at his second desk facing a computer and his CD-ROM. A museum curator was speaking to him from the screen about international artworks that were for sale. Frank could hear the computerized voice as he stepped into the large room.

The wood-lined walls, varnished a deep brown, rose up to a lofty white ceiling. The room was spacious, with enormous windows and rows of bookshelves. Contemporary abstract works of art were everywhere.

The office was on the third floor, and through the nearest window Frank could see a small part of Saint John the Evangelist Church. The window was closed, but Frank could imagine the busy crowds walking down beneath the overcast sky of First Avenue between 55th and 56th streets, in Manhattan.

The cardinal stood and walked over to his large primary desk. He glanced at Frank as he did. "Monet's *View of the Church of Vernon* was sold for $3.7 million last night."

"A bit out of my budget," Frank answered as he sat behind the desk.

The cardinal sat, sizing up Frank's appearance as he did. "You're taking the prodigal son allegory a little too far, don't you think, Frank?"

"The prodigal son returned on his own," Frank answered.

"Well, we cynics always wondered if his motive for returning was love or financial inconveniences, anyway," Cahill grinned.

"You're right, my account dried up," Frank said. He felt a sudden warmth emanating from Cahill. Frank relaxed. They had a history together.

Cahill leaned forward. "Look, we lose priests every year. They find a woman, they fall in love, and then one day, they disappear on us. Is this something like that?"

Frank shook his head. "No."

"Then what is it, Frank?" Cahill asked, dropping the friendly tone in his voice.

"Personal reasons," Frank answered.

"One of my finest priests disappears for over a year and that's the best reason I hear from him? I don't like it. And I don't want it to happen again," Cahill said.

"I apologize," Frank said.

"Good." Cahill then turned to a file on his desk. He opened it. "Now, for the business at hand. I need a postulator. We've received a petition for sainthood."

"Can I decline?"

"I seem to recall one of your vows being the vow of obedience."

"As well as celibacy. I'm simply stating that I don't believe I'm ready for another in-depth investigation," Frank answered.

"Frank, this is more than a simple investigation. And you already did outstanding work in the field for this office. Your handling of the examination of the unnatural occurrences in Willow Lake was extraordinary."

"It was my first case and I was hoping it'd be my last."

"We were all quite impressed with the way you handled the delicacy of the matter."

"I don't believe I handled it well at all," Frank replied, looking at the second file. "I can recommend someone else."

"I've considered others. You're my first and only choice."

"I felt as if I had betrayed those people up there."

"By negating the petition?"

"They loved Father Falcone. They believed that the lake he drowned in was blessed. By finding out what really happened, I crushed their fragile expectations."

"You gave them the truth. How could that be a betrayal?"

Frank took a deep breath. "The truth can sometimes betray. It betrays the innocent. I investigated the supernatural and in doing so I brought dismay."

"I think what you mean is deceit. Deceit betrays."

Frank was silent for a moment, then said, "Of course."

"The important point here is that you're familiar with the duties of a postulator."

"Yes," Frank whispered, feeling an ache in every part of his body.

"Then you know that it is the postulator's duty to investigate each case of unexplainable or extraordinary cures that relate directly or indirectly to the cause of canonization for a particular individual. The postulator meets with everyone alive who knew the person in question. They must document everything they ever wrote, said, or were known to have said," Cahill told Frank.

"It is the duty of the postulator to prove or not prove their 'heroic' virtue," Frank answered.

"Excellent." Cahill opened another drawer, pulling out another file. He placed it on the desk. "This current 'miracle' is occurring in a small parish in Queens. They want to make one of their parishioners a saint. Their petition numbers two hundred thousand names, Frank. I need the investigation to be precise, succinct, and conclusive. You're from this city, you know its people and you've had first hand experience in this arena. Before you make a decision, look the place over. John Beliar and his people will brief you on the details."

Frank watched as Cahill hit a buzzer on his intercom. "I don't think I can endure another investigation," he said flatly.

Cahill eyed Frank closely again. "Suffering has always been God's test for spiritual strength," Cahill answered.

Glib as ever, Frank thought.

"Then perhaps we've made a mistake?"

"Mistake?"

"We've confused theology with the Olympics." Frank stood as Cahill sat back in his chair and smiled.

"One more thing," Cahill said. "Your unofficial absence has not gone unnoticed. And despite what happened there is no excuse for your current appearance."

Frank nodded slightly.

"You'll find your old room just as you left it." Cahill smiled.

Frank turned and walked out of the office. He felt awful.

James was waiting for him outside Cahill's door. He led Frank down the corridor for a short walk, then opened the door to a conference room. In a minute, Frank was sitting at a large oval table under bright lights.

John Beliar, who had been in the room when he entered, stood and shook Frank's hand. "It's good to see you again, Frank," he said warmly. Beliar, like Frank, was a secular priest.

"You too, John," Frank smiled.

"Let's begin, then. This is my assistant, Mark," he said, gesturing to a young man standing behind him. Frank could see the intelligence in the young man's eyes as well as the arrogance of well-educated youth.

They all sat, James to Frank's left, with John to his immediate left. Mark sat to John's right. "A few more apostles and we can have a last supper," Frank cracked.

Without missing a beat, John opened a file. He pulled out a photograph of a woman in her early fifties. He handed it to Frank. "Her name was Helen Stephenson. Hers is the soul in question."

Frank looked closely at the photograph. The woman was soft-featured and attractive. Though there was nothing unique about her, Frank thought he saw a look of serenity in the eyes.

"You won't find any halos," Mark spoke up.

"Too bad. It would have made my job easier," Frank replied. He knew he had seen this face before. Perhaps at the pool only days before? An apparition, a ghost? Destiny, perhaps?

"She died in the convent. Of a heart attack. She had been living there for several years," Mark continued.

"A bit unusual for a lay person to be living in a convent," Frank said, looking up.

"Very unusual. She also was quite vocal in her opinion that women should be ordained. But, all in all, we hear she was a sweet woman," Beliar said.

James seemed confident enough to speak. "She was a registered nurse and created a childcare center in the parish as well as a drug rehab center in the community."

Beliar handed Frank another photograph. It was a black-and-white shot of the Virgin's statue outside Saint Stanislaus. "Since her death this statue of the Virgin cries tears of blood. Only in October and only when it rains."

"You must've heard of the event before, Father Moore?" Mark asked.

"I have. Though I've been out of the loop, as they say. Do you know that in over seventy years the Church has recognized only eleven miracles at Lourdes?" Frank said. He then asked, "Any miracle cures?"

Mark handed Frank a file of medical records. "A dozen claims to date."

"But only one has been substantiated," Beliar said.

"We'll need three to make her a saint," Frank said.

Beliar then placed a photograph of a young girl on the desk in front of Frank. "Her name is Maria Katowski. She was seven years old when this picture was taken. Ten years ago she was cured of lupus after touching the tears of blood."

Frank looked at the young girl's sad eyes. "Who originated the petition?"

"The pastor. Father Philip Kinnely," Beliar said. "Unfortunately, he's turned his parish into a circus. He's sought media coverage and he's allowed parishioners to set up camps in the schoolyard."

Mark grinned. "I wouldn't be surprised to hear he's hired his own public relations firm."

"As long as he doesn't release an album of religious hits," Frank kidded. "What about Satanic sightings?"

James cringed. Frank turned to him. "My dear James, since the early days of the New Testament, our marvelous nemesis Beelzebub, has a way of making guest appearances at our miracles. Or so we are told."

Beliar handed Frank newspaper clippings. "Vandalism, possessions, the homicide rate going up in the community."

Frank looked at the other priests and nodded. "You've done a thorough preliminary." Saying nothing further, Frank gathered up the files and then left the room.

On his way down the corridor, Beliar caught up to him. "How have you been?" asked Frank, in an altogether different tone from his conference-room voice.

"Fine. The cardinal keeps me busy."

"I read an article of yours it must have been a few months ago. You certainly know your Middle Eastern demonology."

Beliar grinned. "I try to keep up. But we still get about a half dozen letters a week addressed to you. About your book. Mostly from theologians. Mostly from all over the world. *The God Within* is still highly respected."

"I wrote that book five years ago."

Beliar sensed Frank's uneasiness. "Was Charles hard on you?"

"He could have been worse."

"You did a great job at Willow Lake. It's a shame that you had to negate the petition."

"It was more than that," Frank said. "I knew Father Falcone."

"I know. It was a shame."

"I studied with him at the seminary. I had never met a man more the ideal priest than he. And they loved him up there, John. They really loved him."

"That makes it more of a tragedy," Beliar said. "And what about all those people who had been cured?"

Frank nodded. "Those people needed to believe in something. They believed so totally they actually cured themselves. It would have taken years of psychological study to get to the heart of it." Frank paused. "John, tell me, what do you really think about all this going on at Saint Stan's? Have you seen it firsthand?"

"A few years ago."

"And?"

"Perhaps the same thing is going on there as it did in Willow Lake. People need to believe in something."

"I don't know if I should thank the old man or curse him for bringing me back," Frank said.

"He has your well-being in mind."

Frank stopped at a familiar door. He hesitated to take out his key and go inside. "Well, here we are."

Beliar extended his hand again and shook Frank's hand warmly.

"I just wanted to let you know that it is good to see you again, Frank. I'm glad you're back."

"It's good to see you, too," Frank said, at last unlocking the door.

"Whatever you need, just let us know," Beliar said, then walked away. Frank then entered his old room.

Frank hadn't seen the place in over a year. Nobody had gone inside to dust and he had to fight a sneeze as he opened a window. His magazines and books were just where he had left them the day he decided to get on a train and find a motel room in Queens. He had decided on the SRO Hotel in Flushing on a whim. He just picked any place because just any place would do. Any place out of the way. Any place he didn't have to be reminded he was a priest.

But now, he was back. There was the desk, the lamp, and the small computer he wrote his articles on. He sat down on the bed and closed his eyes, then thought of Willow Lake and the beginning of the journey that had brought him to where he was.

Frank recalled his first day on the Falcone petition. He drove the two and a half hours up the New York Thruway wondering why Falcone chose such an obscure parish to live in. Frank had been assigned postulator by Bishop Sheeny, from the Boston archdiocese. Father Falcone was from Boston's North End, a tough Italian neighborhood, and when the petition came in from Saint Margaret's parish in Willow Lake, New York, Cardinal Cahill forwarded it to Sheeny. Sheeny then went searching for a postulator.

Frank was chosen immediately. His book had made a big splash in religious circles and Sheeny knew that Falcone had been Frank's mentor in the seminary. Sheeny decided to forgo the ten-year wait petitions usually had to adhere to. He got permission to do this from the Vatican because of the odd circumstances of Falcone's death. The Church didn't want any scandals, and the town was experiencing a religious panic.

Willow Lake looked like it had been lifted whole from "The Legend of Sleepy Hollow." Wooden-framed homes painted white, gray, blue, and brown had lined the one-block main street since the Revolution. Meadows and woods surrounded the town, filled with tall trees that cast long, dark shadows. Mohawk Indians and early settlers could easily be pictured stepping out of the forest.

The mayor, a bulky man in his forties, was a Mr. Hodge. Hodge liked big red bow ties. "This poor town needed a miracle and I think Father Falcone gave us one!" he said to Frank. Frank had immediately met with the priest who sent the archdiocese the petition for canonization. Father Hutton was a thin, balding man in his mid thirties who wore glasses. He was the acting pastor. "We have all read your book up here," Father Hutton told Frank at dinner that evening. "Even the folks up here who don't read much bought copies of it. They knew you were coming and they know you are a brilliant man of the Church," Father Hutton went on.

Frank immediately went through Falcone's things. He found a

small plastic bag in the desk drawer placed there by Father Hutton. In the bag was Falcone's college ring. It was the only personal item found on the body when it was pulled from the lake.

"I thought you should have the ring. In case it is blessed. It was his. They found it on his finger. It was the only finger not eaten away by fish," Father Hutton explained.

Frank looked at the gold ring with the maroon crest on it. He had the same ring. He got it when he graduated from the seminary.

That first night, Frank was brought to the lake where Father Falcone had drowned. Frank stood on the small dock in his black pants and shirt and white collar as Father Hutton said a prayer. Behind Frank, on the bank of the lake, were over five hundred people from the local parish.

Standing on the dock, Frank was told of the dozens of miracles involving the young and old who had been cured of some affliction by praying to Father Falcone and stepping into the lake. From where Frank stood he could see the rise of a small group of hills at the far end. The sky was clear but the headlights from the parked cars lit the dock side of the lake like a nighttime ball field.

Standing in the crowd alone that first night, Frank's eye caught that of a tall black man. He soon learned that the man's name was Royburn. Royburn was in his early forties and lived alone in a big brown house on the outer edge of the lake.

After the ceremony, Frank was following Father Hutton back to his car when Royburn stepped in front him. He looked at him eye to eye as if no one else was there, and said, "You think this lake is blessed, don't ya? It ain't blessed. It's cursed." He then turned and walked away, leaving Frank stunned by the remark.

Chapter 3

When Frank reached Saint Stanislaus, he parked and got out of the car. He knew Maspeth like the back of his hand. He knew well the tree-lined blocks and the old two-story wooden buildings. Alleyways and dead-end streets created vague memories of his own childhood, while the gray October sky enclosed him in a claustrophobic grip.

Walking a short distance, he immediately saw a crowd of people standing in the schoolyard. He made his way to the statue. He stood a short distance away looking at the limestone Virgin.

He then turned and made his way toward the convent. As he did, he had to walk past a six-foot white wall on the other side of which was a large tent. Inside was a makeshift infirmary, like the one at Lourdes: a place set aside for the sick and dying where they and their relatives could rest, wait, and pray. It was a place away from the others. It was private and, at one end, Kinnely had built a small altar facing the statue. This was exactly where Maria Katowski had run, the distance between the convent and the rectory, when she made her way to the church, ten years earlier.

Frank glanced at the entrance to the tent. It was like glancing into a terminal ward at a hospital. He saw burn victims whose scars had never properly healed; he saw those suffering from tuberculosis; those with cancerous growths on their faces; he saw those who couldn't even lift their heads as they lay dying in small cots. Family members, friends, and nurses kept vigil with the sick. Frank also noticed some men with AIDS, looking thin and helpless, sitting in small chairs with hardly the energy to speak, their eyes looking off into the dark unknown.

Suddenly, Frank heard someone shout "Bless me, Father!" It was an old man with a terrible tumor on the side of his face. Several in the crowd heard and turned. Seeing Frank's white collar and his long black coat, it was like viewing Christ visiting the dying, coming to save them from certain pain and death.

An elderly woman, her skin covered with lesions and growths on both her arms, turned in her pillow and reached out to Frank. "Father! Bless me!"

Frank felt all the oxygen escaping from his lungs. He looked around, not sure where to go, when suddenly an angelic-looking young woman grabbed at his coat. She didn't look ill or sickly at all but her eyes were needy and desperate. "Please, Father, bless me!" she said in a fragile voice.

Frank panicked. He pulled up his collar and quickly made his way to the convent door.

The convent was open. Frank walked in and could smell cooking. He saw a stairway and headed toward it. A nun in her Saint Joseph habit, spotted him making his way up the stairs. She was Sister Alice, now the principal of the school. "What are you doing here?" she said to him.

"Excuse me," Frank said, continuing upwards. Reaching the top, he saw a half-opened door. He could see a young woman in bra and panties combing her hair. She was a young nun, not pretty, but her eyes were large and brown. She did not see him and Frank did not linger.

He saw another door which led to a room with a window

above the statue. From reading the file and seeing the photographs, he knew it had to be Helen Stephenson's.

Frank tried the door and it opened. He stepped in and closed it behind him. The room was small and the blinds were drawn. Frank looked around. He could tell that no one had lived in the room for years. He pulled up the blinds and sunlight flooded into the room. There was a bed in one corner and holy pictures and a crucifix on the walls.

Just as Frank sat down on the bed, the door swung open. An outraged Father Kinnely, with a round belly, round face, graying hair, and large blue eyes glared at Frank. Sister Alice was standing behind him.

"What are you doing in here?" he demanded to know.

Frank stood. His coat collar moved, revealing his white collar. "I'm Father Moore," he said.

Kinnely backed off. He was relieved and apologetic. "I'm sorry, Father. I'm Philip Kinnely. We were waiting for you," he said, extending his hand.

"My office is back here," Kinnely said as he led Frank into the rectory, through a dining room and into a small room in the back near the side entrance. The rectory was modest, quaint at best, but certainly clean. Frank noticed a large painting of Jesus of the Sacred Heart. The rest of the room was cluttered with old dusty furniture, books, newspapers, and an old desk under the window.

"Place is a mess, I know," Father Kinnely said.

Frank found a chair nearest the window and sat in it. He reached behind himself, pulling a rosary out from under him.

Father Kinnely took the rosary from Frank with a puppy dog look on his face. "We share this office. Me, Father Paulino and Father Stacey. Father Stacey comes from a wealthy family and isn't used to cleaning. Father Paulino and I grew up with women cleaning the house. The sisters call us male chauvinistic pork chops and refuse to dust for us!"

Frank nodded as he looked over the bachelor office. He now saw why it had no clear identity—it was shared by three.

"Oh, I forgot! Coffee and donuts! I went down to Dunkin' Donuts on Grand Avenue."

Frank held out his hand for the cup of coffee, ignoring the box of creamy donuts, and tried not to smile as Father Kinnely's face flushed with pleasure biting into a Boston Creme.

"My one major vice," Father Kinnely said. "Boston Creme, Jelly, and God forbid, Chocolate Honey Dip!"

Frank sipped his coffee, then sat back in his chair. "I'm glad to hear it's your one vice."

"So, you do talk? I was getting worried there that you were going to stare at me all day!" Kinnely said, trying to make a joke. "Cardinal Cahill said you were born here. Has Maspeth changed much?"

"It still looks peaceful. And Catholic. I had forgotten how many churches there were here. I grew up on the other side of the Expressway. We don't have any churches there."

Father Kinnely reached and grabbed another donut. "That's right. We have Transfiguration down the hill a couple of blocks and then Holy Church at the bottom of the hill. They've been here the longest. Transfiguration doesn't have a school."

"Sounds like a lot of competition for you."

"Oh, me and Father Panowits and Father Kelonski from the Cross are usually at each other's throats, especially during the holidays. The bazaars and bingo games, you know."

"The statue must be giving you an added edge in your competition right now," Frank said.

"An edge?"

Frank sipped his coffee. "I imagine all the attention you're getting here must certainly help bring in the parishioners? Considering that there are three parishes on one small hill."

"I had nothing to do with the miracles of the Blessed Virgin."

"You mean the statue?"

"The statue, if you'd rather." Father Kinnely took a breath. "I know you think I'm an illiterate parish priest, Father Moore. I know you must think that I am enjoying the attention my parish is getting, but I do not have a hand in this."

Frank watched Kinnely closely. "Father Kinnely, the Church gets hundreds of bona fide petitions from bishops all over the world in a single year. That means hundreds of lives must be investigated. And that's not counting all the lives of those who have already been petitioned and that are still under investigation. Even if this Helen Stephenson is found to be a saint, the Church may not decide that fact in our lifetime," Frank said. "At this point, I'm not even sure if I will even recommend a true investigation. The Holy See frowns on any person being considered for canonization who has a cult following."

"I see," Kinnely said slowly.

Frank nodded to the statue. "As the crowd grows out there, so does Helen Stephenson's reputation. Soon, there will be those who will believe that this woman was a saint, despite what is decided by the Church. Superstitions will be created which have nothing to do with the teachings of the Church. And superstitions create gods, not saints."

"And the miracles?" Father Kinnely asked.

"Three are needed for the tribunal." Father Kinnely was the same as Father Hutton, Frank thought to himself. Both were anxious children thinly disguised as men. Men who became priests in hopes of witnessing God's love in action. "Consider me a detective interested only in facts which can be proved. And proof does not come easily. A miracle demands true evidence relating to a petition of Faith, one which I must investigate with the same thoroughness an officer of the law must use. Because *I am* an officer of the law: the law of the Church. The process is best seen as an adversarial procedure. In the eyes of the Vatican, you are guilty until proven saintly." Frank said this with an air of authority. It was all an act to quiet Kinnely.

"What do you mean by true evidence?" Father Kinnely asked.

"Testimony that will be used at the tribunal. Actual witnessed happenings which can only be ordained by the will of God," Frank said, losing his patience. "Father Kinnely, how old is this church?"

"It was built in 1925," Kinnely answered.

"An anniversary? Seventy years? Wonderful way to celebrate, with a miracle in your backyard," Frank said.

Kinnely was relentless. He had dreamed of this moment for ten years and he wasn't going to let it get away from him. It was going to live up to his fantasy. "Because of Helen's presence here I've acted with courage and conviction surprising even myself! I call that a miracle!" Father Kinnely said. "I was a street punk! I grew up in Hell's Kitchen but thanks to the grace of God I became a priest!"

Frank felt the need to breathe fresh air.

"Please, give us some time here. A few days? A week?" Kinnely pleaded.

Frank stood up. "I am here to do a preliminary. It probably will take a few days."

Father Kinnely beamed. "We've prepared a spare room! I was so excited when I heard that you were coming here I went out and bought new sheets and pillowcases. I'll show you!"

Frank followed the bulky frame of Father Kinnely up a flight of old wooden stairs. Frank felt uncomfortable in the quiet, old-fashioned surroundings of the rectory.

"We do have a pretty decent cook here. She makes wonderful pasta and Chicken Française! The other priests here are Father Stacey, and Father Paulino, as I mentioned. And the principal of our school, Sister Alice, she's dying to meet you. Of course, her vow of humility prevents her from telling me this. But it's in her eyes."

Frank stood in the hallway as Father Kinnely opened the door to a small bedroom.

"It's small but very quiet. See, I even had a little desk brought for you. I hope you'll be comfortable here." With that, he left Frank alone.

Frank looked around. The room was small but quaint. The walls were painted white, but since the window didn't receive direct sunlight, the room had a pale hue to it. The bed was against one wall, allowing its sleeper to face the window. Frank glanced down to the yard below, realizing the room was well chosen, since its only window faced the schoolyard right above the statue.

Frank then opened a small bag he had been carrying. He opened it and took out a prayer book, a chalice, and a Sanctus bell. He placed them on the desk.

He then removed a camera, a white cloth, and a plastic bag for gathering blood. It had "sterile" marked on it. He placed them on the desk beside the more arcane tools.

Frank then left the room, finding Kinnely waiting at the bottom of the staircase. Kinnely walked Frank to the rectory door and opened it. Frank walked onto the stoop, turning his collar up to the chill in the air. "Father Kinnely, out of all the thousands of petitions the Church receives, there have only been three saints canonized in this country in the last hundred years," Frank said as he walked out onto the sidewalk. "John Newman was a nineteenth-century bishop. Mother Cabrini founded several religious orders, and Mother Seton, who founded this country's first religious order, died in 1821. What do we learn from those three saints? We learn that if you are not a bishop, you'd better be a nun who founded a religious order or, at the very least, have been dead for over a hundred years. It doesn't look promising for a gentle woman from Queens."

Father Kinnely did not lose his look of determination. "You don't have to be a priest or a nun to be a saint, Father."

Frank saw the sincerity in the man's eyes.

"Father, the sick and dying asked if you would say Mass for them. Whenever you have the time. We have a small altar near the statue," Kinnely said.

"Of course," Frank told him, feeling a tremendous sinking feeling as he did.

Father Kinnely was about to close the door but stopped. "There is one other thing. If you hear the sound of someone outside your room tonight, I better explain now," he said.

"Explain what?" Frank asked.

"There's been a presence in the rectory since the miracle. I have even seen it with my own two eyes. Two Octobers ago. The figure of a man. I woke up in the middle of the night and saw him standing in the hallway. He didn't move and he said nothing. And then he was gone, as quickly as he appeared," Father Kinnely said.

"And who do you suppose he was?" Frank asked. "An angel?"

"A dark one. Satan. I have no doubt," he said.

"If Satan happens to knock on my door tonight, I'll be sure to let you know," Frank said with a grin. He then walked to his blue-gray rented car which was parked on the corner. He took one last look at the quiet rectory, then got into his car and drove away.

Frank hadn't driven very far when he stopped and pulled the car to the curb. Up ahead was a tall elm tree with a large branch which hung across the entire street. The tree looked like a tree back in Willow Lake, and the association struck Frank so hard he pulled the car to the curb and parked it. He sat and stared at the tree's long limbs, watching how the sunlight fell through the gold and yellow leaves.

Frank stood in Father Falcone's room. Outside the window was a large, old elm tree, its shadow falling across an old photograph of the priest's parents. They were smiling Italian immigrants, full of pride, standing beside their son in his priest's robes. Other photographs included one which showed Father Falcone in a college football uniform, and another which showed him in cap and gown at his graduation day from Columbia University.

Frank sat at the desk and found all the old newspaper clippings he had asked for concerning Falcone's work with the poor of Willow Lake and Lakewood Township. He was not surprised to see article after article showing Falcone's tireless dedication to church activities, including working with the growing number of homeless and drug addicts.

In another photograph Falcone stood at a picnic table with a dozen black kids smiling shyly for the camera. A banner reading "Lakewood's Champion Chiefs" in red and white was spread out and held by the children. Frank also noticed a plaque with the inscription "To Father Joseph Falcone and his selfless duty to our town of Willow Lake." Next to the plaque was a photograph of Falcone, then a tall, confident priest.

It was then that he found an old suitcase. This was filled with clothes and was ready to be given to a local orphanage. Curious about its contents, Frank opened it, finding a copy of his own book, and Father Falcone's personal journal.

Frank couldn't wait to read the journal. He expected it would give him further reasons to continue the process and bring Falcone's case all the way to Rome. But right before he began to read the first entry, he turned to the copy of his book and opened it.

It thrilled him to know that Falcone, his mentor, found solace and possible instruction in his book. Frank was excited when he noticed pencil markings throughout the book. Falcone had underlined certain passages and placed exclamation points in the margins beside particular paragraphs. Frank's excitement quickly turned to confusion when he saw the words "crap" and "childish" written in the margins.

On the last page of the book, Frank was taken aback when he saw the line, "my ex-student wallows in duplicity!" written in black ink in Falcone's handwriting.

Frank remembered how odd he'd felt as he put down the book and looked up at a small mirror which hung in Father Falcone's room, above the desk. Frank could still recall the look of anguish on his face as he replayed that line again in his mind.

He placed the book on the desk and picked up Falcone's journal. He noticed that the last entry was made the day Falcone died.

He turned to the last entry and read it. The handwriting was clear, bold, and confident:

"Today, I will go to the lake and never come back."

Frank turned to the entry made the previous day.

"When I pray, I hear my own voice and no other. Last
night I decided that I will not bear witness anymore to any
false hopes. I'm sick of pretending. I'm tired of lying.
People come to me for advice? They should pray to a wall!
Because that is how I feel—like a wall of nothing. There is
a feeling in my gut that I cannot shake. A feeling that
none of this matters. I can almost say that I feel my body
dying. I feel my mind grow numb and my heart cold. The
boys at the school will all one day give in to drugs and
greed. I'll stand over their graves offering nothing but
moronic prayers. I can no longer be a witness to their cor-
ruption. Does the cycle never end?"

Frank had a tough time reading on. He couldn't believe that it
was the same Father Falcone that he knew. He read each entry
working his way back to the beginning of the journal. In the
diary Falcone called Father Hutton a "pious homo" and he
called the people of Willow Lake, the same people who were
going to the waters to pray to him, "insipid, dirty people who
enjoy watching Bugs Bunny more than they do reading a book
with more words than pictures in it."

Frank read on. One particular entry read:

"For the pure hell of it I'd like to open a whorehouse in
this town. These people need money, lust, dreams, and
fantasy more than nauseating prayers, solace, crap! I'm
not their spiritual leader—I'm more their caretaker, the
superintendent of their emotional puke! If I had true
courage, I'd tell them that God is a joke! If he exists at all,
we're nothing to him but worms under his feet! I'd rather
drown in the lake and forget this world than go on lying
to myself."

Frank read on.

> "I despise Sundays. After Mass I had nothing to do so I
> read *The God Within* crap book. Frank should be beaten
> for the junk he wrote. Who can believe a word of it? I
> hear he's being lionized! I should go see him and spit in
> his face. God is indifferent to our plight. I have little faith
> in His ability to help us."

After reading that entry, Frank went to see Sheriff Crowley.
The sheriff was a heavyset man in his fifties. He had a full head
of gray hair and a pudgy baby face. Frank sat across from his
desk. "I believe Father Falcone committed suicide."

"What makes you think that?" a stunned Sheriff Crowley
asked.

Frank told him what he had read in the diary.

"You're going to have one unhappy town if you're right."

"Take me to Royburn's house," Frank told him.

The sheriff drove Frank to the house. Royburn came to the
door looking suspiciously at the sheriff.

"There's no problem with you, sir," Frank told him. "I came
here to talk to you alone."

"About what?"

"About the priest," Frank told him. "Father Falcone."

"I got nothing to say."

Crowley stepped closer to the door. "This is a police matter
now. If you don't talk to this padre here, I'll have to bring you
down to the station and then you'll have to get a lawyer."

Royburn stepped away, allowing Frank to enter the house.
Frank turned to the sheriff. "Give me some time alone."

Once in the house, Frank could feel the solitude of a dwelling
where one man lived alone: a stillness permeated from every
room. Frank was familiar with that silence.

"Why do you want to know?" Royburn asked.

"I have reason to believe Father Falcone did not die in an accident. I have reason to believe that he took his own life." Frank

looked out the window facing the lake. It afforded a great view of the lake and the hills beyond, and the mountains beyond that. Though the lake was aglow with sunlight, Frank could picture it under a cloudy sky. Nothing on that lake could hide from the view.

"Did you see him that day in the boat? Were you home?"

"Yes."

"What did you see?"

"I saw the priest take the boat out. I saw him row it to the middle of the lake like he always did. I watched him like I always did when I was home."

"Did you see anything else?"

"I saw the storm coming. It came down from the hills. But that was later."

"What happened before that?"

"I saw him stand. He then took off his shoes. I saw him in that white jacket he wore. I saw him look over the side. I saw him . . ."

"You saw him what?"

"I saw him stand at the bow. I saw him stand there and look up at the hills. Then I saw him jump into the water," Royburn said.

"You saw him go in for a swim?"

"No, I saw him step out of the boat and push away from it. I saw him jump into the lake like a man who knows he ain't comin' back."

"What else did you see?"

"I saw him go under."

"You did?"

"I saw him drown. It happened quick. Nothing I could do."

"Why didn't you tell anyone you saw this?"

Royburn talked slowly. "I knew it wasn't what they wanted to hear. And anyway, you're the first person who's asked."

Frank looked back at the lake.

"There ain't no saints out there. Now you have to live with what you know, don't you?"

Frank couldn't answer.

"It pains me to know what I do. I never asked nothing of God and He never did anything but take from me. But still, I'm sorry that I have to share what I know. I was hoping I'd die with it. Until you came to this town. Then I knew you'd find out. In a way, I wanted you to come here."

Frank thanked Royburn, and left the house.

Back in the car on the way back into town, Crowley looked concerned. "I'll have to bring Royburn in and question him officially. I'll tell you this, Father, there ain't nobody in this town who is going to want to hear this. God save this town."

Frank went back to the rectory and packed. Father Hutton found him standing over his suitcase. He told Father Hutton what he had discovered.

There was a long silence. "Are you sure?" Father Hutton asked. He was pale.

"I read his journals."

"I feel so empty inside," Hutton said.

"That is not the Church's concern." Frank had to hide behind something. He felt his heart sink, his breath being taken away. He needed to turn away. He had to survive. "I'm going back to New York to finish my report."

"What about our people? What about the parish?"

"I came here for the truth and that's what I'm leaving with," Frank told him.

"You're abandoning us?" Father Hutton asked.

Frank said nothing and left. He drove back to the city feeling like a coward. But he had to escape. Everything he had believed in had been shattered. He wondered if any of it could ever become real again.

Frank drove to the university to see his friend, Father Sam Corey.

The expansive Saint John's University campus lay between Utopia Parkway and Union Turnpike. He left his car on the street and walked onto the campus, looking for Bent Hall. He took the elevator to the top floor, where he found the entrance to a lecture room large enough for nearly a hundred students. The seats sloped down to the floor, where the lecturer stood looking upwards at his students.

In the center of the room, with thick blond hair, bright blue eyes, and a winning all-American smile, was Sam Corey. Just twenty-seven, he had a certain aura about him. He exuded charm, warmth, piety, and exuberance: a most charismatic priest.

He was just ending his lecture. "Finish reading chapter four and have a good weekend. Being a good Catholic doesn't mean you have to be a sanctimonious bore. Remember Saint Augustine. He had several torrid affairs before he became a priest at the age of forty-two. The night he took his vows he found himself in deep anguish and prayed: 'Make me chaste, oh Lord, but not just yet!'"

The students laughed as Corey dismissed them. As he did, he noticed Frank standing at the top of the room. Corey was silent for a long moment. Frank turned away and walked outside.

Corey was quickly surrounded by students of both sexes. Some of the young women were very pretty and Corey, handsome and charming in his white collar, must have seemed an anomaly to them.

Frank waited outside in the bright sunlight, feeling the tranquility of the campus. He missed it terribly but he no longer felt he could teach. He didn't have the passion for the subject matter anymore.

Corey stepped out of Bent Hall and walked right up to Frank. "Hello, Sam."

"'Hello, Sam'? That's all I get after a year of absolutely nothing?"

"I needed to get away."

"You didn't return one phone call. I left you a dozen messages."

"I cut everyone off," Frank told him. "The archdiocese didn't even know where I was."

"I would have expected more from you," Corey said.

"And you were right to do that. You, of all people, I should have called. But I just wasn't up to it, Sam. Believe me."

"I was worried."

"I know," Frank answered.

"You look pretty good."

"Thanks. You look great up there. Your students love you," Frank smiled.

"I wish I knew you were coming. I have another class at Fordham in twenty minutes."

"It's fine. I'll walk you to your car," Frank said as the two men headed to the parking lot.

"What brings you back to the fold?" Corey asked.

"The archdiocese. They have another soul for me to examine. Right here. At Saint Stanislaus."

"Take a pass," Corey told him.

"I told Cahill I'd do a preliminary," Frank said. They walked into the parking lot, and Corey gestured to Frank that the car was at the other end.

"Have you been to the parish yet?" Corey asked.

"I just met the pastor. He's convinced a piece of heaven has landed in his schoolyard."

"That's a lovely thought for him," Corey smiled.

"People want to believe so badly that they're not alone in the universe. They look everywhere for signs: a cloud formation is the Hand of God! A ray of afternoon sunlight on a window is the face of the Virgin Mary!"

"And you have to tell them what it really is," Corey said.

Frank nodded slowly. "I'm the miracle-killer."

Corey could see the look in Frank's eyes. When he walked, he walked looking down.

"In the Middle Ages," Frank said, "they drove stakes through the hearts of those who killed themselves. Bodies were mutilated and the Church was allowed to confiscate goods and lands belonging to suicides," Frank continued. "The Church feared despair so much they ripped out the hearts of the dead who they suspected of having committed suicide."

Corey said seriously, "We've come a long way from that."

Frank stopped and looked at Corey. "This pastor asked me to say Mass."

"If you're not in state of grace you'll be putting your immortal soul in jeopardy," Corey replied.

"I know."

"Do you want me to hear your confession?"

Frank walked on. "Bless me, Father, it has been two years since my last confession. I'm lost in the wilderness, amen? I don't think so, Sam."

Corey looked serious. "Don't abandon Him yet."

"You're a dying breed: a priest who took the vows to serve his God," Frank said sarcastically.

"So, I hear," Sam smiled. "But don't forget I had an excellent teacher."

Frank stopped again and turned to Corey. His eyes suddenly came alive. "I'll need your help."

"You'll need the blood analyzed," Corey smiled. "I have a friend right here on campus who runs the lab."

"Good. The statue only cries when it rains. I don't know how long we'll have to wait." Frank looked up at the beautiful blue sky.

"Not long," Corey answered. "Don't you feel that?"

"Feel what?"

"It's going to rain tonight." Corey smiled again, this time it was a wide, infectious smile. "Life is a miracle, Frank! Nature, the wind in your hair! The sunshine! Stop hiding in a labyrinth with your religious journals. A priest should be with the people, with nature, with upheaval!" Corey stopped and took out his keys as he stepped over to a candy-red Corvette.

"That's yours?" Frank asked, surprised.

"I'm a priest for the nineties," Corey kidded. "I love being a Vencentian: no vow of poverty."

"Just be careful," Frank said.

Corey nodded to a Saint Christopher's medal he had hanging on the rearview mirror. "For good luck." He opened the driver's door. "Do you know what the first thing you told me was when I was studying with you in the seminary? You said there are no perfect priests."

"That's all I ever wanted to be." Frank paused for a long moment.

A wave of understanding washed over Corey. "Remember what Chesterson said, 'The strange thing about miracles is that they do happen.'" He got into the car. "And remember Augustine's advice, 'Doubt is a part of faith.'"

"I know," Frank joined in. "He also said we should always remember that one thief was saved and that we should never presume that the other thief was damned."

Corey smiled. "I like that. Thanks for reminding me of it. I'll use it for class next week."

"Sam?"

"What, Frank?"

"I want it to be a miracle."

Corey nodded then drove away.

Chapter 4

Frank went back to the rectory to have dinner. When he saw them all sitting there at the large wooden table in the dining room staring up at him with wide-open eyes and happy smiles, he wanted to turn and run. He had a headache and all he wanted to do was go back to bed.

But he was also hungry and his whole attitude changed when Kinnely placed a good bottle of Italian wine on the table. After three quick glasses Frank felt warm inside and did his best to allow the other priests at Saint Stanislaus to offer their homage.

The dinner guests were the priests from the parish. Father Paulino was nearly the same age as Father Kinnely but was darker skinned and wore his hair short and slicked back. His face was round, with a large mouth and brown eyes. He had a habit of looking at you directly most of the time, usually with good reason. Frank found out later that Father Paulino was blind in one eye. He was also much shorter than both Fathers Kinnely and Stacey.

Father Stacey was the thinnest in the group and his clothing looked ironed. His jaw was square and his face clean shaven. His eyes were a gray color with eyebrows that were dirty blond, like his graying blond hair. Though in his late forties, he had the jump to his walk that suggested a young man in his twenties. His speech was slow and somewhat dispassionate, the exact opposite of the intense, manic speech of Father Paulino. Father Stacey was also from a family of priests. His uncle was a Franciscan missionary in South America. Frank noticed a few signs of affection between he and Father Paulino. The more wine they drank the more obvious it became.

"You're a celebrity to us," Father Kinnely said with his round face jolly and robust, sipping the wine like a pro.

Throughout dinner, Frank watched the priests. It occurred to him that they must contain an abundance of tolerance to be able to absorb the relentlessness of their jobs. There could be nothing more monotonous than listening day in and day out to the simple, petty difficulties of ordinary people. Parishioners sometimes had exciting dilemmas, but usually trite ones.

"You must be more used to dining with bishops than ordinary priests like us," Father Stacey said with a smile.

"Not recently," Frank grinned, feeling the wine.

"I've always envied the wealthy. It will probably keep me from entering the gates of heaven," Father Kinnely said.

"Helen will get you in," Father Paulino said.

"I guess you all knew Helen Stephenson well?" Frank asked, trying to act interested in the conversation.

"She was a friend to us all," Father Paulino answered.

"And she brought us a miracle," Kinnely said quickly.

"Father Kinnely, for discussion purposes, let's remind ourselves that we live in a world of television, nuclear weapons, satellite communications, prefabricated food, McDonald's, Dunkin' Donuts! If the Lord God wanted to show His Hand to the multitude, I wonder if He would have chosen Queens," Frank said.

"He chose Fátima, and Lourdes," Father Kinnely said with the clear, unaffected voice of a man educated by his own personal culture. "He could have chosen Paris or London!"

"God would choose a humble place because He is changeless, omniscient, and all-powerful," Father Paulino said.

Frank nodded his head in agreement. "Of course He is. But there is a theologian, a priest named George Tracy, who has published a book which questions your point. He speculates about whether the God we pray to is affected by our prayers. If He were, then He would be a God of pure unbounded love, struggling, suffering, achieving with humanity."

"And your argument is?" Father Paulino asked.

"There's a lot more world and a lot more humanity out there, needing His presence, than there is existing on this hill," Frank responded. He then said good night to the priests and went quickly to his room. On his desk he found the petition but barely glanced at it.

He stepped over to the sink, took off his collar, leaned down, and turned on the faucet. A blast of ugly brown water filled with worms and slugs flooded the sink. Frank jumped back. There was an explosion of thunder. Lightning flashed across the sky. Frank rushed over to the window. He looked down on the yard. There were tiny points of light everywhere. From where he stood, Frank could see thousands of people making their way into the schoolyard clutching flashlights under their umbrellas.

"Father Moore!" shouted Father Paulino from below. Frank saw him in the crowd below his window. "The rain!" He smiled, his face wet with it.

"Get under an umbrella, Alfred!" Father Stacey yelled at the drenched priest.

Frank put on his pants, shirt, and collar, and with his coat thrown over his back, raced down the stairs and out into the schoolyard. Everyone was facing the statue. At the front of the crowd was Father Kinnely, down on his knees with his head bowed in prayer.

Frank looked at the statue. It stood bathed in light from the dozen or more flashlights the people held up to it. With its arms outstretched and its face aglow from the light, it took on dramatic proportions in the rain.

And then there was the blood. Frank could see the dark liquid flow freely from the face of the statue. He pushed his way through the crowd, seeing how the crowd parted when they saw his priest's collar.

"Bless us, bless us!" the old and young demanded alike as Frank walked closer to the statue. He waved his hand in blessing as he passed them, and when he reached Father Kinnely and Father Paulino, he looked up into the rain.

"Her tears!" Father Paulino said, his voice cracking with emotion as he stepped over to Frank.

Frank quickly took his clean handkerchief from his pocket and held out his hand, allowing the dark liquid to fall into the white cloth. It was thin and wet like the rainwater, and in the darkness it looked like wine. Frank folded up the handkerchief and carefully placed it in his breast pocket. He then looked around and saw that many of the faithful, the sick, the dying and the healthy, had bottles, cups, and glasses in their hands. Though the tears of blood were so small, the people were still fighting their way to the statue to see if they could get a portion of the blessed blood to take home with them. The crowd slowly edged forward. Frank could feel the tenseness in their movements. They all wanted to be at the statue's feet and collect the precious tiny drops of blood.

Frank stepped back and looked up again at the statue. Nearly five feet high, it was right below a window. It was gray and tarnished and weather-worn. Frank had a clear view of the statue's features in the glow from the flashlights, and could see the soft lips, cheekbones, and eyes. Long hair under the veil fell to both sides of Mary's face, and her long slender arms reached down as her open hands, palms up, pointed to a small globe at her feet.

Frank could also see where the dark liquid was coming from. The best he could make out was that it was flowing, with the rain, from the statue's eyes. From that part of its face, it ran down her breasts and then divided into three streams—two running down her arms and one down her thighs and onto her feet. Some red flowed off freely to the small globe.

"Father Moore," Frank heard. He turned to Father Kinnely, who was now standing. "I knew Helen wouldn't disappoint us," he said, smiling.

Frank turned to the crowd of parishioners. In the dark, he could see their eyes nearly ablaze with belief. Like the faces he had seen at Willow Lake. Faces old and aging and faces young and innocent. He saw an old man painfully raise his hand, deformed by some horrible disease, as he prayed to the statue. He saw a woman on her knees look up to the Virgin and remove a veil from her face, revealing an awful scar that looked like it had been suffered in an accident. In the bright sunlight, or like now, in the dark of night, the believers stood with eyes upraised. Frank watched them with his own heartfelt wonder, though there was no proof to them that the statue of the Virgin was crying as a human being cries. Though there was no proof, they believed the blood cried was for them and for their salvation.

With his hair wet from the steady rain, Frank left the school-yard, desperate for the shelter of his room. Once inside it, he sat in the dark. He felt terror as he had never felt before. He sat at the edge of the bed with his hair wet and his clothes dripping water. He felt the wetness of his pants legs, his shirt, and the water running down the side of his face but still, he couldn't move.

It was happening again. The people, like children, praying in the rain. Praying, hoping, needing a miracle. Frank couldn't stand it anymore. He couldn't stand their weaknesses. He couldn't pity them anymore. He only had enough pity for himself.

The next morning Frank had breakfast with the other priests.

"We're sorry," Father Paulino said.

"We've had the pipes checked a dozen times. No one can find a reason for it," Father Stacey chimed in. "We think it's some paranormal thing."

Father Kinnely said nothing, but his face revealed a gravity Frank hadn't seen before. "It's happened before?" Frank asked.

The priests looked to each other, then turned to Frank. "Right before the Virgin cries," Father Paulino replied.

"Are there any other odd happenings I should be aware of?" Frank asked. "Besides the man Father Kinnely saw in the hallway?"

Father Stacey nodded. "The cemetery."

Frank noticed that Father Paulino and Father Kinnely looked uneasily at Father Stacey when he spoke. "What about it?" Frank asked.

"Not long after the rain, we find graves are dug up. Tombstones are overturned and even small animals are found decapitated," Stacey said.

"Satanic rituals?" Frank asked.

"That's what the police have told us," Father Paulino answered.

"And there are the rapes," Father Kinnely said.

"Rapes?" Frank asked.

Father Kinnely looked at Paulino and Stacey, then at Frank. "Since the first of October each year there has been at least one woman raped in the parish each of the last ten years."

Frank looked around the room. Each priest, including himself, was wearing his black cassock and slacks. "Do you have any newspaper articles, any reports of the events?"

"We've saved everything," Father Kinnely said.

Back in his room, Frank called the archdiocese. "It's Frank Moore, Charles," he said when he heard Cahill's voice. "I want to see you this afternoon."

Frank stood on the other side of Cahill's desk realizing for the first time how small the man looked in the large room. "So, you believe it warrants further investigation?" Cahill said, looking up at Frank. John Beliar stood on the other side of the desk, to Frank's left.

"For the moment," Frank answered.

"Frank, since this 'event,' our office has been inundated with petitions for sainthood. There are 980 million Catholics in the world and no doubt every one of them would like a bona fide miracle in his backyard," Cahill said with a grin.

"As I recall, the Church's foundation was built on miracles: the loaves and fishes, the resurrection."

Beliar spoke up. "That was nearly two thousand years ago. The Church has since been struggling to get out of the dark ages."

Cahill stood up. "We're afraid that pastor out there is making a mockery of the process," he said, then looked at Frank directly.

"Maybe he is. But maybe like Augustine he believes the ends justify the means."

"Don't hide behind rhetoric!" Cahill said loudly.

"That wasn't my intention."

"Then what is your intention? Do you want the Church to do pagan rituals next? Perhaps we should sacrifice some virgins or firstborns? Do you think it was superstition that helped Pope Paul destroy the Communist Party in Poland? The Church has real power, Frank. Power based on fact, muscle, diligence." He stopped himself. He felt that he had said enough.

"I don't need a lecture on theology or Church politics," Frank said sharply.

Cahill decided to change his tack. "What makes this event different than Willow Lake?" he asked.

"*Opus contra naturam*," Frank answered.

"'Sometimes a deviation from the usual is a revelation of the truth,'" Cahill translated.

"I was there. I saw the tears," Frank said, and the room was quiet.

Cahill looked at Frank, then Beliar. "All right. All right. Let's see it your way for now. Push on. You have my full support. And remember this. This year marks the thirtieth anniversary of the Second Vatican Council. Also, Pope Paul had decreed 1975 as International Woman's Year and now we have a twentieth anniversary of that! There are some important clergymen in Rome who believe that there is no coincidence that the person you are investigating was a woman," Cahill said.

"This is also the thirtieth anniversary of the canonization of Mother Elizabeth Seton, the first native-born American saint. Also a woman," Frank added.

"Precisely," Cahill replied.

"And there's one more thing," Beliar chimed in with his soft, melodious voice. "This Helen Stephenson was very vocal about women participating in the vows of the priesthood."

"I see," Frank said.

"So, it is a very delicate matter," Cahill said, his voice cool and detached.

Frank still wasn't sure that everything had been brought to light. He thanked Cahill for his confidence and turned to walk to the door.

"Oh, Frank, the annual Bishop's Dinner is at the Plaza this Saturday night. I'd like to see you there. And bring this young protégé of yours. I'd like to meet him," Cahill said.

"It's a dressy affair if I remember correctly," Frank said.

Cahill grinned. "We're priests. Be humble. Dress down. Oh, and I may ask you to say a few words. If I remember correctly, you were a wonderful dinner speaker. So be prepared."

Frank was dismissed and left Cahill's office. Walking down the corridor toward the elevator, he found Beliar suddenly behind him. "You think my conclusion is wrong, don't you?" he asked him.

"I admire your enthusiasm," Beliar said discreetly.

"But you distrust my judgment."

"I would never suggest that. But I do believe we're in danger of looking foolish no matter what the outcome. Our reputation is treading on thin ice with this case."

"And we can't walk on water. Can we?" Frank said.

Beliar smiled to himself as they continued walking. "I'd rather not mix metaphors with you. I'd lose."

Frank stopped. "John, why didn't you get this assignment?"

"I asked Charles not to consider me. In fact, I suggested you right from the beginning," Beliar told him.

The elevator door opened and Frank stepped in.

Before he went back to Saint Stan's, Frank went to a local hardware store and bought a small flashlight. When he did return to the rectory, he found the door to the cellar and went down into the darkness.

Once in the cellar, he looked around for the hot water pump and the large water pipes that ran through the rectory. He thought to himself how easily one could pollute the running hot water.

Back in his room, he took a nap.

Chapter 5

Upon waking, Frank went down to the kitchen for a cup of coffee. It was nearly three-thirty. Kinnely had just finished his late lunch and was sitting at the table when Frank entered.

"Usually after this happens I don't sleep for a few days," Father Kinnely told Frank, his eyes still ablaze from the experience of the night before.

"I've decided to investigate," Frank told him.

Father Kinnely nodded his head. "Thank God."

"You know the procedure. The petitioner will pay for all expenses concerning the investigation. Once I decide to bring the case to Rome then my office, in my name, will take over the expenses incurred."

"I understand."

Frank poured himself a cup of coffee. "I see that you've included Helen Stephenson's birth certificate in the petition as well as the schools and churches she attended." Without another word, Frank went back to his room, picked up the file and his own notebook, then got into his car and drove away.

Frank drove to Maria Katowski's address. The woman who answered the door was dressed in a dull green housecoat. Her hair was long and prematurely gray. Though she was a plain-looking woman, Frank could see that she looked older than her years. "I'm Father Moore. I'm looking for Maria Katowski," he said.

The woman was startled to see a priest at her door. "I'm her mother," she said awkwardly, then asked Frank into the house. She quickly pushed her hair back over her ear, trying her best to look presentable to the priest. "Please excuse me. I was about to do some cleaning today," she said to Frank.

The apartment was a railroad type and it looked like it hadn't been painted in years. Everything in the three rooms looked worn, like the look on Maria's mother's face.

"Is your daughter at home?" Frank asked.

"Why are you here, Father?"

"There has been a petition of the Ordinary Process of Canonization for Helen Stephenson. That petition was set forth by Father Kinnely, the pastor of Saint Stanislaus parish. Your daughter's name appeared on the petition concerning a miracle that occurred to her because of direct intervention by Helen Stephenson." Frank saw pain in the woman's deep blue eyes as he spoke to her.

"It is a miracle, Father!"

"Mrs. Katowski, I may need firsthand testimony from your daughter. Does she still live here with you?"

"No."

"Is she living with her father?"

Mrs. Katowski's eyes betrayed no emotion. "I haven't seen him in eleven years. Neither has she."

Frank sensed the uneasiness in the woman's voice.

"Bless my house, Father," she asked.

Frank glanced around the tired, empty, lonely apartment muttering phrases half remembered as he blessed the house.

"Bless my daughter," she asked.

"Where is she, Mrs. Katowski?"

"Bless her soul, Father," Mrs. Katowski said, getting to her knees.

"Mrs. Katowski."

"Bless me and forgive me for all my sins, Father," Mrs. Katowski begged. She even reached up for his hand as if to coax a blessing from him.

Frank looked at the woman kneeling before him and wanted to hold her, comfort her, release her from the tremendous pain he saw in her eyes, but all he could do was raise his hand and pretend to douse her with a spiritual remedy.

Mrs. Katowski bowed her head, accepted the blessing, then spoke softly. "She ran away."

"When?"

"Last year. She turned seventeen and she ran away. She said she hated me, Father. She said she hated everything about me and the life I gave her."

Mrs. Katowski did not see the blank look in Frank's eyes. "Does she call? Have you seen her?" Frank asked.

"In the park. With the others. She stays down there. I tried to get her back. I asked her to forgive me. She has a boyfriend. He's been in jail. He's older than her. People in the neighborhood tell me that she does drugs. That's what the kids in the park do. All those drugs. The police come once in a while to chase them but they keep coming back. When she sees me coming, her boyfriend stops me. I'm her mother! He stops and threatens me! I love my daughter, Father! I love her!" Mrs. Katowski shouted. Frank nodded, muttered that he understood, then left the house as quickly as possible.

Back in his car, Frank sat behind the wheel before he decided to see the doctor mentioned in the file on Maria Katowski that Father Kinnely had given him. He drove past the park, only a few blocks from the Katowski apartment, but he saw no one there, so he drove on.

Dr. Meyers had his small, neighborhood office on Grand Avenue, which was the business section of Maspeth. Frank placed Maria Katowski's file on the doctor's desk, then explained why he was there.

"Sure, I remember that little girl," the thin, gray-haired doctor said.

"You diagnosed her as having lupus?"

"Certainly did. Here," he went on, "you got her blood test right here in your file."

"Did you treat her?"

"I didn't have to."

"Why not?"

"She cured herself."

Frank watched as the noticeably fragile doctor fidgeted behind his large wooden desk.

"She came in with her mother after a fainting spell one morning. Must have been a good ten years ago, yeah, there it is in the file. The poor girl looked pale and near exhaustion. I ran some blood tests, the works. A few days later, I think it was, I got the tests back but I was busy and by the time I read them I was frantic. Called the girl's mother right away. They were living in the neighborhood, so they came here in a few minutes. I sat them both down and told them that I was going to get the little girl into Booth Memorial and I already had a bed waiting." The doctor stopped.

"Yes?"

The doctor looked at Frank with a faraway look in his eyes. "Oddest thing, you know. As soon as she walked in she had a big smile and everything about her looked so healthy. I saw this as soon as she walked in. She had such color in her face."

"What did you do?"

"I went ahead and had her checked into the hospital, of course. But I decided to ask them to run some more tests. And the strangest thing! She was fit as a dollar bill, like we used to say."

"Was the first test accurate?" Frank asked.

"I checked it. I did. I spoke to the doctors and technicians who ran the tests. I didn't see anything out of the ordinary. It was all done properly."

"What do you think happened?"

The doctor shrugged his shoulders. "She cured herself."

"Is that possible?" Frank asked.

"I didn't cure her," the doctor said.

"Have you ever seen anything like it in your practice before or after Maria Katowski?" Frank asked the doctor.

The doctor answered quickly, "Nothing as drastic as that little girl."

"It is possible that she cured herself, biologically or medically, then?" Frank asked.

The doctor grinned wisely. "What do we know about anything medically or biologically? Every day these young doctors are finding out things we never dreamed of. Of course it can happen."

"Do you remember anything else about her or her mother?"

The doctor took his time. "I suppose you could say they acted in a religious way."

"How?"

"The little girl spoke about the statue. The one over at that parish on Grand Avenue."

"Saint Stanislaus?" Frank said.

"She touched the statue's tears and her hands glowed. That's what she said. I had seen her just a few days after that happened."

"Did you examine her hands?" Frank asked.

"Of course."

"And?"

"Nothing," the doctor said, matter-of-fact. "But then I wasn't surprised. I'm not a religious man."

"Would you sign a notarized statement concerning everything you just told me? And would you please send me the lab reports?"

"Who is it for?"

"To be used at a tribunal in Rome," Frank told him.

"But I'm Jewish!" the doctor said.

Frank smiled back. "That won't affect the testimony." Dr.

Meyers stood and shook Frank's hand. "Sure. Send me over something to sign and I'll sign it." The doctor led Frank to the door. "You're talking about a miracle, aren't you?"

"Yes."

The doctor rubbed his face and eyes, trying to rub away the tiredness. He thought for a moment, then spoke. "It might have been a miracle." He smiled. "It certainly was unexplainable."

Frank left the doctor's office and drove to Maurice Park. He had to find Maria and talk to her himself. Her firsthand account of the events of that rain-filled October would be of tantamount importance to the tribunal if the process got that far.

Frank parked his car and walked around. Growing up in Queens, he knew teens hung out in the park. Usually where there were benches far from the prying eyes of adults.

Frank saw a small crowd of teens near the handball courts. It was nearly dinnertime and they were hanging out way too early. He figured they had to be the druggies.

He walked across a large, asphalt softball field eyeing one particular young woman with long brown hair. There was a glow about her. Perhaps it was the setting sun. There was an aura about her and he found himself drawn inexorably toward it.

She didn't see him coming. Four teens stepped up from behind their bench and faced Frank.

"What's your problem?"

Two white kids, one black kid, and one Latino. They looked stoned, angry, threatening.

"I don't have a problem," Frank said. "I'm looking for Maria Katowksi. I'm Father Frank Moore."

"He's a priest," the Latino kid said.

"Who gives a shit," the white kid said loudly.

Frank was trying to get the attention of the young woman he thought might be Maria when he saw the white flash of a knife. He froze.

"We's the Master Race from Bayside," the black kid spoke up.

"That's right. And nobody messes with our women, man," the second white kid said.

"He's a priest, man, he can't do women," the first white kid drawled.

Frank watched as they all walked toward him from different angles. He saw a razor blade in the black kid's hand and the Latino kid had something else in his. Frank also spotted a cross around the Latino kid's neck. The white kid noticed Frank looking at the cross. "I guess the Lord's gonna have to forgive us, huh?" the white kid grinned.

Frank sensed evil. Not in the young teens' baby faces, and not in what they said or how they menaced him, but in the air itself in the park around them. It was intangible. As if there were a Satan and he had left just his shadow in the park and nothing else. As if he had left his voice, like an echo, or perhaps he had only left a thought in their minds. "Destroy what isn't yours." That was a powerful idea. And a powerful one for those who had nothing.

Frank stepped back, his own gold crucifix dangling from his neck. He was ready to fight, but they were a pack, and though he was bigger and stronger, he knew they could hurt him if he took them all on. "I didn't come here for a problem, but if that's what you want, you'll get it. I won't get all of you and you'll get me bad, but at least one of you is going to the hospital. So come on!" Frank shouted.

They didn't move. Frank looked at each of them full in the face, but none moved forward. Frank said nothing. They all seemed transfixed. It was as though time and motion just came to a dead stop. They were looking at him but their eyes were blank. Dead. Or was it fear he saw? "I said, come on!"

"Fuck you, man!" the first white teen said.

"Come a little closer," Frank told him. "I'm standing right here."

The first white teen stopped. The black teen stepped up to him. "What's up?"

"Nothin'," the white teen said. He lowered his knife.

"You okay?"

"Yeah, it's him, man. He's freaky," he answered.

The Latino teen spoke up. "Forget it, Jimmy," he said.

Seizing on the break in the tension, Frank took a step back and slowly walked away from them. As he did, he looked around for Maria, but she was gone.

"Weird," the black teen uttered as the four boys watched Frank walk across the asphalt ball field and back to his car.

❖   ❖   ❖

Frank immediately returned to the rectory. He was angry at what happened in the park and frustrated at the direction his investigation was taking.

He sought out Kinnely. Father Stacey told him that he was in the church. Frank found Father Kinnely at the altar, just closing the tabernacle.

"Father Kinnely?"

The two priests stood in the middle of the large, empty church. Its size was exaggerated by the stillness. Frank felt uncomfortable in the midst of it.

"Can I see Sister Alice now?"

"I'll get her."

Frank stepped in front of the older priest. "I saw Mrs. Katowski. Her daughter ran away. Did you know that?"

"Yes."

"Why isn't it in the petition?"

"I didn't think it was important," Father Kinnely said.

"Her mother says she has been seen in the park."

"She has?"

"Did you know that?"

Father Kinnely closed his lips tightly. He turned away from Frank. "Yes. She runs with this terrible gang. A bunch of tough kids. Dangerous, too."

"Why didn't you tell me?" As Frank spoke, he saw Father Paulino in the corner of his eye step out of the many shadows in the dimly lit church.

"Helen saved Maria! The little girl would have died!" Kinnely cried, nearly hysterical.

"What are you hiding?" Frank asked him.

"Nothing," Kinnely answered, then walked away.

"Father!" Frank called after him. But just as did, Father Paulino stepped up to him.

"Forgive him."

"For what?" Frank asked.

"For keeping certain things from you."

"Father Paulino, I cannot make an accurate investigation if relevant facts are deliberately withheld. What's going on?"

Father Paulino took Frank gently by the arm and led him away from the altar. "He feels that he failed Helen. You see, Maria Katowski became addicted to drugs and, worse, we learned that about a month ago she was arrested for prostitution. She was just released. Does this discount the petition?" Father Paulino asked.

"The tribunal is much like a court of civil law here. They weigh facts, not assumptions. Some saints had families. Some saints had sex throughout their lives, some saints didn't. I'm not looking for 'good' or 'bad' facts, just the truth."

"I respect your desire to find the truth," Father Paulino said, handing Frank a folder. "These are all the newspaper articles you wanted," he said.

Frank glanced through the documents, noticing how the headlines were about how the cemetery had been rocked by vandalism which some saw as a sort of reaction to the "miracle."

Frank thanked Father Paulino and went on his way.

Sister Alice was round-faced with white, unblemished skin. Her smile was infectious, like a little schoolgirl's. Frank met her in the parlor of the convent and was served tea and cookies by other nuns. It was already after dinner. Frank hadn't eaten yet, and devoured the cookies.

The convent was much different from the rectory. Where the rectory windows nearly always had their shades drawn, the convent was flooded with light. Lace curtains hung from each window exposing the car-lined street, where large maple trees cast long shadows.

Frank also noticed how brightly painted this room was. The parlor was a light blue with yellow trim. The furniture, though modest, was perky, with little knickknacks placed on wall shelves and end tables. Frank sat on a comfortable but plainly decorated dark blue couch flanked by twin ceramic lamps.

"Sister, what did you know of Helen Stephenson?" Frank asked.

Sister Alice's face lost its mask of innocence. Suddenly, the quiet, unassuming nun looked impatient. "Not very much." She poured herself more tea. "She ran the children's day care center we had. She had helped us set up a shelter for the homeless in our parish. She was a dedicated woman." Sister Alice noticed that the sun had come out again. "It was, as they say, 'her show,' Father."

"It sounds like Helen Stephenson was a strong individual. They say Mother Cabrini was a forceful woman." Frank smiled.

"I imagine she was," Sister Alice responded. "She founded fifty convents in eight different countries, bringing over a thousand sisters into our Church. That's not counting all the schools and hospitals she founded. She also founded the Missionaries of the Sacred Heart. We are the order of Saint Joseph, in case you wondered," Sister Alice told Frank.

"Thank you." Frank smiled, looking over the sister's habit. It consisted of a black blouse and a long black gown which reached down to her ankles. She wore a white band across her forehead with a black veil which fell down behind her neck, touching her shoulders. On her feet she wore simple black Victorian boots with a small heel. A rosary with wooden beads was worn as a belt. Frank thought how bothersome it must be during the warm days of summer. Vatican II had given religious orders the option to make their dress code more contemporary and less severe, but the Sisters of Saint Joseph who taught at Saint Stanislaus had continued to resist change.

"Are there any other questions I can help you with?" she asked.

"Just one more. Helen Stephenson lived here in the convent. Why?" Frank asked, sharply.

"Father Kinnely thought it best she lived close to where all her work was. She received no pay for her efforts, so we gave her room and board," Sister Alice replied.

"Thank you, Sister, you've been very helpful," Frank said.

Sister Alice gave Frank a long look then bowed her head. "You have a difficult task ahead of you. I pray that you accomplish it without too much suffering," she said.

Frank left the convent and was about to go back into the rectory, when he saw the side entrance to the church. An impulse sent him inside.

It was dark in the church, but the October moon was out early and it filled the large building with streaks of white light.

Frank knelt at the rail, looking up at the altar before him. He felt small in the presence of so much darkness, and so much emptiness. The church had been closed for hours and a cold draft brought the chill of the night into the place. The pews, lined up row after row, looked strange without anyone kneeling in them. Frank smelled the melting wax from burning candles and the lingering odor of incense.

"*Credo quia impossible est,*" Frank said out loud. "I believe because it is impossible," he repeated. Just words, however. Clever words. What'd they have to do with faith? With God? With his life, to be exact. Was that what all this was about, finding a reason for his life? To Frank, his life looked like it was spread out toward the horizon without any purpose: there was nothing for him to believe in, or accomplish, and there was no one he loved. God was something of the past: a childhood memory.

Frank stood and bowed his head. His loneliness tore through him like an ax. He felt it cutting him in two. He thought about Falcone. A failed man. A loser like himself. The difference was that Falcone couldn't fool himself anymore. He couldn't walk through the day pretending that when he faced his final hour he would think of something smart to say that would negate all the years of wasted motion, wasted tears, wasted thoughts and actions.

Frank lifted his head and rubbed his eyes. He thought of Father Falcone once again. This time he recalled to memory the afternoon he went to the lake with Lang, the sheriff's deputy. It was the smell of the church that brought him back: the smell of ritual, the smell of death.

Officer Lang was in his early twenties and had only been a deputy for a year and a month when he found Father Falcone's body floating in the lake.

"Found it right there," he said, pointing to a shaded section of the lake nearly one hundred yards from the road. Lang was dressed in a light brown uniform and beige hat. He wore a large .357 on a clean-looking belt and holster.

Frank walked through some tall grass, following the deputy until they reached the body of still water where Father Falcone had been found.

"He was facedown, you know? I noticed real fast because of the flies. Must have been hundreds, maybe thousands buzzin' around the shade right over him," Lang said.

Frank walked closer to the dark, murky water. The deputy stopped walking and stood on the only dry-looking patch of ground in the shade. Frank had been given a pair of boots for the swamp by the county sheriff's office and was glad he'd worn them.

"He must have been there in the spot for a week or more. And we got a lot of fish in this here lake, you know. That's why I wasn't too anxious to turn him over. But when I saw that ring on his finger, I knew that was him. We all knew that ring."

"You did?"

"Sure. Whenever we received the Eucharist at Mass, we would see it on his finger," Lang said.

"Of course," Frank said.

"The whole town knew that ring," Lang said.

Frank recalled the police photograph which showed Father Falcone's face just about eaten away by the fish. The ears, the eyes, the lips were the first to go. The only dead person he had ever seen before Falcone was his own father. His mother had died when he was just a kid in school. He never saw the body; only at the wake did he get a final glimpse. But he was fifteen then. He had as much of a relationship with his mother as he would have had with a friendly aunt. He had his friends in school and his great ideas about the world and his place in it back then. He also had a stronger, more innocent idea about God. He truly believed that when his mother died she was going to heaven.

When his father died, Frank had administered the last rites. Suddenly, he remembered his father, unconscious for several hours before taking his final breath. Alone in the room, Frank could hear the gasp and then the silence. The head tilting down, the eyes already closed, and suddenly the body, always so quick and energetic, becoming stone. After administering the sacrament, Frank had leaned down and kissed his father's face. But he was lifeless already and the skin felt like rock; and when he touched his father's thin shoulders in a gesture of good-bye, he remembered how heavy to the touch they felt. In death, bodies didn't fly up to heaven as the Renaissance painters portrayed them, on the contrary: they stuck to the earth like boulders.

"And the boat?" Frank asked.

"The rowboat we found on the south shore in about six feet of water."

Frank looked over the cool, brightly lit lake. "The water always so calm?" Frank said.

"Calm now, padre, but you should see it when we get one of those mean squalls in the summertime! The waves reach up about six feet or more!"

Frank could see Father Falcone taking the boat out early that evening. He was a strong man and Frank could picture him rowing across the lake, and how when he got to the middle the world around him erupted with fierce winds and rains.

"A squall like that could last a few hours or a few minutes!"

Frank looked around the lake. Outside of Royburn's, there wasn't a house in sight. "Was there a storm warning that day?"

"Nope. It was just one of those things."

Frank followed the deputy back to the car, which was parked near the dock. Frank took a last look at Royburn's house. "Anybody ever talk to Mr. Royburn? You know, ask him if he saw anything?"

"Nobody that I could think of," Lang answered.

Frank then nodded and got into the car. He was planning to go back to Falcone's room and rummage through his things. He was hoping to find a diary or journal of some kind.

Frank remembered all this as he stood up in the pew, and walked out of the church and back to his room in the rectory. It had been a long day and now all he wanted to do was sleep. But before he went to his room, he went back into the convent and visited Helen Stephenson's room again.

An elderly nun let him in. Telling her where he was going elicited a big smile from her face. Frank then walked up the stairs and into the room.

He put on the light and sat at the desk. He could see a pen, a dictionary, and a small pad—clean and untouched in the center of the desk.

He then opened a drawer. The first one at his right hand was empty. He opened another drawer and found another pen, a date book with nothing written inside, and more pens.

Frank then turned in the chair and looked around the room wondering what it must have felt like to be Helen Stephenson. He tried to put himself in her bones, in her flesh, in her mind. He saw the books on the shelves and knew she was an avid reader. He then got up and went looking for Kinnely.

Frank found Kinnely in his room. Frank had knocked and

Kinnely came to the door. "Who's been in Helen's room?"

"The nuns clean it, but no one else."

"Did she have a family?"

"Her husband died of cancer right before she moved in."

"Children?"

"A daughter. But she was young."

"I want to talk to her."

"I don't know where she is."

"I want her last known whereabouts."

"But we haven't seen her."

"I don't care. I want her last known address on my desk by noon tomorrow," Frank told him before walking out.

Chapter 6

The next morning after breakfast Frank sat at his desk and called information for Roxanna Stephenson's phone number. There was no listing under the address Kinnely had given him. So Frank took the address to the local post office on Grand Avenue and found there had been an address change.

"The last name's been changed," the clerk told him.

Frank went to the address. Now Roxanna Woods, she was renting the first floor of a home on 53rd Avenue. The house was halfway up a winding hill. The street was very pleasant looking, with trees, small front lawns, and a fork in the road right above Roxanna's home, which led to another, shorter hill.

Frank rang the bell and when there was no answer, rang the upstairs bell. A man in his sixties answered the door. Seeing Frank was a priest, he congenially answered his questions. Frank learned that the man, a Mr. Walsh, was Roxanna's landlord. He learned that she had been living there only a few months and had just returned from living somewhere in Rhode Island. Frank also learned that Roxanna worked for a construction company that had a main office only a few blocks away on Maurice Avenue.

At Santora Construction the priest's collar was a big help once again in getting people to respond to his inquiries. Frank was told that Roxanna was the foreman at an electrical job being done on a medical center less than five minutes away on the Long Island Expressway service road.

The medical center was nearly complete and there was a crew laying in the electrical wiring. Frank parked his car and walked up to the side of the building. A young man in a hard hat took notice and asked Frank what he wanted. Frank told him that he was looking for Roxanna Woods and was directed to go into the building. "She's on the second floor," the hard hat told Frank. "But you can't go in without one of these." He tapped his head. "I'll get her for you."

A few minutes later a woman emerged from the building. She was of medium height and was wearing a hard hat, construction boots, and a red vest over her blue work shirt.

She walked over to Frank. "You have to wear a hat," she fairly shouted at him.

"I'm looking for Roxanna Woods," Frank told her.

"That's me. This way," she said. She then turned to another worker. "Jimmy, take over!"

Frank followed her around the back of the building, where she took out a key and opened the door to a shanty. She pushed open the door as Frank followed her in.

Closing the door behind him, Roxanna put on an overhanging lamp and sat behind a small desk. On the desk was a computer. It was clear that the shanty was her on-site office. Maps and blueprints covered the walls.

Roxanna sat and seemed to have a hard time taking her eyes off his collar. He took a long look at her. Her eyes were oval and blue. Her hair was light, like her mother's, and her face was round and pale in complexion, also like her mother's. She looked like she had just turned thirty. There was something hard in her eyes when she at last decided to talk.

"Does this have anything to do with my mother?"

"Yes, in fact. I'm Father Frank Moore," Frank started to say, but was cut off.

"How did you find me?"

"One of your neighbors told me," Frank said.

"Sure, who doesn't trust a priest," Roxanna said sarcastically.

"You're married now?" Frank asked.

"I was married for a long weekend a few years ago. But I decided to keep the name when I got divorced. Why all the questions?"

"There's been a petition for your mother's canonization and I've been assigned postulator."

"My mother, a saint? That's a good one," Roxanna said.

Frank could hear the sarcasm in her voice, which threw him again for a moment. "That is what the process is all about—to answer that question."

"I don't think I can do anything for you."

"But you are her only surviving relative."

"What do you want from me?" Roxanna asked quickly.

"I need to find out if your mother had any journals or if she kept a diary or anything like that."

Roxanna interrupted him. "Look, Father, I really don't have the time for this and I really don't care what the Church thinks when it comes to my mother."

Frank tried to analyze the hostility in Roxanna's voice. "Fine. But it is important to the investigation that you answer some questions, if you don't mind?"

"Is there a law that will force me?" she snarled. The hostility had turned to anger.

"Of course not."

"I don't like the Church, or anybody, for that matter, butting into my mother's life, Father Moore," Roxanna said quickly. "Excuse me, if you don't mind. I have plenty of work to do!" She shot another look to Frank that made him want to run out of the room.

But Frank stood his ground. He was very curious about her

behavior. "You look a lot like your mother," Frank said.

"You knew her?" Roxanna asked.

"No. I've only seen a photograph." He tried not to notice that there was a certain sensuality to her full, thick lips. Frank could see how her hair swept along the side of her face. Frank noticed something else about her: there was a tinge of sensitivity to her manner. He couldn't place exactly how it revealed itself, but he had seen it before in others. It was the tiredness in the eyes, the faraway look that overcame a person when they were momentarily alone. Frank could also recognize another trait, a more hidden one, because he had it himself: hysteria that seethed just under the surface. It was a nervousness that hid itself behind the facade of self-control. Even though she was now fighting to maintain her composure, Roxanna Woods was not the threatening woman whom she first appeared to be. She was now someone else entirely.

She stood up and opened the door. "I have to get back to work. Good-bye," she said. She then handed him a hard hat off the rack. "That collar doesn't protect you around here." She put on her own hard hat and walked out of the room, leaving Frank dumbfounded.

Frank quickly drove to Calvary Cemetery, only fifteen minutes away. He had asked Sam Corey to meet him there. Sam had left a message with Father Paulino earlier that he had the results from the lab tests on the blood.

He took the Long Island Expressway service road down to the main entrance of Calvary Cemetery. Father Kinnely had set up a meeting with the gatekeeper for the cemetery. The power of organized religion, Frank thought. The Catholic Church owned the cemetery and employed the cemetery workers.

Frank entered the tall cast-iron gates to the cemetery's entrance, passing a small one-story brick house on the inside of the graveyard. The gatekeeper and his family lived there.

Frank noticed a small bicycle near the back door. He thought how odd it must be to shut your lights off at night and have the last thing you see outside your window be a row of tombstones.

As directed, he drove on toward a small truck. A large-boned man in his late forties, with thin brown hair and a hard, weather-worn face stood in the middle of the road in a dark gray windbreaker and gray overalls.

"Mr. Sandowski?" Frank asked as he got out of the car.

The gatekeeper nodded. "This way," he said. He started to walk, but Frank interrupted with, "I have an associate on his way."

"I don't have all day," Sandowski muttered. He looked annoyed. Just then Corey's sports car pulled in through the gate.

Frank smiled at the gatekeeper to calm him down as Corey jumped out of his car holding a file.

"Hey, Frank," he smiled as he walked over to him. Sandowski turned on his heels without even acknowledging Corey.

"Our guide is a bit impatient," Frank said quietly as he and Corey followed him.

Corey took one look at the gatekeeper, then whispered to Frank, "Dante gets Virgil and we get Herman Munster."

The gatekeeper headed across a narrow walkway which led down a thin row of tombstones. These were all sizes, with different types of lettering and all kinds of names and sayings written on them. As Frank and Corey walked, they looked across the horizon at weather-beaten rows and rows of gravestones.

Corey handed Frank the file. "It's blood, all right," he said.

Frank opened the file as he walked.

"Human blood," Corey finished.

"Type O," Frank read. He then turned to Corey. "Helen Stephenson's blood was type O."

Corey felt a chill run up his spine. He closed the file and, with Frank at his side, caught up to Sandowski, who had disappeared, momentarily, behind several trees.

When Frank and Corey caught up to him, they had passed several rows of mausoleums and trees and reached an abruptly treeless hill. They stopped at the crest.

"Biggest cemetery in the world, some say," Frank said.

Tombstones stretched in all directions through acres of elm, maple, birch, and willow trees. It seemed like a lot of land to give to the dead.

"Over here," Sandowski said. His voice was harsh and low. Frank noticed how his eyes were hooded and his forehead wrinkled as if he had squinted in more rainstorms than a dozen men his age. "That's her grave."

Frank and Corey walked over to a plain white stone at the end of a row. Only the name Helen Stephenson and the birth and death dates were written on it.

"See how the grass grows in nice and green?" the gatekeeper asked. Frank could see how the grass around the stone was golf-course perfect. "But nothing grows here," he said, pointing to the rest of the section. The surrounding grass was dull, burned, nonexistent.

Corey stepped over to Frank and whispered, "He should try a novena or a Vatican-sanctioned rain dance."

Frank fought down a laugh, then followed Sandowski down the hill. "Where are we going now?"

"To the bad stuff," Sandowski answered.

Frank and Corey followed the gatekeeper downhill and stopped abruptly when he did.

Frank saw a small clearing with several freshly dug graves. Mounds of earth were piled a few feet high on top of the grass beside several recently filled holes.

"Here's where it starts," Sandowski said. He stopped walking and pointed to a row of tombstones a few yards further up the hill. Frank and Corey stopped dead in their tracks. Out of a row of eight stones, four had been vandalized. In red lettering, "Mary is a whore!" and "The Virgin sucks cock!" had been sprayed carefully across the soft gray stone and marble. Whoever did the writing apparently wanted it to be read and understood.

Frank felt uneasy looking over the desecrations when he felt Corey touch his shoulder and nod to a particular stone. It read: "Frank Moore is a homo." Frank was stunned.

"That's you, no?" Sandowski asked.

Frank nodded slowly. He felt as if someone had kicked him in the gut. He felt violated and hadn't a clue as to the identity of the violator.

"What else?" Frank asked, dry-mouthed.

"From here to section twenty-one, I counted forty-seven statues busted. You know, people leave statues on the graves. Some are cheap and made of plastic. Some are made of better stuff. Anyway, this morning I counted forty-seven smashed to bits. And that ain't countin' the nine decapitated Christ heads I found. They find a crucifix and then they rip the Christ head off of it. When I heard you were coming I figured I'd wait to fix it all up again. But people started complaining. That's why I was in a hurry. I can't leave this like this." Sandowski shook his head. "What kind of world we livin' in?" he said to Frank.

Frank noticed a large green bag sitting in the middle of the aisle. Sandowski opened it, showing Frank the destroyed statues and smashed crucifixes.

"And the graves?" Corey asked.

"They dug up these two. We just laid them in yesterday. They got to the coffin, then tried smashing that with a shovel," Sandowski said. He then nodded to a shovel leaning against a stone. "You can buy that in any hardware store." He turned to Frank. "And then you got the dead animals."

Frank and Corey followed him to a small slope several rows away. Inside a small circle made of wood were the still stretched-out bodies of a small cat, a rat, and a bird. Their heads had been ripped off and were missing from the circle. Written in red on the side of a large tombstone was, "Frank Moore is the Antichrist."

Reading it made Frank shudder. He stepped up to Sandowski. "A satanic cult?" he asked.

"Yes."

Frank then saw something else written on a stone. "It is impossible to believe."

"What's that from?" Corey asked.

"It's a play on words. The original quote is 'I believe because it is impossible.' Tertullian. Second century. I used it for the title page of my book."

Corey was pale. "Not a place I want to run into Beelzebub. Let's get out of here," he said. The sun seemed anemic and was fading in the distance.

Frank nodded to Sandowski and he quickly led them back to their cars at the gate's entrance. Sandowski told Frank that he was getting in a crew the next morning to clean everything up.

That night Frank sat at his desk staring at the lab report. He was still not sure what it all meant. Later he tossed and turned in bed, fighting to get the images of the cemetery out of his head. Unable to sleep, he went back to his desk to finish a draft of his speech. A copy of his book sat on the bed. He hadn't opened it and didn't want to. He glanced at the quotes on the jacket cover. Reviewers had called the book "the deepest thinking from a theologian since Paul Tillich's 'God Above God.'"

Frank recalled the nights he read Teilhard de Chardin's *The Divine Milieu* and thought how all the grief and loneliness he felt were the gifts of his calling. He believed that all the doubts were drowned out of his mind because he was able to write them down. The thin book in his hand was, at one time, his salvation.

Frank thought of the bottom of the pool he swam in, then thought of what the bottom of the lake must have looked like to Father Falcone. Every bottom of the pool looks like every bottom of every lake: vast, peaceful, and dark.

He crumpled to the floor and knelt at his bed. "I believe because it is impossible," he prayed. He looked up at some imaginary heaven. And nothing.

"I believe because it is impossible," he prayed again. Again he waited, but all he heard was silence in reply.

The next morning, Frank had breakfast alone in the kitchen, then went back to his room, about to work on his speech for the ceremony at the Plaza when he happened to glance out the window. A young woman caught his eye. She was standing alone staring at the statue. Frank knew who she was instantly. He had no idea why he knew it was she, but he did. She was looking at the convent, the window, and then the statue. She ignored everyone else and stood alone, nearly trembling. It was clear she was reliving an intimate personal experience.

Frank ran down the stairs and out into the schoolyard. He walked up behind the girl. "Maria?" Frank asked.

The girl looked over to Frank. She wore sneakers and jeans, as well as a blue-jean jacket. Frank could hardly see her face with the wind blowing her hair across it.

With one hand she moved it away and as soon as she did, he could see there were acne scars on her left cheek, and that her eyes were glazed.

"Huh?" she said. All of her motions were slow and awkward.

"Maria Katowski?" Frank asked, stepping over to her.

Maria looked at Frank's white collar before looking at his face. Frank tried to put a comforting look in his eyes. "My name is Father Frank Moore," he said.

"Are you the priest that's looking for me?"

"Yes, I am," Frank said softly.

Maria looked relieved. "I came here to tell you that you shouldn't be asking for me. Somebody told the people I hang with. They said that they heard you were going to take me away. They told me that they'd kill you—"

"Hold on! I'm not taking you anywhere! And who was going to kill me?" Frank asked.

"My boyfriend. He loves me. I told him that you were only a priest and that they should all leave you alone," Maria said, struggling with her words. "How come you want to talk to me?" she asked quickly.

"I'm investigating the life of a woman that you once knew."

Maria grew attentive. "You mean Mrs. Stephenson?"

Frank nodded to her. "That's who I mean."

"People around here say she's a saint. And she was!" Maria said quickly. She then turned and looked back at the statue. Her long thick hair covered her face again.

"Why do you think she was a saint?"

"She was a good person," Maria answered.

"Why do you say that?" Frank asked.

"She was good to people."

Frank saw how pretty the girl's face really was. When the wind blew the hair away from it, he could see the blue-green eyes still keen and full of youth. The face, though distorted by the slow movements of the jaw, actually looked innocent. "She saved my life."

"I heard."

"She cured me. I had lupus. I was going to die. And after I touched the statue, it bled on my hands and on my face. Helen Stephenson's blood." Maria said it all with complete honesty.

"Her blood?" Frank had to question deeper.

"Who else?" Maria asked.

"The Blessed Virgin's blood?" Frank suggested.

Maria looked distant. "I never thought of that."

"What makes you think it was Helen's blood that cured you?" Frank asked.

Maria looked at Frank. "Don't know. People said it. My mother said it."

"Did you know Mrs. Stephenson at all? Did you talk with her, Maria?"

Maria scratched her nose, lifting her hand slowly to her face. Her baby blue sweater was pulled around her wrist, held tightly by her fingers. "I wanted to know her. She was a nice lady. All the kids liked her. I liked her. I wish my mother was like her."

Frank edged closer to the girl. "You should go see your mother, she misses you." Looking at her, the image of a frightened deer in the woods came in his mind.

"I can't stay long," she said softly, looking over her shoulder to the street beyond the schoolyard.

Frank put his hand out to her. "Want to get up closer?" Maria took his hand and walked toward the statue with him. She took slow-paced, cautious steps. Suddenly, Frank felt as if the whole world had stopped. The morning sun was bright, and though the yard was filled with people, it was as if they were the only two people in the world.

"Do you remember Helen Stephenson's room?"

"Yes."

Frank watched the young girl make her way past the white stone fence, stopping a few feet from the convent. "Do you remember that morning, Maria?"

"I remember the rain and how cold it was. I remember the wind."

The open space of the schoolyard allowed gusts of wind to blow through his hair. "What else do you remember?"

Maria raised her head. Frank couldn't help but notice the dryness of her lips, and the paleness of her complexion.

"I walked around from there," Maria said, pointing at a gate aside the convent, opening to the street. "Then I walked up to Mrs. Stephenson's window."

"What were you looking for?"

Maria shrugged her shoulders. "Nothing. I just wanted to look inside."

"Then what happened?"

"Thunder. Thunder crashed and there was lightning!"

Frank watched her closely. He could see her relive that morning in her memory. He also noticed how high she seemed, either from drugs or self-induced euphoria.

"Then I felt a hand on my shoulder. I was looking at the lightning and I felt it."

"A hand?"

"Like someone touching me," Maria answered.

Frank could see her eyes nearly glowing. He saw that aura about her, the same he had seen when he saw her sitting on the bench, not even knowing who she was. "Then what did you do?" he asked.

"I turned to the Blessed Virgin."

"Go on," Frank said, like a teacher prodding his student.

"I began to pray," Maria said softly.

"To pray?"

"Yes," Maria told him, nearly joyously.

"Whom did you pray to?" Frank could feel Maria tremble when she spoke. She then turned to the statue.

"I prayed to the statue." Maria looked to the concrete replica.

"To the Blessed Virgin?"

"Yes. I prayed to the Virgin and to Mrs. Stephenson."

"You prayed to Mrs. Stephenson?" Frank asked.

"Yes. I prayed to her the night she died and went to heaven. I knew she had gone to heaven so I prayed to her again that day."

"What did you pray for?" Frank had to hear everything.

"I prayed that I would die," Maria said.

"Why?" Frank asked.

"I prayed to die! I prayed to die in my sleep so my father would come home." Maria remembered her father, and suddenly Frank remembered his.

Frank put his arms around her, pulling her close to him. Maria allowed him to hold her. She leaned her face against his shoulder. "I prayed and that's when I saw it. That's when I saw the blood!"

"The blood?"

"The blood dripping down."

Abruptly the wind stopped. There was a sudden eerie silence for a schoolyard packed with people talking and praying. Frank felt the sunlight on his shoulders.

"Where was the blood coming from?"

"From her eyes." Maria's voice was growing smaller.

"And then what did you do?" Frank asked.

"I couldn't move." Maria's eyes closed tightly.

"Yes?" Frank asked, not giving up.

"I saw the blood drip down her face. I saw it fall down her hands."

"And then?"

"I heard a voice."

"A voice?" Frank asked.

"Yes. Like she was talking to me." Maria turned to Frank.

"Who?"

"Mrs. Stephenson," Maria said strongly.

"What did she say?" Frank continued.

"She told me to touch it. To touch the blood."

"So what did you do?"

"I put out my hands," Maria said, reaching out her hands.

"And?" Frank asked.

"The blood fell all over my hands. I felt it on my fingers," Maria said, her voice rising with every moment she relived.

"Then what happened?"

"It fell some more." Maria was feeling the blood run through her fingers.

"Where?"

"On my face!"

"And what did you do?"

"I don't remember."

"Yes, you do," Frank persisted.

"I tasted it!"

"You did?"

"It was sweet and warm," Maria remembered.

"Do you remember what you were thinking, Maria?"

"Yes." Maria grew sad.

Frank edged closer to the fragile figure standing dazed in the bright morning sunlight. "What were you thinking? Please, tell me."

"I was thinking—"

"Yes?"

"That I wanted my father back." Maria looked away from Frank.

"Yes."

"I was thinking how much I missed him being with us."

Frank saw a tear run down the young girl's face. "You must have loved him very much."

"I did."

Maria's sad, round face turned to his.

"I loved him." Maria played absently with her hair. Her fingers twisting long strands.

"I'm sure he knew that."

Maria shook her head. "He never knew how much I loved him."

Frank put his hand on her shoulder. He squeezed it. "It wasn't your fault what happened between your parents."

"It was."

"You can't say that. You can't hurt yourself for something you had nothing to do with."

"He would have stayed with my mother if she didn't have a kid," Maria said angrily.

"Who told you that?" Frank questioned her.

"My mother did! She told me that I ruined her life! She told me that if it wasn't for me, my father would have stayed!"

Frank felt Maria tremble. The sky suddenly closed, as gray clouds appeared. The wind grew cold.

"I wanted to die, Father. I wanted to die."

Frank felt her tears on his fingers as he patted them away from her face. He wanted to protect her from the demons of loss she was carrying with her but he was unsure how.

"We all feel that way sometimes," Frank began.

"I prayed to Mrs. Stephenson to help me. I prayed to her to help me find a way to get my father to come home to me."

"You thought she could help you?"

"Yes." Maria pushed back the hair from her face, stepping away from Frank as she did. "Then I walked to the church. I guess because everybody was there for the Mass for Mrs. Stephenson."

"You still had the blood on your hands and face?" he asked
"Yes."

"People said your hands and face were glowing, shining. Do you remember that?" Frank needed to know.

"I felt so weak. I felt so tired. And I was scared, too."

"Do you remember being in church?" Frank had to help her and himself.

"She was calling me," Maria told him.

"Who?"

"Mrs. Stephenson." Maria tried to imagine the woman she hadn't seen for years.

"Calling you?" Frank asked.

"I heard her."

"From where?" Frank looked around the schoolyard.

"From the church." The red brick building stood only yards away.

"But she had passed away? Are you sure it was her?"

"I heard her calling me. I heard her, so I walked down the aisle to the altar," Maria said, as if Frank should have known already.

Frank gently turned Maria's face to his.

"What was she saying?"

"She said," Maria strained to recall, "'It'll be all right.'"

"And you remember your hands with the blood on them? How did they feel?" Frank touched her hands, feeling her long bony fingers.

"Like when I get high," Maria said gently.

"I don't understand," Frank said carefully.

"Like when I shoot smack. I feel so warm inside. That's how that blood on my hands felt. Warm. I could sleep and be at peace, you understand me, Father?" Maria said pleadingly.

Frank nodded. "Yes. I do."

Maria stepped away from him, and with a shaky hand, she reached up and touched the statue where the Virgin's feet stood on the globe. "She saved my life," Maria told him.

"The statue?" Frank asked, eyeing Maria's blue-jean jacket as it covered her light blue sweater. She still seemed a child.

"No, Mrs. Stephenson. She sent the blood from the statue to cure me of lupus."

"How do you know that?" he asked.

"I just know," Maria said, as a tiny smile crossed her mouth. She gave Frank the strongest look of clarity she had shown so far. "It was a miracle. That's why."

Frank was silent.

"I better get back to my boyfriend Jimmy before he gets up. He nodded out on some smack last night. I did some coke to stay awake so I could see you."

"You're hurting yourself. That boy is no good for you. Go see your mother. She's worried about you," Frank said.

"I won't lose Jimmy!" Hysteria flashed across Maria's face. "My mother couldn't keep my father. That won't happen to me. I won't lose Jimmy," Maria said, stepping back from Frank. "Would you see a doctor for me?"

Maria was walking backwards. "No."

"For Helen Stephenson?" Frank pleaded.

Maria looked up to the statue. "I can't," she said, continuing to walk backwards.

"I'm worried that you might be ill."

"She *is* a saint," Maria said loudly. "Not like my mother. Mrs. Stephenson loved me."

"Your mother loves you," Frank said.

The last thing she said to Frank before she walked away was, "She didn't even know me. She didn't even know who I was and she still loved me."

Part Two

Chapter 7

The bright lights of the Plaza Hotel and its surroundings dazzled the two priests. Horse-and-buggy carriages, walking tourists up and down Central Park South, stretch limos pulling up to the hotels that lined the avenue, and the excitement of the moment slid across Frank's mind like a sweet drink. Frank loved the glamour and intensity of the Church's power.

Frank and Corey entered the Plaza from the main entrance and took the central elevators to suite 900R.

When the door opened, Frank and Corey saw the suite filled with priests in conversation and businessmen in tuxedos. They walked through the room shaking hands and making quick introductions. There were secular priests, Jesuits, Marists, and Franciscans.

Frank was dressed in a stunning tailor-made black suit he had worn on his book tour, and instead of a tie, wore his priest's collar. Glancing around the room, he noticed that he was among the elite of the various orders. Some faces he had met briefly before, some had names he recognized from journal articles, while others just looked impressive.

Through the floor-to-ceiling window, Frank could see Central Park, in all its nighttime splendor, glowing with the light of its sturdy lamps. The world of power didn't mind showing its enormous wealth here, in the center of the city, Frank thought to himself. Everything looked rich: the men in this room, the sprawling park outside, the glistening lights of Central Park South, and the other hotels below.

"So what do you think of our suite here?" Frank heard from behind him. He turned and saw the cardinal standing there. Frank could see the light of power in the man's gaze. He seemed charming but aloof, intelligent but not reflective, cunning but not blatant. This was his arena, and Frank could almost feel the man's heart pounding with excitement.

Cahill was wearing a red robe and glittering jewelry. He wore large rings inset with gold and purple stones on every other finger and around his neck he wore a crucifix that was at least six inches long and studded with diamonds and emeralds. On his head he wore a red velvet cap. "So introduce me to your protégé," Cahill said to Frank.

Frank introduced Corey, who stood in awe. All he could do was bow and kiss the cardinal's ring.

"Does opulence offend you?" Cahill asked a shaking Corey.

"Huh?" Corey stammered.

"I hope not, but it does offend some of us here," the cardinal said, then nodded to the Franciscans, who stood in the center of the suite in their long brown robes. "I understand the vow of poverty, but if we left it up to orders like the Franciscans, we'd be a Church without a home, without influence. I despise the argument that the 'people' are our home. The 'people' are our flock and we are their shepherds! And without money the shepherd dies! I'm suspicious of those who argue for poverty. We have to deal with governments. And faith may impress the needy easily enough, but the wealthy need a little more."

Cahill brought Frank and Corey aside as he smiled at the businessmen who could not stop looking at him as if he were a famous movie star. "There are over five hundred men here tonight. All businessmen paying $5000 a plate! All for Catholic charities. And every one of them could afford $10,000 if we asked!" The cardinal grinned. "All the money they make makes them feel guilty. When they give a little of it away to charity, they feel refreshed, reborn! It's better than confession for them. Hell, most of them haven't been to church or heard Mass since they received their first communion!"

Frank enjoyed the tenacity of the older man. "So, we're back to selling indulgences?"

"Why not? It worked then! Some of them think I walk around all day in this hideous outfit! I wear it for them. They want to see power on display. They want to see pomp and circumstance! They want to see performance! Religion is based on ritual and celebration! God has called on us to continue those traditions for his Church and that is why your book is important, significant!" The cardinal leaned closer to Frank. "Evil is not just cruelty in action, it is also misunderstanding. Misunderstanding ideas has done more evil in the world than all the work of Satan. The Tower of Babel was mankind's real curse!" The cardinal leaned back. "After this miracle nonsense is over, you should go back on the lecture circuit with your book!"

"I'm not sure I can stand all the attention anymore," Frank said.

"Come on, I can't believe you don't like to be treated well. I know men, Frank, and I see in you a man who likes it when people make a big deal of him!" the cardinal said.

Just then Beliar walked up to them. He quickly shook Frank's hand and introduced himself to Corey, who asked, "Are you the John Beliar who wrote *The Malevolent Darkness of the East*?"

Frank chimed in. "The very one. John knows his demons. He spent several years in the Balkans, studying in ancient churches by candlelight."

"I got very little sleep," handsome, soft-spoken Beliar responded.

Corey cringed. "I don't blame you. It's not my favorite topic."

Beliar smiled. "You're frightened of Satan?"

Cahill spoke up. "Of course he is. Lucifer always frightens the pious. It's the wicked who don't quiver at the mere mention of his name." Cahill exchanged a look with Frank.

"I don't believe in Satan," Frank said.

The small group grew quiet.

Beliar spoke first. "Then how do you explain that there's been an appearance of Satan at every miracle recorded by man since Christ rose from the dead and the Devil appeared at his tomb?"

"The more publicity for Satan, the more for God," Frank smiled.

"I believe in Satan," Corey chimed in.

"Good for you," Cahill smiled.

"Then do you believe that there's a Satanist out there who wants to pervert the investigation of a miracle?" Frank asked.

"Yes, perhaps. A demon or possibly the spirit of an evil man, a ghost condemned to eternal suffering," Beliar replied.

"Like Father Falcone?" Cahill said.

Frank was silent. So was Corey.

"Then you don't believe in evil, Frank?" Cahill asked.

"Oh, on the contrary," Frank answered. "I believe there's an evil energy in the world, but it's created by men. There are evil men in this world and they don't wear black hats nor do they have eyes burning with hate all the time. They're sometimes veiled in righteousness, sometimes in duty, sometimes in cloaks of power. They usually act to satisfy their own desires, their own needs, despite the destruction they bring upon others. Evil men always feel they are defending themselves from the attacks of others. They are morally bankrupt personalities. Some cynical, some devious, some ignorant. And they like nothing better than to tempt the innocent and destroy the good. They are also charismatic. Look at the Nazis or any street gang or even serial killers. They are sometimes highly intelligent and dynamic. But they turn away from love, and that makes them ugly inside."

Cahill frowned. "Frank, sometimes you are so pompous."

Beliar then spoke up. "By the way, we received your lab report on the blood today."

Cahill, with his eyes still riveted on Frank, said, "Yes. Fascinating. Are we now to believe that the statue is bleeding Helen Stephenson's blood?"

"It certainly isn't mine," Frank shot back.

"We'll be interviewing those who claimed they were cured next week," Sam Corey said.

Satisfied, Cahill said to Corey, "Enjoy yourself. There's plenty of food and wine—" he then lowered his cracking voice while keeping his eyes on the rest of the suite. "Stay away from the Franciscans!" He then walked to the door, surrounded by a dozen admirers in tuxedos.

The main dining room at the Plaza was a ballroom that looked the size of a football field, with high ceilings and fifty tables of ten seats each. Frank instantly felt the magnificence of the event. Something this grand and obviously established could not have happened in the sixties or seventies. Back then rich kids were joining ranks with the poor, positioning themselves in direct conflict with the Establishment. Though a child, he remembered those turbulent times, wondering if they would ever end, and they did. Not with a bang, but with the eighties: the money generation. And now the nineties, where the motto is, "help give power to your side and your side alone."

Frank thanked the heavyset bishop for showing him to his chair on the dais, which spread so far to both sides of the room that he couldn't see those sitting at the far end. He searched for Sam Corey down in the seats and managed to see a hand wave. It was Sam with a big smile on his face. Frank would learn later that Corey had a wonderful time networking the ballroom. Even though he knew many of the clergy there, he enjoyed himself by telling them all that he was a personal guest of the cardinal.

Frank sat back and surveyed the room. Bright lights from the ceiling lit the dais as the waiters hurried back and forth filling and refilling glasses amid the near roar of the seated crowd. Most of those at the tables were wearing black ties and tuxedos, giving the already elegant room a look of naked aristocracy. Priests sat side by side with rich laymen.

And there wasn't a woman in the entire place. All those serving dinner were also men. This was a dinner similar to those in the Middle Ages, when the entire monastery came out for roasted pig as tables lined both sides of the fireplace. Monks and priests ate side by side, and not a woman was to be seen. Now, instead of the abbey, it was the Plaza.

And what was just as important was that the businessmen seemed comfortable in the presence of priests who looked manly and capable and not overtly religious. The cardinal, a shrewd politician, knew this well.

Frank took notice of how healthy and tough the faces of the bishops and priests at the tables looked. They could pass for hunters and military officers! The laughter that filled the room was the laughter of hearty men ready and able to sink their teeth into tender prime rib and wash it down with a glass of Scotch!

Frank could see that most of the faces of the priests that sat at the tables below him were Irish: big, round, effusive. Most of the talk centered around the Vatican and how displeased most of the priests in the ballroom were with Rome. The Pope was usually Italian, though most recently Polish, while the Church's power base in America, especially in New York City, was Irish. Irish Catholics, Frank had learned, considered themselves apart from the Italians who ran Rome. Perhaps that was why Cahill was fond of Frank: Frank was Irish. Maybe that was why Cahill preferred Frank over Beliar, he thought to himself, even though Beliar was always at his beck and call, always doing his bidding.

Frank got himself another glass of wine and fell into light conversation with the archbishops at either side of him. He enjoyed taking part in the zestful atmosphere surrounding him. He felt like he was at a hunting lodge or a boys' night out; the wives stayed home while the boys played. This was the side of Frank Cahill liked to see. This is why Frank was seriously beinging considered for the position of bishop. There was a side of Frank that loved power. A side driven by amibition and confidence. He enjoyed the spotlight. He even relished it once. But all that changed since Falcone, and never again would it rule his existence.

As Frank looked around the room he thought to himself how there would be no go-go girl jumping out of a cake this night. Women weren't the issue; money was. Money, and the smell of it, permeated the room. From the sleek corporate businessmen to the millionaire entrepreneurs who made their fortunes selling hamburgers and pizza pies, the conversation underneath the laughter and the booze was about money. Fat faces tied into their tuxedos smiled like good parochial schoolboys who no longer feared the wrath of the parish priest who sent them home with a note to be signed. No, these businessmen felt like equals with the priests at their tables, and enjoyed the donations that they were making to Catholic charities. Souls weren't the issue, bankbooks were. Frank doubted if the word *religion* would ever come up in any of the hundreds of conversations going on below him.

Knowing that he was the first speaker, Frank cleared his mind of his own personal thoughts. He knew that this dinner was no place for him to discuss the anguish he had been struggling with. He knew that he was asked to speak of faith, but not question it. He was there to affirm for the room full of the Church's wealthy followers their choice of religion.

His book raced through his mind as well as the reason he had taken the time to write it. He was confirming what the Church had ordained centuries ago—that Jesus Christ was a man and that he died for the sins of Man even though he was God. Jesus Christ was God. And if you followed God and his teachings, you were saved. Your soul was brought to salvation upon death. Good works alone did not assure a place with God in heaven, but faith did. Good works were important, but not enough. *The God Within* stated that faith was intrinsic in everyone; that faith was there inside the person and all that person had to do was allow faith to germinate. Faith was a major step in finding God. If one had faith in God then His will would eventually make itself known to that soul during his time on earth. That was Frank's proposition in *The God Within*. If Frank had been a dishonest man, it wouldn't have mattered. But his quest for the validity of faith was sincere. He truly wanted to define faith as something natural and he did think that he had found a formula.

Hearing his named called, Frank walked to the podium amidst applause and flashing camera bulbs. He could see, from the corner of his eye, Cardinal Cahill smiling as he faced the joyous crowd. When Cahill had made his short speech, moments before, the crowd was hushed and Cahill played his status to the hilt. He was royalty, religious royalty. He talked to them like the nuns and brothers talked to them in high school. He was Patton leading the charge against the enemy: poverty, idleness, indifference. Whatever they wanted to hear, he said. When he was finished with his short speech, they applauded with reverence.

Then Cahill introduced Frank. Just before he did, he smiled to no one in particular but Frank knew what the smile meant. It was as if to say to the crowd at his feet, "Look, you see, we have this good-looking priest with us. He could have had girls, and football scholarships, but he decided that we were the right choice. Not all priests are wimps or closet gays! We have intelligent, handsome guys, too! So you see, boys, you're on the right side!"

Frank acknowledged the applause at his introduction, then walked to the podium. He knew what every man in the room was thinking: what happens that day when the ambulance comes for me, when my life is handed over to some indifferent, wealthy doctor? Whose hand will I hold? Some strange nurse, some distant relative, or even some son or daughter waiting for me to pass away so they can get the grieving done and dig their hands into all my loot? I could have been a priest! Frank could hear them say to themselves: If this good-looking heterosexual made that choice, it couldn't be so bad. He probably gets laid, he probably has his own car and money in the bank. Nobody says he has to wear that collar all the time!

Frank decided to keep his speech short. He knew his appearance spoke volumes, so all he said to them was—"In college I played varsity baseball, second base, and I wasn't sure what I was going to do with my life until one day my father said to me, 'Frank, marry a rich woman.'" Frank paused, then said, "And so I did." A loud applause filled the room. "Tonight, as I look out across this wonderful room and see so many heavy wallets, it makes me think of something an adversary of ours once said. It was Martin Luther who put it so wisely, 'God commonly gives riches to those gross asses from whom he expects nothing else.'"

The room was silent. Suddenly, Cahill laughed. Everyone at the dais turned to him, watching his face contort with laughter. They joined in. Soon, the whole room followed his lead. Frank stepped back from the podium as Cahill stood to shake his hand. "They love you, Frank," he said. "Can't you now see all that self-torment and that hiding in the SRO was nonsense?"

Frank was taken aback by Cahill's candor. He turned to the crowd, permitting their admiration to flow through him. In so doing, he realized why Cahill wanted him to speak: if the Church could clone Frank, they would. They'd put Frank's handsome face on posters, like the Army does: CHRIST WANTS A FEW GOOD MEN. And, JOIN THE CHURCH. BE ALL YOU CAN BE! BE CATHOLIC! Recruitment would go up a thousand percent.

After his speech, Frank heard a heavyset bishop mention that it was raining cats and dogs outside.

"It's raining," Frank told Cahill.

"So, you have the limo all night."

"The statue," Frank said. He saw the recognition of the thought in Cahill's face. Corey was in earshot. "We have to get back," he told him.

Frank and Corey left the party and made their way to the waiting limousine.

Chapter 8

As the limo pulled up in front of the schoolyard, Frank and Corey jumped out. The schoolyard was packed with people standing facing the statue. Umbrellas by the score dotted the yard as several police cars stood between the crowd and the sudden emergence of camera crews.

Frank opened his coat to expose his collar as he pushed his way through the rain-drenched crowd. People were praying and joining hands as he and Sam Corey reached the white, brick fence that separated the schoolyard from the convent. Through the rain, Frank could see Father Kinnely kneeling at the foot of the statue saying Mass at a makeshift altar. The Eucharist was in the air, commanding the entire schoolyard to kneel on the wet pavement. Only the police and the camera crews continued to stand as the crowd said out loud, "The Body and Blood of Christ!"

Frank turned and saw Sam mesmerized by the flow of tears. "I've never seen anything like it," he said.

Frank remembered the feelings he had his first night in Willow

Lake. He remembered the spotlight hanging from the tree limbs and the hundreds of people standing on the dock praying to the priest who had died in the horrible storm. He remembered watching them as they waded into the lake filled with anticipation. They would sit in the water or stand in it. Some would go deeper and dunk their heads in it, hoping to heal their ailing bodies and souls.

Frank recalled watching the faithful, who had left behind their evening television and trips to the bowling alley and bars, march to the edge of the lake praying to a God they had never seen in the name of a man they had loved and respected.

Frank remembered thinking to himself that before that night he had never had true faith. The validity of his scholarship, travel, and celebrity was called into question. He felt a surge of emotion, a leap of faith that startled him out of a life of pretense, avoidance, and white lies. "I have never believed before," he said out loud.

Kinnely's booming voice jolted Frank back to the schoolyard. "But what happens if it's not God?" said Frank. "What happens if none of this has anything to do with the Almighty? Sam, at Willow Lake I saw the deaf able to hear again, I saw the dying rid their bodies of cancer. And it had nothing to do with the sacred or sanctified," he said.

"Then perhaps humanity has more power than it realizes. Good and evil are our own invention. And we're touched on every level by our choice: love elevates us, evil disgraces," Sam answered.

Frank felt as if he were in the eye of a storm: there was chaos all around him and yet he was the living center of silence. "'To reach what you do not know, you must go where you do not know,'" he said.

Sam nodded in agreement. "Some are cured, Frank. Maybe it doesn't really matter why."

Frank saw Kinnely looking at him, and turned away. He motioned toward the priest, when a bright camera light lit up the schoolyard. Frank noticed a TV video camera taking footage of a tall, blond reporter. Frank stepped over to her, listening to what she had to say.

"This is Dotty West and we are back at Saint Stanislaus School in Maspeth, Queens. We are standing only a few feet from the statue itself. As you can see there are hundreds of people here—Catholics and non-Catholics from all over the world. They are here to pray to Helen Stephenson. However, there is a controversy surrounding this long-deceased woman. Some say that the Catholic Church won't canonize her because she worked to reform the Church and believed women should be priests. Others say that's nonsense."

Frank watched as she turned to him. She was looking at his collar as she did. "Keep the tape going!" she shouted to her cameraman.

Frank felt as if all eyes in the schoolyard were on him. That's when he saw Roxanna in the crowd. She was standing under an umbrella only a few feet from him when the camera lights flashed in his direction. He saw her there and she saw him. She took off and Frank made a move to follow her.

"Rick, more light over here! Father Frank Moore? You are Father Moore, aren't you? Father Kinnely described you for me. I'm Dotty West from *National Scoop: America In Perspective*, and we are doing a story on recent unexplained phenomena in the world. You're the official postulator representing the Church here concerning this miracle. Do you have any comment about the miracle?"

"What miracle?"

Dotty West was taken aback. "The blood, you know, from the statue's eyes when it rains?"

"No one in the Church has officially called what happens here a miracle. If you want to call it a miracle, fine. I'll call up the Pope and tell him. I'm sure he'll take it into consideration."

"But what about the blood?" she asked.

"It'll wind up on an episode of *Unsolved Mysteries*, I'm sure."

"But what about the other cases of miracles—the girl who was cured of lupus ten years ago?"

"Her doctor's reports are being looked into for verification. For all I know, she might have just had the flu."

She waved the cameras off. "Hold it, Rick." She then looked directly at Frank. "Look, if you don't want the publicity just let me know."

"Lady, what I don't want here is a circus."

"I can't believe your Church can't use the coverage."

Frank's voice grew sterner. "If you want a story about the miracle on the mount where seven loaves of bread and a few small fish fed a multitude—read the Bible! This is not a horror movie made to sell tickets for your particular enjoyment! The Church has no official comment at the moment, thank you." Frank allowed his big brown eyes to open widely in the light of the cameras that drenched his face.

Keeping her composure, Dotty West saw another priest standing behind Frank. She thanked Frank, then turned to Sam Corey. "In your opinion, is this a miracle, Father?"

Corey smiled and looked right into the camera. "I'm Father Sam Corey. How is everyone out there? Did you go to Mass last Sunday?"

"In your opinion, is it a miracle, Father?" Dotty West asked again.

Frank was about to say something when he saw Sam take control. Seeing that, he slipped away. "Here's how I'll answer you," he said, looking into the camera. "Would it change your life if it was? And if your answer is yes, then I ask you this—why do you need a miracle to change what you're not happy about?"

Frank walked toward Roxanna's home. He knew where she lived, and he knew Maspeth. He was hoping that she hadn't gone in. The rain had stopped as he walked along Maurice Park. A warm air mass had moved up from the south, shifting the wind from the northwest to the southwest.

It was the northwest wind that brought the small cold front

and the rain, and now the southwest wind was bringing with it warm air and fog. The fog settled slowly and noisily after the rain had stopped. It was one of those fall fogs that flattened the air, carrying with it a sense of enclosure which made the world on the ground seem more dense and made every sound echo with an eerie weight.

Frank was only a few blocks from Roxanna's house when he got the feeling he was being watched. He looked around, but saw nothing through the fog. He could make out the tall trees in the small park and the tips of the high cyclone fence that surrounded it, but there wasn't anyone around. Frank walked on. He felt the dampness of the night air and he felt a desolation, not only of a man who was lost in wandering, but of a soul lost in its wandering too.

He suddenly felt the urge to find a woman. He wondered if that was how rapists thought. Did they wander aimlessly along until they happened upon someone alone? Or did they plan it? Frank stopped walking. He felt disconcerted that the awful thought had crossed his mind and wasn't going away. He turned and looked at the small bungalow standing at the corner. In the lit window, he could see the shape of a woman in the kitchen on the phone. The curtain hadn't been drawn and Frank could make out the outline of her figure, her face, her arm holding the phone.

He walked on. He forced the dark thought from his head but it kept coming back. He wondered if the woman was alone, he wondered if the doors were unlocked. He wondered how easy it might be to get her to let him in if he just walked up to the front door, rang the bell, and stood there in his priest's collar. She would let him in no matter what excuse he had for being there. A woman would let a priest into her house without concern.

Frank turned away from the house and headed for the avenue. It was nothing more than a scar that ran through the neighborhood along Mount Zion Cemetery. From where he stood, he could see the small rise of hills come at him from the fog. He could see the gray and black stones shimmering under the streetlamps' yellow light.

Frank walked toward the cemetery and stared at it. There was so much he could do to destroy the hope of a miracle. This time he wouldn't need a priest who committed suicide to ruin it. All he had to do was tell Cahill that nothing holy was happening in that schoolyard.

Frank then decided to turn and go back to the rectory. It was clear that Roxanna wasn't still on the street, that she had gone home. He half wanted to ring her bell and ask her why she was at the schoolyard, when he saw a woman sitting on a park bench near the ball field.

He slowly walked over to her. It was Roxanna.

"That was the first time I had been that close," Roxanna said. She didn't even look up at Frank. It was as if she had been sitting on the park bench having a conversation with herself until he came along. She took a quick slug out from a flask. "I know it's not ladylike, but who gives a shit?" she said.

"I was surprised to see you there," Frank told her.

"You writing a book?" she asked sharply. "Look, Father whatever, I'm going home—"

"Frank Moore," Frank said. "I need to know if your mother kept a journal or if she had any writings—"

"You ask questions like a cop."

"I am a cop. In a way. For the Church," Frank answered.

"And that gives you privileges, doesn't it? You wear that collar and you think you have some right to open up someone's heart. And so what if you do some damage—just throw a little holy water on the suffering soul and that'll make her feel better," Roxanna said.

"Father Kinnely told me that he wasn't aware of any written material so I only have you to ask—"

"Oh, Kinnely! There's another winner! The man danced around my mother like an overaged Romeo!"

Frank was silent.

"Oh, I see your wheels turning. You're wondering if they had a relationship or not. Get what you can on the woman, right? I mean—'if we can't make her a saint, then let's make her a whore!' You priests are all the same." Roxanna got up and walked to a car parked a few feet away. Frank followed right behind her. "Look," she said, staring right at him this time, "I want to be left out of this crap of yours. I don't like saints, holy men, or soul-savers. I don't believe in forgiveness and I love the sinner as much as I love the sin, thank you very much." With that, she took the flask out of her bag again and took a slug. She looked at Frank, daring him. "Want a slug? I'm being polite. I know you priests only drink wine—"

Frank didn't even hesitate. He took the bottle and took a slug. It felt good going down. "Don't tell the Pope," Frank grinned.

Roxanna looked Frank over. She felt that official air that he had the first time they met disappear. And she liked it not being there. "You're sharing a drink with an atheist, did you know that?"

"Is that a confession?" Frank asked.

"You trying to get me alone in the dark?" Roxanna took out her car keys and opened the door.

"Let me buy you dinner."

"Why?" Roxanna asked.

"I'm hungry. And maybe you are too," Frank answered.

"I never ate with a priest before and I certainly never shared a drink with one."

"Be careful, you might turn into a religious zealot."

"The world has enough of them already, I'm sure."

"It probably does."

"Though you're better-looking than most," Roxanna said.

"Well, don't worry, I'm not one. I'll take an oath."

"That'd make me feel better. You can never tell these days," she kidded.

"What about getting something to eat? My treat."

Roxanna looked at Frank a long moment. "There's a diner on Grand Avenue. They have a bar."

"I like a good diner," Frank said, gently taking the keys from her.

"I like a man who takes control," Roxanna whispered teasingly.

"You shouldn't drive. You've been drinking."

"I thought it was souls you saved—not lives," Roxanna said.

"We do a little of both," Frank said, opening the car door for her.

They drove to the diner on Grand Avenue. It was a small place with several booths. They slid into one facing the window. The Long Island Expressway was in full view, as was the Manhattan skyline off in the distance.

Frank couldn't take his eyes off her. In the bright light, she was even prettier than the first time he saw her. She was also feminine, and her blue eyes didn't miss a trick. She managed to be interested in everything around her. Frank felt that she was especially interested in him. "Your mother must have been very pretty when she was young," Frank told her.

"She was," Roxanna answered.

Frank noticed her white blouse under the blue-jean jacket. He liked the dark skirt she wore, and the black-heeled boots.

Roxanna glanced out the window. "Good ol' Maspeth. I like it when I'm drunk. I tolerate it when I'm not. I find myself being drunk more often these days." She looked at Frank. "So, what do you really do, Frank Moore?" She smiled and sipped her drink.

"I'm a troubleshooter. They send me where they need me: a distressed parish, an investigation, an international conference on a controversial issue."

"Or if they need a miracle checked out," Roxanna interjected.

"That sort of thing."

"So, you're nothing like Bing Crosby in *The Bells of St. Mary's*?"

"Nothing like him. In certain cities my singing voice has been registered as a deadly weapon."

Roxanna sat back, holding her drink with two hands. Frank noticed. "So, you had one of those glorious 'callings'?"

"Something like that," Frank answered.

Roxanna discreetly moved her hand back, knocking her spoon off the table. She then leaned over, picking it up and flashing her thigh at Frank. She was wearing panty hose and she had fine, long legs. Frank looked. She noticed him looking. "Just what I thought," she smiled.

"It's what I had to give up. I'm not a virgin, if that's what you're asking," he said.

"And you wanted to wear the white collar."

"I considered myself a theologian."

"How lucky for God. Where did it hit you, this glorious vocation? On one of those retreats the nuns made us go on?"

"No," Frank answered. "Junior year in college, actually. I was in the chapel one afternoon praying for help with a final exam when it struck me how tranquil the chapel was. Then I started thinking how being a priest might be an interesting occupation."

Roxanna was serious when she asked, "Any blasting trumpets?"

"None, actually. It was a subdued calling. I struggle with it. But I'm still here." Frank sipped his drink. It was his first, and it felt good.

Roxanna could see he was still struggling with something. "You're a member of my club, aren't you?"

"And what club is that?" he asked.

"The club of misplaced party animals. It's a lousy club to pay dues to," she said.

After several drinks and a light dinner, they went back to the park. They sat on the bench, enjoying the fog as it descended even further. Frank glanced around the park and could see the fog slowly drift down to only a few feet above the lampposts. The park was empty except for a man walking his dog in the ball field in the distance.

Frank had had two drinks in the diner and they made him feel loose, comfortable and relaxed. He was talking to Roxanna but looking into the fog ahead. "People see the collar and they say—'he knows.' The collar signifies that God has chosen you to administer the sacraments. He has picked you to be this divine lightning rod delivering His grace to the suffering. But then, one day, something happens: you can't say Mass; you can't bless the needy. But the collar is still there." Frank felt a sense of relief telling this woman sitting beside him things he hadn't told anyone except perhaps Sam. But she was a stranger.

"Would you like to hear my confession?" Roxanna asked.

A feeling of emptiness rushed through Frank.

"Afraid I'd bore you? You must wallow in the glory of other people making themselves naked in your shrouded presence."

"I never thought of it that way," Frank answered.

"Around here, there were no movie stars, no astronauts. We had priests! You people have the power to bless! You're the judge! The umpire! The big shot who knows all the rules and regulations! I think that's what my mother loved about them—her priests! Their confidence. She moved to the convent right after my father died. I was nineteen years old. She cooked for her priests, she cleaned for them—she didn't give a damn about what happened to me." Roxanna stood up. Propelled by the unpleasant memory, she walked away.

"Where are you going?" Frank asked. "You should go home."

"I'm a big girl, or didn't you notice?" Roxanna said, walking through the fog.

Frank followed her. They walked along the Long Island Expressway service road and toward the overpass. The overpass rose two stories up and over the expressway.

"Hey!" she said when he stepped up to her. "Let's walk across! I like it up there!" Roxanna pointed to the walkway connecting the two sides of the community.

Roxanna grabbed Frank's hand, hurrying him across. When they reached the other side, they climbed the concrete stairs leading up and over the six lanes of cars that sped by underneath them in both directions. Through the steel fence, that rose over nine feet high, encasing the overpass, Frank had an even clearer view of the skyline, of the city bursting across the star-spattered sky.

"This is great!" Roxanna shouted over the din of the cars racing by below. She raised her hands and collapsed on Frank's chest. "This is the only place I know where nothing matters. I don't have a problem in the world up here. So, you really think God made us?"

Frank looked at Roxanna. "It doesn't matter, either way."

"Why not?"

"Because all that matters is that we exist," Frank said.

"Right," Roxanna said, looking off into the distance.

"Of course, unless we're dreaming this," Frank said.

Roxanna gave him one of her rare smiles. "I like that. This is all a dream."

"Why do you like that?" Frank asked, playing along.

"Because in a dream," Roxanna said slyly, "you can do whatever you want and get away with it. Because it's only a dream." The glee quickly left Roxanna's voice. Her look was immediately distant and introspective. She said nothing, but just kept walking. Frank followed her.

"I think I'm drunk," Roxanna said, cutely.

"You should go home—"

"Don't be a holy roller. Come on, follow me," she told him. She threw her arms around him, and lifting her head up, she smiled at him. "I haven't had this much fun, Father—" She stopped herself. "I'm going to stop calling you Father from now on!"

Frank smiled back at her. "What are you going to call me?"

"Frank! I like the name." Roxanna tilted her head, enticing Frank with her smile.

Frank could see the lines in her face as she stood in the harsh glare of the overpass lights. He could also see the circles under her eyes. She would not let go of the past, and it would not let go of her.

"I like being with you," she told him.

"Thanks," Frank said.

"I feel like I'm out on a date. In fact, I can't tell you the last time I had a good time with a guy. A time as good as this."

"Maybe you don't give yourself a chance," Frank interrupted.

Roxanna glared at Frank. "Don't patronize me. I'm a grown woman. I have been for some time. I don't need to hear that I don't give men a chance."

Frank sensed that Roxanna was going to step closer to him. He was anticipating it. He was watching her every move closely, waiting.

"Are you afraid that I'm going to try to kiss you?" Roxanna teased.

"I might be," he smiled.

"Oh, really?"

"I kiss you and the heavens will open and Michael the archangel will ride down from the sky on his white-winged horse and strike me dead with one blow from his righteous sword. Of course I'm scared!" Frank said. Frank could see her lips in the harsh light. He could smell her perfume, and he could see her eyes already giving herself to him.

"If I kissed you and that happened? I'd join a nunnery on the spot!" Roxanna said.

"You would scream, 'I believe!'" Frank said. He then felt her hand on his collar. He felt how soft her fingers were on his face as she touched him there.

"I don't think I could believe, even for you."

"Oh," Frank said softly.

"I'm what the Baltimore Catechism calls an 'occasion of sin,' aren't I?" she asked.

"You are," Frank answered softly.

"You are a handsome man. And more intelligent and sensitive than any I have ever met around here." Roxanna made a motion as if to hit him. "Why the hell do you have to wear that collar?"

Frank wanted to taste her lips and hold her close. "I don't have the answer to that question, not anymore."

Roxanna leaned over and kissed Frank. She then put her arms around him, pulling him closer to her. "I feel like I'm kissing a priest."

"You are," Frank answered honestly.

Roxanna gave Frank a sarcastic look, then stood back. She

twisted her hips, grabbing hold of the railing as cars flashed by only twenty feet below her.

Frank turned her around, took her in his arms, and kissed her passionately, feeling the wind on his face as he did. He felt the sensuality of the moment connecting him to somewhere else. He felt the tenderness of her touch, the passion in her lips, the need she had for him. He then felt her push her hips closer to his, felt her edge one leg in between his. He felt her put her arms around his waist.

Roxanna looked up at him. "You want me, don't you? I feel that you want me."

"I do," Frank told her.

"Come back to my apartment," Roxanna said.

Frank looked at her. He could see the desire on her face. But he pulled away. He looked down and closed his eyes. He could feel her holding him tightly with her hands on his open coat. "I can't."

"Why not?"

"It wouldn't be good for either one of us."

"I'm offering myself to you!"

"I know."

"What's wrong? I'm not good enough?"

"I didn't say that."

"You're cold. You're ice. I don't think you could feel anything," she said sharply.

Frank felt the chill in the air. He could see his breath in front of his face.

Roxanna grinned. "I thought you might be able to help me. Was I kidding myself? You can't help me. You can't care enough to help me."

"That's not true," Frank told her.

"A dead woman interests you more than a living one," she said, then turned and walked away. Frank didn't move. He just watched her cross to the other side of the overpass and walk along through the park, her light hair shining under the street-lamps. He imagined her crying, hating him, hating her mother, hating all the priests she knew, and mostly, hating herself.

Frank waited until he could no longer see her. He then walked back to his room in the rectory. "A dead woman interests you more than a living one," he could hear Roxanna say over and over as he tried to sleep.

Chapter 9

The Mass had changed considerably since Frank was a kid and an altar boy. He never liked the change from Latin to English but did enjoy, from the very beginning, the saying of Mass. He liked what it meant. He liked its drama and mystery.

He saw it as a celebration and a ritual with a long tradition that encouraged the feelings of community and togetherness all celebrations contain. But as he stood in the vestibule, dressing with two altar boys at his side, his estrangement from the duties and their meaning pained him.

The vestments were originally ordinary garments of the ancient Roman world. First, he put on the amice, a square of white linen wrapped around the neck and covering the shoulders. In the Middle Ages, the amice was worn as a hood to protect the head in cold churches. It symbolized the "helmet of salvation." It is the virtue of hope which helps the priest overcome the attacks of Satan.

Frank then put on the alb, a long white garment reaching

down to his feet, which symbolized the innocence and purity that should adorn the soul of the priest who ascends the altar. The cincture is a cord used as a belt, symbolizing chastity. He placed the maniple, an ornamental vestment of colored silk, over his left forearm as a symbol of the hardship the priest must expect in his duties. He then placed the stole around his neck. The stole, a long scarf, is a sign that the priest is occupied with an official priestly duty.

With everything else in place, Frank put on the chasuble. A full garment shaped like a bell and reaching to the feet all the way around, it symbolized the virtue of charity. Frank looked in the mirror. Standing before him was a priest dressed in the green and white liturgical colors of the October Advent. Frank had worn all the colors: the white of Christmas and Easter; the red, the color of blood, worn on all the feasts of the Lord's cross and passion and feasts of all martyrs; old rose worn on the third Sunday of Advent and the fourth Sunday of Lent; gold, when the vestments are made of real cloth of gold in place of white; and black, the color of death, used for services of Good Friday and funerals.

Hearing the organ player in the balcony in the back of the church stop playing, Frank knew it was time. He bowed his head and walked out to the altar. He sensed immediately the fullness of the church, hearing the congregation rise as he entered the altar area. He dreaded the moment, even coming close to telling Father Kinnely that he was struggling with the act of leaving the priesthood altogether.

Frank's decision to say Mass was based on a hope that maybe he would find his faith as he commemorated the sacrifice of Christ's body and blood.

The Mass had also changed in a subtler way—it was a lot less formal than it had been for so many centuries. Now, before Mass started, the priest serving it would step up to the side of the altar and say a few words to the congregation about his interpretation of the gospel for that day. This particular Sunday, the gospel of Christ coming upon the leper would be read.

Frank faced the packed church. He knew that those who were there came to hear his Mass because of his role as the outsider who might threaten the wonder of their statue. Frank did not want to encourage them, nor did he want to crush their fragile hope. He decided not to speak about the statue at all.

"Today's gospel is about Christ and the leper. And I believe in many ways we are all lepers. We all feel isolated, at times, from the community, separate from our friends and family." Frank had planned to go on, but he stopped. He felt ludicrous lecturing the faithful.

He turned to the congregation and they sang a song of greeting.

> "Blessed are they who are poor in spirit,
> Theirs is the kingdom of God.
> Blessed are they who are meek and humble,
> They will inherit the earth . . ."

After the song, Frank sat down at a chair placed for him at the side of the altar, as Sister Alice stood from her seat in the first pew and walked to the ucterr, where she read from the Epistle from the Missal.

When she was done, Frank walked to the altar and looked down at the crowded church. "In the name of the Father, and of the Son, and of the Holy Spirit," he said.

The congregation followed by making the sign of the cross and repeating along with Frank.

"The grace of our Lord Jesus Christ and the love of God and the fellowship of the Holy Spirit be with you all," Frank said loudly.

"And also with you," the congregation answered.

"The grace and peace of God our Father and the Lord Jesus Christ be with you," Frank said to them.

"And also with you," they answered again.

"The Lord be with you," Frank told them.

"And also with you," they said.

Frank walked to the pulpit where a large maroon-covered

book with gold trim sat waiting for him. Frank opened the book and looked to the pews. "This is the word of the Lord," he said. "Thanks be to God," the congregation replied.

Frank read the gospel of Jesus and the leper, listening to the words himself as he read it. "If you desire to heal me, I shall be healed," the leper told Christ. Christ then healed him.

Frank completed reading the gospel then turned to the congregation to give his sermon. He felt every eye in the church on him. "You may have been thinking, 'if only Christ himself was as visible to us as he was to the leper. That way, there would be no need for faith. It would be so clear to us.' If you weren't thinking this, I was. And it is a reasonable thought. However, despite living proof, I wonder how many of us would still question His existence? I wonder how many of us would still pursue false gods, would still deny love and hope? If Christ were standing here right now, in this church, how many of us would rationalize His presence and call what we saw an apparition, a ghost? And when we went back to our friends, how many of us would feel stupid when telling them what we saw? Especially when we were met with odd looks and disbelief. My point is this—faith does not come from what we can see or touch. If it did, there would be no value to it, no importance. Christ knows this. He knows that His invisible presence is worth more than if He took a walk down Grand Street every day and ate dinner at the local diner. You know why? Because He knows that eventually we would question the very thing we saw with our own eyes, or touched with our own hands, and it would lose value. We are human. We are frail and unable to cope with or understand the mysteries of life and death. That is why we pray and that is why we need to believe when there is no proof. 'It is easier to move a mountain than it is to have faith,' says the gospel. Those are not idle words. To love God is to love the mystery. And to find proof that you can touch or see or even hear with your own ears, is not proof at all. It is not Christ's way. That is why true faith is valued. Any one of us here could move a mountain if we really wanted to, but how many of us could say that we truly know God?" Frank stepped away from the pulpit and back to the altar, where the altar boys, carrying the tray of water and wine, offered them to him.

Frank took his gold-plated chalice, holding it with both hands but allowing his thumbs and forefingers to hang over the lip of the cup. Then the altar boy holding the wine poured some over Frank's finger and into the chalice. The same was done with the water.

Frank waited for the altar boys to kneel at the altar steps, then he turned to the kneeling congregation. "Blessed are you, Lord, God of all creation. Through your goodness we have this wine to offer, fruit of the vine and work of human hands. It will become our spiritual drink," he said to them listening closely to the words he was saying.

They answered, "Blessed be God, forever."

Frank walked to the tabernacle, opening its gold-plated door. He took out the large ciborium, which held the tiny wafers, the consecrated hosts, and carried them over to the altar table. There he emptied them on the paten, held one in between his fingers, then raised it for all to see. "Blessed are you, Lord, God of all creation. Through your goodness we have this bread to offer, which earth has given and human hands have made. It will become for us the bread of life," he said.

"Blessed be God, forever," the faithful responded.

Frank turned to the rows of pews and said the Lord's Prayer. The congregation followed. "Our Father, who art in heaven, hallowed be thy name; thy kingdom come; thy will be done on earth as it is in heaven. Give us this day our daily bread; and forgive us our trespasses as we forgive those who trespass against us; lead us not into temptation but deliver us from evil. Amen."

Frank broke the host, saying, "Lamb of God, you take away the sins of the world."

The congregation replied in unison, "Have mercy on us."

Frank said again, "Lamb of God, you take away the sins of the world."

"Have mercy on us," the congregation answered.

"Lamb of God, you take away the sins of the world."

"Grant us peace!"

Frank took the Eucharist to his lips. "Before he was given up to death, a death he freely accepted," Frank said, "He took bread and gave thanks. He broke the bread, gave it to his disciples, and said: Take this, all of you, and eat it: this is my body which will be given for you. When supper was ended, he took the cup. Again he gave thanks and praise, gave the cup to his disciples, and said: Take this, all of you, and drink from it: this is the cup of my blood, the blood of the new and everlasting covenant. It will be shed for you and for all so that sins may be forgiven."

The sanctus bells rang as the bread and wine were changed to Christ's body and blood. The church was quiet and solemn. Frank prepared to take communion himself. Frank felt his throat dry and hard. As all priests knew, he was well aware that what he was doing was not a symbolic act, but he was actually turning the bread and wine into the body and blood of Christ. Just as Christ had done according to the gospels. Given the powers of a priest, it was his duty to administer that sacrament to the faithful.

"I'm performing a miracle," Frank thought to himself. "The miracle of changing the bread and wine into the body and blood of Christ."

Frank raised the Holy Eucharist so that all in the church could see. "Do this in memory of me," he said with his eyes raised to the ceiling and a heaven he tried to imagine.

"Lord, I am not worthy to receive you, but only say the word and I shall be healed," Frank said with his hands trembling. He then bowed his head and pretended to place the wafer in his mouth as if swallowing it. He felt a tremendous disgrace—he could not receive communion, the body and blood of his savior. He had not gone to confession, so his soul was tainted with sin. It was better to disgrace himself, if caught in the act of pretending communion, than to blaspheme God and endanger his immortal soul.

"Hallelujah, hallelujah!" the chorus of worshipers sang out as Frank held back the trembling that grew from his hands to his arms and shoulders. He quickly walked to the altar railing to meet the hundred or so who were waiting to receive the Eucharist.

With an altar boy standing at his side and one step ahead of him, Frank placed the small white wafers on the tongues of those waiting on their knees at the altar railing. Receiving the host purified them and they would be in a state of grace until they sinned again.

Frank could not look at the faces that looked up at his. He rushed through the giving of the Eucharist, touching the white wafer, hoping for a sensation, anything, that would make him feel that it was something more than just a wafer. But he felt nothing. Though he loved the drama of the words and the glory of the act itself, it was all just a concept to him, neat and logical.

Frank watched the altar boy who was holding the gold-plated paten placed under the chalice in case any of them fell. Church law prohibited any hands touching the wafers after they had been transformed into the body and blood. The responsibility that only his sanctified hands were allowed to touch the Eucharist reminded Frank even more of how hollow a symbol of the Church he had become. To him, even his gold chalice, which shone brilliantly in the light, was only a gift from his parents and not the blessed vessel the Church said it was.

"Let us affirm our faith," Frank said, still trying to hide the duplicity in his own heart from all those eyes that were looking upon him. Frank spoke loudly with the rest of the church, "We believe in God, the almighty creator of heaven and earth. We believe in Jesus Christ, his only son, conceived by the Holy Spirit and born of the Virgin Mary. He suffered under Pontius Pilate, was crucified, and was buried. He descended to the dead and on the third day he arose again. He ascended into heaven and is seated at the right hand of the Father. He will come again to judge the living and the dead."

Frank felt beads of sweat on his brow and more of them running down his collar. He could see the altar boys watch him with confusion.

The congregation continued—"We believe in the Holy Spirit, the holy Catholic Church, the communion of saints, the forgiveness of sins, the resurrection of the body, and the life everlasting, amen."

Frank sought to find his voice. "The Lord be with you."

"And with your spirit."

Frank raised his eyes to the glittering twilight beauty of the candles and lamplight outstretched before him. "Go in peace," he said, then quickly walked off the altar to the vestibule.

His thanked his two altar boys and hung the borrowed vestments onto a hook in the vestibule closet and put on his coat. He could hear the crowd milling around the vestibule door.

"Is there another way out?" Frank asked the altar boy.

"There is, Father."

"Which way?"

"Out that door," the boy said to him, pointing to the far corner of the room.

Smiling at the boy, Frank put his finger to his lips, then opened the door and followed its long, winding path behind the altar. The back way out the vestibule led Frank to the other side of the altar and the pulpit. Frank walked past the altar and headed down the center aisle of the nearly empty church. Just as he reached the door a woman stepped out from a pew.

"Would you bless me, Father?" the elderly woman asked.

"No," Frank said, looking at her with blank eyes. He walked away, leaving the woman stunned as he stepped out the back door, feeling like the Antichrist.

Frank then went up to his room and vomited into the toilet. He knew he had just committed a mortal sin.

There was a knock on Frank's door. It was Father Paulino. "Father Frank, we just got a call. Maria Katowski is in danger!"

Frank cleaned himself up, then opened the door. A pale Father Paulino quickly explained to him that a young boy called the rectory asking for Frank and left an address. The boy said that Maria was very sick.

Father Paulino drove Frank to the address, which was only minutes away. They drove past Maurice Park, continued on under the Long Island Expressway and down a road that grew more deserted as he followed it. Father Paulino drove past a Federal Express office, several truck lots and eventually he found the address. Parked in front of what was clearly an abandoned factory was an ambulance. There was a hustle of activity around it.

Frank had arrived just as paramedics were carrying Maria Katowski out on a small wheeled metal stretcher. She was wrapped in several blankets and a large safety belt kept her from falling off. Frank could see that her eyes were closed and her face was pale.

"How is she?" Frank asked a young blond boy.

"She had a needle in her arm," he answered quickly.

"I'm a priest!" Frank shouted to a short woman whose blond hair was tied back under a green cap. "I know this girl! Can I ride to the hospital with you?" he asked.

The woman nodded and Frank watched as Maria was placed quickly into the ambulance, then he jumped into the truck. Father Paulino was told that they were going to Saint John's Hospital and he drove there as quickly as he could. Inside the ambulance was a unit that was prepared to handle drug overdoses.

"We got an OD!" a bearded paramedic shouted into the ambulance radio as Frank held onto the handgrip bolted into the side of the paneling of the ambulance—just to keep his balance.

"What's her pulse?" the woman asked with a tone of authority in her voice.

The baby-faced blond boy in the white and orange colors of the paramedic's outfit held Maria's motionless arm as he looked at his watch. "It's way down," he said to the woman.

"Oh, man, we're gonna lose her," the bearded paramedic said to the black man driving the ambulance through the narrow congested streets around Grand Avenue.

"Give 'em the horns!" the woman shouted.

Frank watched Maria lie perfectly still as the siren blasted from the ambulance's roof. Her eyes were still closed and her face grew more and more rigid in its appearance despite the flash of the red lights outside the window.

Frank felt helpless as the paramedics worked around him.

"She's young, she's got to have the strength," the bearded paramedic said with desperation in his voice.

"The stuff may be bogus," the woman answered back. "They mix rat poison in some of it. I saw a dude go down in Brooklyn last month. His eyes were bulging."

The baby-faced boy looked up at the long-haired woman with his eyes wide open. "No vitals!"

Frank was pushed out of the way as the bearded, taller man threw both his fists hard on Maria's chest. "CPR!" he shouted.

"Move this damn truck!" the woman yelled to the driver, who was already speeding through red lights.

"She's blue!" the baby-faced boy shouted. As he did, the woman moved him out of the way and began to slap Maria's face hard. When she saw no reaction, she took a bag of ice and shoved it under Maria's blouse. She then pulled Maria's pants down around her ankles, shoving another bag of ice between her thighs. As she did, the bearded paramedic continued to punch Maria's heart, hoping to get it working again.

"What's her pulse?" he shouted to the baby-faced boy.

"No change!" the boy shouted back.

The bearded man turned to the defibrillator and got it set up. He then placed it over Maria's heart. "Ready! I'm not losing this one!"

Frank watched as the woman hit the switch and electric currents blasted through Maria's body.

"Again!" shouted the bearded man.

"Ready!" shouted the woman. Maria's body jerked.

The crew waited for a reaction. There was none.

"What's her vitals?" the bearded man asked.

"No change," the young boy answered.

Frank looked at the woman as the baby-faced boy stared at Maria's lifeless body.

The bearded man looked at Frank without emotion. "She's gone. She's dead," he said, as if Frank didn't understand him the first time.

The woman pushed her hair away from her face and turned to Frank. "Shouldn't you do something?"

Frank just looked at her.

"She's Catholic," the woman said, gesturing to Maria's gold cross lying motionless on her chest.

Frank looked up at the bearded man, who was now writing in his chart. The woman was looking right at him as the baby-faced boy sat back, stunned.

Frank mumbled some words in Latin as he made the sign of the cross on Maria's forehead, then touched her cold lips with his forefinger and thumb. "Blessed are they that mourn, for they shall be comforted," he said, remembering a quotation from Matthew. He then held Maria's hand and whispered to her, as if she could hear him, "May the souls of all the faithful departed, through the mercy of God, rest in peace."

Frank moved away from Maria, taking in her pale, now nearly blue young body, and shook his head slowly.

That afternoon Frank did nothing but sit in his room watching the sun slowly fade into a sad twilight.

He was numb.

He put on his civilian clothes: plain blue shirt, jeans, and sneakers. Wearing a windbreaker over it all, he got into his car and drove aimlessly for twenty minutes until he came to Queens Boulevard. At the corner of 56th Avenue stood the slope of a large hill. Above the hill and to the south was a larger grassy hill and the northernmost arm of Calvary Cemetery. At its crest, in between large elm trees, was a scene of the crucifixion played out by ten-foot white statues of the Blessed Virgin Mary, Mary Magdalene, and Christ. The Virgin Mary was standing looking up with her arms reaching out for her son who was hanging on the cross with his head tilted upwards as his eyes searched the sky for God, his father. Mary Magdalene was the audience of one with her hands at her sides and her eyes glued to Christ.

The statues gleamed white in the early evening darkness, two spotlights adding to the dramatic effect. Frank stood across the street from the cemetery after parking his car. He recognized the setting from his youth, nearly forgotten. He looked at the haunting drama being played out on the hill by the large statues and noticed all the cars driving by on Queens Boulevard, oblivious to the human drama represented.

It shook Frank deeply to face the symbol of his own delinquency. After having said Mass with the corrupt soul of a heretic and now being confronted with the enormous symbol of his faith, it was too much. He turned around and looked for a bar. But there were none in sight. He was standing by a deserted gas station and realized that he was at the edge of a small industrial area near the residential homes of Jackson Heights.

He walked up the block thinking he might find a bar at the top of the hill when he came upon a large painted sign that read NAKED CITY. He walked up to it and saw a large bouncer with a Mohawk haircut standing at the door.

"Ten bucks to get in," the bouncer said.

Frank handed him the ten dollars. "What's inside?"

"Anything you want," the bouncer grinned.

Frank shook his head and entered the noisy club. He was immediately hit by a loud blast of music and the swirl of colored lights. He followed a small crowd that led him through a hall of mirrors and up a few steps that led up to a long bar. The bar had been turned into a platform and on the platform were eight young women—all nude. Frank was stunned but was quickly jolted back to reality when a nude woman stepped up and took him by the arm.

"Hi," said the pretty blonde, tall, thin and wearing nothing but sneakers, smiling.

Frank nodded a hello, then felt the girl's hands on his chest.

"You have to tip me, handsome," the blonde said to him.

Frank took out his wallet and handed her a dollar. She smiled and ran her hand across his waist as she quickly moved to the next man.

A topless waitress walked up to him, offering to get Frank a drink from the small bar in the corner of the room. Frank ordered a Scotch and walked to the platform. He found a seat and a pretty, dark Eurasian girl quickly stepped over to him. She wore a tight-fitting miniskirt and heels. Her round breasts were exposed and her dark eyes revealed neither a smile, nor an expression of any kind. She touched her breasts, and looked at Frank. He felt a surge of excitement race through him. She then turned around and slowly bent over. His eyes were glued to her legs as she slowly slipped her miniskirt up her waist until she was revealing everything to Frank, from the cheeks of her bottom to her labia.

Frank was immobile. She then placed her hand on her ass and slowly caressed herself. Frank took a bill out of his wallet and quickly gave it to her. The expression on her face never changed. Her eyes remained fixed on him and his on hers but nothing was said. She then moved down the platform and another girl stepped up to Frank. This one had a big smile. She lay down on the platform in front of him and spread her legs. As she did, the waitress gave Frank his drink. He tipped her, then tipped the smiling girl a dollar and knocked down the Scotch.

Frank went through three drinks at the bar and then stood up. He saw a sign that read VIP LOUNGE and followed it. The sign led him down a stairway, where he found himself on line. He was already dizzy from the drinks when a waitress brought him another as he waited. Up ahead he saw several bouncers bringing the men one at a time to a wall, where the nude girls danced privately for them. Small spotlights fell solely on the women, leaving the men in darkness.

Frank sipped his drink as he was led to the basement and directed to a folding chair. He sat in the folding chair in front of a stark naked young woman with steel-blue eyes and dirty blond hair. Barefoot, with nothing on but a tiny pink ribbon in her hair, her skin seemed to shimmer from the makeshift lamps that hung from the ceiling, placing her in a shadowy underworld.

Drunk, Frank handed her whatever small bills he had left in his wallet and she leaned over him, dangling her breasts in his face. Frank felt her breath on his face and saw her nipples just out of reach. She then turned around and bent over, showing him her perfectly shaped rear, then leaned over and sat down on him.

"Touch me, doll," she said in a strong voice.

Frank tentatively touched her hips with both hands and was surprised to feel her grab both his hands and place them firmly on her breasts. He hadn't touched a woman there in years. Her nipples were erect as he fondled them. The girl then turned and kissed him on the cheek. As she did, she pressed one hand down on his right leg and her other hand down on his crotch. She squeezed his penis briefly, then stood up.

"Next!" a bouncer shouted from behind Frank. Still dizzy from the booze, he turned and felt himself being lifted up and into the darkness and out of the VIP lounge. Moments later, he was back on the street, walking to his car. The headlights from the traffic put on a show for him as he grinned to himself, feeling too drunk, elated, and numb for any deep reflection. When he found his car, he also found himself looking up at the crucifixion scene. This time its haunting presence was dissipated by his drunkenness. He smiled at the scene which looked less dramatic and more or less sterile in his estimation.

Though he couldn't be the perfect priest, he'd be the perfect sinner. So, he saluted Christ on the cross with an exaggerated gesture, got into his car, and drove off.

Frank found himself parked in front of Roxanna's apartment. He got out of the car when he saw that the light in her living room window was on. He walked up the stoop and rang the bell. He turned and from where he stood he could see the entire Manhattan skyline glimmer over his shoulder.

The door opened and Roxanna stood with the light behind her. She stepped out onto the stoop, facing Frank.

"What?" she asked. Her face was drawn and tired. Her sharp blue eyes frowned at Frank. She was wearing a light blue T-shirt and jeans, and she was barefoot. Frank knew that a glass of Scotch couldn't be far away.

"I couldn't go back to that room—alone. I had no place else," Frank told her.

Roxanna watched him for a moment. "Do you want coffee?" He nodded. Roxanna let him in.

He walked in as Roxanna closed the door. He stood silently with his hands at his side. He tried to push away the faces and bodies of the girls he had just watched in the den of iniquity he had just come from; but they wouldn't go away. So, instead, he concentrated on Roxanna's face and how it seemed to mirror his: the loneliness, the dark circles under the eyes, the distress.

He followed her into the kitchen. The side light was on but it wasn't too unbearable. The coffee was brewing as Roxanna washed out two coffee cups. She tried to pass him but stopped. "Move, please," she said. He stepped back. "Where were you?" she asked him.

"Paying my dues," he answered.

Roxanna seemed to understand. The coffee was ready and she turned to him. "Sit inside. I'll bring it in."

Frank walked into the living room. A small lamp was on. He found the sofa and sat. His head was spinning.

Roxanna entered the room and sat on a chair across from him. She placed his coffee down on a table beside the sofa. Frank looked at it. "You're not wearing your collar," she said.

"I know," Frank told her.

"Did you come here for pity?" Roxanna asked. "Because if you did, you can turn around and go. I don't have any pity for any priest."

"No. I didn't come here for pity."

"Then why did you come here?"

Frank didn't answer. He tried standing but felt dizzy. He

managed to get up. He stepped over to Roxanna.

"What?" she said again, like someone who knows the answer but needs to hear it. She stood up and placed her hand on the back of his neck. She caressed him for a moment then stopped. Frank leaned toward her. He took her in his arms and then gently kissed her on the lips. Her lips were wet and soft. "I thought you didn't want this," she said to him.

He didn't answer. But he held her tightly and kissed her again. He felt her tongue in his mouth so he gave her his. They pushed toward one another tightly. Frank felt her hand on his belt as she pulled it to open his pants. Though he was drunk, he managed to pull up her T-shirt and pull down her bra, not even waiting to undo the straps. Roxanna pulled his pants down over his hips and Frank felt her hands on his erect penis. His mouth was on her nipples as she pulled his penis back and forth with one hand, caressing his ass, his legs, and his back with the other.

Frank then turned to her jeans, but before he could undo them, she had already slipped them down from her waist. Seeing a glimpse of her white panties made him yearn for her even more. He saw her pubic hair, vagina, and he wanted to touch it, taste it, forget all of his problems just by being that close. He slid her panties down over her hips, pulling her to the floor.

He wanted to enter her, make love to her, pull her closer than anyone had ever done before. He was losing himself in her, feeling the sensation overwhelm his senses. He kissed her mouth, her earlobes, her neck, her breasts. He felt her firm, round bottom in the palm of his hands. He felt her hand touching him below his penis, pushing him forward, making a thrill of sensation rise up to the top of his head, promising the white heat of sex and the overpowering pleasure of release.

But then he stopped. He pulled himself away from her. He had to. He was sweating and his mouth was still wet from the kissing, but knew he had to stop.

He could see her lying back on the floor looking up at him. Her blue eyes and their black pupils were big in the shadows. He could see the outline of her thighs and her breasts—but he knew he couldn't go on.

Though he was still high from the drinks, he knew he had to get dressed. He circled the room looking for his pants. He found them. Clutching them in his hands, he sat back on the sofa feeling foolish, childish, alone. Roxanna watched him. "What happened?" she asked.

He looked to her. He could see the outline of her pretty face. "I took a vow."

"You broke others. I know you have," she told him.

"But they only involved me. This would involve you, too," he said. "Anyway, it wouldn't do us any good."

"And you decided for the both of us?" Roxanna asked.

"I came here because I couldn't stand being alone over there. But by coming here, I'm asking too much from you."

Roxanna looked at Frank a long moment, found her clothes, put them on, then sat in the dark.

"I don't understand you. I'm confused," she said.

"I shouldn't have come here," Frank told her.

"You want this thing to be a miracle, don't you? So you can be a hero and announce to all the bishops and cardinals that Frank Moore has found proof of another saint?"

"No. That's not why."

"Then what is your reason?" Roxanna asked.

"We both know what a world without hope is like. But if I can help prove that there's a reason to believe . . ."

"You want to justify your life. You need a miracle to do that?"

"Yes," Frank answered.

"It's the here and now that matters to me."

"I understand that more than you think," he told her.

"Then have faith in that."

"It isn't enough." Frank stood and looked for the door. "I have to get back."

"You can't drive like that," she told her. "Stay."

"I can't," Frank answered. He looked for his coat. Finding it, he made his way through the semidarkness to the door. He looked for Roxanna, but he couldn't see her. He then followed the light as it spilled out from the kitchen.

"Is this what you want?" he heard Roxanna say from the light. He entered the kitchen and saw her sitting at the table facing a book. "It's my mother's diary," she told him.

Chapter 10

They sat at the table facing cups of coffee. Frank was reading the diary, entry by entry. One particular passage, written on July 19, read:

> "Roxanna has been on my mind today, all day. But Philip Kinnely has reassured me of my choice. Sometimes, when we speak of my daughter, I feel as if he and I are husband and wife discussing the life of someone who we both love so much. Philip doesn't know it—but he is my strength, and in many ways my partner."

"Read the passage of July 29," Roxanna said to him. Frank turned to it and read.

> "Philip came to my room last night with a pained look on his face. He sat down like a hurt child in the chair by the window, telling me that he fears losing me. I was so

moved by his words. He didn't stay long. When he left, I had such a lonely feeling. I wanted him to stay."

"Now read August 14," she said to him. Frank turned a few pages forward and read aloud:

"August 14. Saturday night. This summer has been hot and I feel tired all the time. . . I am writing this entry in the middle of the night . . . near three o'clock and though the streets outside are empty, I hear every noise, every cat that walks, every car that drives by. It is on nights like this that I miss someone sleeping beside me. My husband was so good on nights like this when I couldn't sleep . . . he would listen to my worries and concerns . . . Philip is like that . . . so much like my husband . . . I know he has so much affection for me . . . I know that he does . . ."

Frank stopped.
"Go on," Roxanna told him. He did.

"August 28. Saturday night. About one o'clock there was a knock on my door. It was Philip. He was sweating . . . his eyes were on me as soon as I opened the door. I was half asleep and only wearing a thin nightgown . . . he said something about not being able to sleep . . . I know I should have left the convent . . . I told him that I was tired . . . he looked at me so sweetly. Lord . . . I have not been held by anyone in so long. . . . please give me the strength to forget how much I long to be kissed as a woman is kissed . . . to be desired . . . to be touched and to touch . . . I have tried to eliminate the physical from my life . . . for you, Oh Lord . . . but I . . . crave the closeness of another human being in my arms . . . I was with a man most of my life . . . the memories are so difficult to forget . . . Oh, Lord, please hear my prayer . . ."

Frank stopped reading. He closed the book.

"They made love," Roxanna said.

"It doesn't say that they did," Frank replied.

"What is it with you, Frank?" Roxanna asked. "Can't you accept that she was lonely, that she needed someone? Do you find it so repulsive when someone acts like a human being?"

Frank said nothing.

Roxanna stood up. "She was a human being, goddamn you! Frail, lost, confused."

"If she made love to Kinnely, then she clearly sinned. And if she sinned, she wasn't a saint," Frank said slowly and deliberately. "I don't interpret this passage the way you do."

Roxanna sat back down and looked at Frank with sharp, accusing eyes. "Go try and prove that God exists in somebody else's life, not mine."

"I became a priest to prove that there wasn't a God," he told her. "I know that now. I wanted to prove that a loving God didn't exist. Why? Because the God I believed in was the mirror image of me. A God too good for the world. A God who only cared about the proud, the powerful, the intellectual," Frank told her. "And then when I investigated Falcone's death I proved that a caring God doesn't exist," he said.

Roxanna was confused. "I don't understand."

"I'm here to disprove this miracle, Roxanna. They don't want your mother to be a saint."

She listened and said nothing.

"I'm the miracle-killer." Saying that, Frank walked back into the living room and sat down on the sofa. He closed his eyes. He was so exhausted and drunk, he didn't hear Roxanna walking into the room behind him. He didn't feel her taking off his coat, helping him lie back, and he didn't feel her gently covering him with a blanket.

When Frank awoke it was after seven and Roxanna had already

left. There was no note, nothing. Frank got himself up from the sofa and locked the door behind him when he left.

The sky was a murky purple with spots of light filtering through it as he sat at his desk by the window in his room at the rectory. Stretching just a bit, Frank could see the blue-gray color of the Manhattan skyline. In front of him was the diary and he was reading it page by page.

Frank found something extraordinary in Helen Stephenson's journal, especially in her last year on earth: there was the talk of hope, and what should be done to form new charities, new guidance counseling, and ways of forming new bonds of friendship between neighbors in the parish.

Frank turned page after page, reading the woman's determination not to allow her life to be a meaningless one. She called upon her God every day, asking Him, pleading with Him, cajoling Him to bring love and peace to those her life touched. She wrote about the parish, the nuns and laity she came across in drives to raise funds for orphans, the handicapped, and the underprivileged. She wrote about the children in the school across the yard from her modest room in the convent. She wrote about her prayers to God the Father and especially the Blessed Virgin. Yet her prayers were never for herself. She never asked the God to whom she prayed to give her anything but the strength to continue what she called over and over—"His Will." All her prayers were for others and their needs.

As Frank read deeper and deeper into her life, turning the pages as the book grew thinner, he realized that Helen Stephenson never mentioned her daughter more than a few times. When she did mention Roxanna, she always wrote of her daughter in a painful way. She would write how she thought so much of her daughter, wanting to call her and asking to see her, but also refusing the thought. Always afraid that if Roxanna came back into her life, her love for her daughter would distract her from serving her Lord fully. Helen Stephenson wrote how much she felt she had failed as a mother. That was her sole grief. And at times, that grief was revealed with a blunt denial of

Roxanna's importance in her life. Her God was the significant factor in her day-to-day thoughts, and not her daughter.

Frank wondered how deeply this must have affected Roxanna when she read it. It was clear that her own mother had chosen God over her. And since Helen Stephenson was not an educated woman, that choice was made bluntly and awkwardly, without the intellectual capacity to justify it. It was a decision as brutal as any decision when survival of the heart and soul is at stake. In the end, Helen Stephenson believed that she could do more good in the world by giving herself wholeheartedly to the parish and its faithful than to the needs of one individual—her daughter. It was a remarkable choice, as devastating as it was courageous. The woman sacrificed her own longings as a mother for the needs of strangers.

Frank was sure, as he read and reread the pages, that Helen Stephenson did not make the choice for the glory, or to escape the responsibility of her motherhood. She made it because she felt that it was the way she could do the most good. It was a moral and emotional choice. It was an inspired choice, and a severely painful one. Both mother and daughter suffered. Both suffered so that Helen Stephenson's love of her God could flourish unchecked.

As he read on, Frank found that the one person mentioned more frequently than anyone else in the journal was Father Kinnely. His name appeared at least once on every page. And the further the journal went into that last year of her life, the closer Helen Stephenson grew to the man she began to call "Philip."

This "Philip," Father Kinnely, did everything with Helen Stephenson and she planned everything with him. From charity functions to the special Masses and the toy drives and orphan funds, they were inseparable. Helen would come up with a plan to raise money and then go about cajoling, prodding, and pushing Father Kinnely, knowing that his authority as pastor would get the project through.

Frank read on, experiencing the severity of her missionary zeal. He also began to learn, through her words, what was happening between her and Father Kinnely. When she mentioned Father Kinnely, the tone of the entries changed: they were no longer about events and plans; they now had a personal edge to them.

Besides the entries he had read with Roxanna, Frank found others concerning that period of time.

"August 1. Philip walked me back to my room laughing as we both joked about the way Father Paulino was so surprised with the party we had thrown for him. Once in my room, I wanted to change the conversation to something that had been on my mind. I wanted to speak to the archbishop about raising funds for a drug clinic. We needed one in the neighborhood. . . . Philip was too jolly for such a serious discussion . . . I told him that he should go to sleep . . . but he kept talking about how much fun he had . . . and he started looking at me . . . I am a grown woman and I do know the feelings men have . . . I began, for the first time, to fear that I may be creating these feelings in Philip . . . I mentioned to him that maybe I should move out of the convent . . . He was furious! He was so hurt and then he got mad at me! His mood shifted so quickly . . . I never saw him so angry . . . when he asked me why I would even think about moving . . . I lied. I told him that I needed more privacy . . . he got up and left so quickly, he didn't even shut the door . . ."

Several entries after that were missing. Frank found the next long one, dated August 28. It was part of one he had read earlier at Roxanna's house. He reread it.

". . . Labor Day weekend. Father Paulino and Father Stacey are visiting relatives. I have managed to stay away from Philip most of the day. The school is empty and though the place is lonely, I must admit that I like having all of this room to myself . . . I have enjoyed each day

though the heat is nearly unbearable. Waiting for the rain.
Wanted to see Roxanna but she called to say she was
going to the Jersey shore with friends for the weekend.

The next entry simply read:

"Philip came to my room last night."

And the next entry was a list of quotations from the Bible,
mainly from the Old Testament. The handwriting was getting
harder to read and the entries began to grow less consistent.
Several days were skipped, and when an entry was made it only
dealt with matters of business. Helen Stephenson's obsession
with the drug clinic grew.

By the end of September the mention of an illness appeared.

"It is Monday, September 23. I awoke out of a deep sleep
last night from a sharp pain that ran through my chest.
My left arm had very little feeling. I have told no one of
this . . ."

An entry made on September 26 was the most difficult to read.

"Left side of my face . . . is stiff and hurts. Speech is
slurred . . . I sleep so little Lord, I am ready for Your
hands . . . *Confiteor Deo Ominoptenti . . .*"

The last entry in the journal was made on September 29.

"Lord . . . please protect my daughter who I love with all
my . . . Philip is my deepest concern . . . my shame . . . I
have . . . without you, My Lord . . . there is no hope.
Please, let all my work not be in vain . . . it is all I can
offer to you . . . I am not worthy but only say the words
and I shall be healed."

Frank reread the last passage then closed the book. He walked out of his room, down the dimly lit hallway finding Kinnely's door open and Kinnely sitting at his desk with his head in his hands.

Chapter 11

Frank knocked on the open door. Kinnely turned to him.

"Do you have a minute? I have some questions to ask you," Frank said.

"I was going to go to Helen's grave. Can we speak there?" Kinnely asked.

"Yes," Frank said. They got their coats, got into Frank's car, and drove to the cemetery.

The bleak gray sky stretched out in all directions above them as they stood over Helen Stephenson's grave in Calvary Cemetery. Her grave was on top of a hill near a gully that was hidden by a thick row of trees. A cold wind blew east from the city skyline, which rose up over the East River. Frank could feel the thick, damp air in his nostrils and his eyes as he looked down at the simple marble gravestone which read "Helen Stephenson, 1933-1985." The stone was speckled and dark gray. Father Kinnely had brought along a bouquet of flowers and he forced them down into the hard-packed earth. They stood, red and yellow against the bare, brown earth.

"She was a young woman," Frank said, breaking the silence.

Father Kinnely didn't move. His eyes were watery from the cold and dampness and he hardly took them off the gravestone at his feet.

"How often do you come up here?"

"Whenever I get the chance," Father Kinnely answered.

Frank watched the overweight, round-faced priest stand with his hands at his side and his knees bent just enough to keep his balance in the strong shifting winds. Like the schoolyard, the cemetery hill created a funnel for the wind as it blew up from the river and from northeast of the city.

"I remember the day we put her here. It was just as gray out. It was the longest walk of my life—up this hill. Everyone was here. The nuns, the kids from the school, her daughter, the whole neighborhood. I said the usual prayers and the usual things were done. We all held a rose and threw it on the coffin as we walked past the grave." Father Kinnely glanced to the long stretches of highway which ran like a swirl of zigzags off in the distance. "Cars were driving by just like they are now. The world was going on with the things that the world goes on with—but there was such a silence."

Frank could hear the quiet hum of the highway in the distance. He could also see rooftops brown and black on the horizon beyond the steel gray of the roadways. The rooftops belonged to Maspeth.

"No one cried. We all knew that she was in God's hands," Father Kinnely said.

Frank felt the knifelike wound cut through the warm comfort of his coat. Reaching for the journal, he touched it with his gloved hand then pulled it out of his pocket and showed it to Father Kinnely.

"You recognize this?" he asked.

Father Kinnely looked at the journal then looked up to Frank. "No. Is it her journal? The daughter gave it to you? You found it?"

"You lied to me. You told me you didn't know it existed."

"I wasn't sure."

"Have you read it?"

"No."

Frank kept his eyes on the priest standing in front of him. He watched as Father Kinnely huddled himself in the long black coat that he wore. "Here. Are you curious? Do you want to look at it?"

"I don't know if I can."

"Why not?" Frank asked.

"I don't know if I can take it. Hearing her voice. Reading her words, her thoughts."

"Why not?"

Father Kinnely silently glared at Frank.

Frank passed the book between his fingers as he held it. "I read it last night. And there are some things in here I must ask you about. Unsettling questions."

"I'm not afraid of what Helen wrote." Father Kinnely grew rigid in the cold wind. "Ask me anything."

Frank waited a moment, then spoke. "She wanted to leave her room at the convent and find a place outside. Why didn't you let her?"

Father Kinnely looked dumbstruck; as if someone had just seen a movie of his most secret moments. "She was concerned. Concerned that I was developing feelings for her."

"Were you?" Frank asked.

"Yes," Father Kinnely answered quickly.

"I want to know what happened between the two of you."

"Nothing of that nature ever occurred."

"Were you aware of the feelings she had for you?"

Father Kinnely gave Frank his puppy dog look. "I'm cold."

"Answer me."

"I was her pastor. She obeyed God's law and the Church. We spent time together. We planned things together."

Frank grew impatient. "When you were alone with her, what went on between you?" Frank demanded to know.

Father Kinnely snarled at Frank. "You have no conscience, do you? No shame! You twist her words to create something false!"

"Did she let you sleep with her, Father Kinnely?" Frank screamed, loud enough to frighten a handful of sparrows from the limb of a bare oak several rows of tombstones away.

Father Kinnely turned and walked down across the path of dead grass to the sidewalk where the car was waiting. Frank followed quickly behind him.

"That's what happened, isn't it?" Frank shouted.

"No!"

"That's the fact you've been hiding from me ever since I got here! You didn't want me to know that something corporeal, something intimate happened between you two! It would negate everything good that she had done! That's why you can't stop telling me what a good person she was! You're doing this out of guilt, aren't you, Father Kinnely?"

Father Kinnely was white-faced. He leaned against the door of the car, catching his breath.

"She allowed you to make love to her! She loved you and found herself unable to resist those feelings that she had! That Labor Day weekend when the two of you were alone! You went to her room and you wanted her!"

Father Kinnely pushed Frank violently away. He leaned over and gagged. Frank took hold of Father Kinnely as the priest vomited in the side of the road.

"Kinnely?" Frank said, controlling his voice.

Father Kinnely pushed Frank away again. He threw his bulky body to the hood of the car, leaning on it for support.

"She was a human being," Father Kinnely said, wiping his mouth.

"I know that. I don't judge her."

Father Kinnely shook his head wildly. "But she never let me."

"Never let you what?"

"Touch her."

Frank shook his head. "Stop protecting her."

"Let God be my witness! She never let me touch her!"

Frank stepped back. He gave Father Kinnely room to breathe. He could see how faint the priest looked. "Then what happened that night?"

Father Kinnely tried to balance himself on his own feet. He closed his eyes as the wind picked up and pushed through his thin gray hair. "I went to see her. I did. I couldn't get her out of my mind. I have always desired women. But never, Father, never have I ever approached a woman as I did Helen that night. I loved her, damn you!"

Frank saw the rage in Father Kinnely's eyes as the priest turned to him.

Father Kinnely's voice grew louder as he spoke. "She knew what I was feeling. She didn't want to hurt me. We never spoke about the tenderness we felt for one another. I even considered leaving the priesthood for her. But she wouldn't hear of it."

"Why not?" Frank asked.

Father Kinnely gasped for air as he spoke. "She loved God! She loved the Church! Not me!"

"What happened that night?" Frank asked.

Father Kinnely was breathing easier. He shifted his weight to the door of the car again. "I tried to kiss her. It was a foolish gesture. I just wanted to hold her. It wasn't just the sex. It was how I felt about the woman."

Frank saw the disappointment in the priest's eyes.

"She backed off from me. She was scared at first. I saw how confused she was. She didn't know what to do. I felt so damn cruel! I couldn't control what I felt for her and it was wrong for me to put so much on her! She saw me as her priest! Her confessor! The pastor of her church and here I was, a lecher! A filthy-minded old man!"

"But you loved her?" Frank said.

"I loved her. I also felt lust and love combined."

Frank thought of Roxanna. He thought of how she put her lips on his and how it made him feel alive, wanted, no longer lonely. "Did anyone witness this event on Labor Day?"

"No. Not that I know of," Kinnely said. Father Kinnely

relaxed. Frank could see him shrug his shoulders letting the air out from his lungs. "It was so hot in her room. I was sweating. I didn't want to go back to the rectory alone. It was such a long, empty night," Father Kinnely said.

"You're telling me that you never touched her?" Frank asked.

"I'm telling you that I wanted to but she wouldn't let me. She respected my collar more than I did!"

Frank bit the inside of his lip. "Why did you stay a priest? After she died?"

"Because that's what I am. I may be a bad priest, Father Moore, but it's all I know! I won't write an important book about God but I believe in His will, and I love Him," Father Kinnely answered.

"You didn't stay in the priesthood just to try to get a petition going for her?" Frank asked, trying to corner the pastor.

"No!" Father Kinnely shouted, looking visibly upset.

"Out of guilt?" Frank wanted the truth.

"No! You have to believe me! I know Helen was touched by God. I saw it that night I went to her room. I saw how she handled me." Father Kinnely's voice suddenly became softer. "She loved me. She did. I know she did. She loved me and was reaching out for me. She was a human being. But she refused to give into her own loneliness."

"I don't know if I believe your story—" Frank interrupted.

"But you must!" Father Kinnely pleaded.

"Why? Ever since I've been here you've kept the truth from me. Every time I learn something of significance in this case it has to be despite you!" Frank shouted.

Father Kinnely's eyes portrayed the look of a man who was not immune to the idea of punishing himself even more so than he had already done. "You can't take vengeance on her when all of this was my fault."

Frank slowly placed the journal back in his pocket. "You would swear to all this?"

"Yes," Father Kinnely answered quickly.

"And what about the desecrations in the cemetery?"

"I paid the gatekeeper to do it. All of it."

"And the polluted water?" Frank asked.

"That too."

"From the pipes under the rectory? The hot water pump?" Frank asked.

"Yes," Kinnely answered slowly.

"Are Paulino and Stacey in on this with you?" Frank asked.

"No! They know nothing about it!" Kinnely was adamant.

"The cardinal will have to hear your testimony and you will no doubt have to answer his questions, too." Frank felt the sympathy in himself grow. "I doubt that you'll be allowed to remain pastor if they accept what you say as the truth."

"I'm not a very good pastor," Father Kinnely said with a frown.

Frank pushed his collar up. The morning sky was none the brighter. If there was a sun in the sky it was warming some other world. It cast no shadow on the rows of gray and brown marble tombstones.

"Everything I have told you here today is the truth," Father Kinnely said.

"I believe you desired her. That is all I believe right now," Frank told him.

"Was that so wrong? Even for a priest?" Kinnely asked.

"Yes," Frank answered. "For a priest who believes in his vows, you know it is."

"I was lonely," Kinnely said mumbling his words.

"I understand the excuse."

"You do?"

"More than you know. I understand it and I empathize with it. But I cannot condone it," Frank said.

They then drove out of the cemetery in silence.

Mrs. Katowski wore a simple black dress with a black hat and veil for her daughter's funeral. Alone in the first pew, she hardly took her eyes off the altar; except when she glanced at the small plain coffin in front of her. All the classes from the school, from the first grade up to the eighth were required to attend, along with the nuns and Father Paulino and Father Stacey.

Frank watched how ashen and drained Mrs. Katowski held the wooden railing of the pew in front of her to stop herself from trembling. Her pale blue eyes, swollen from tears, were charged as if wired to every nerve in her body. Kinnely told Frank that Maria's father could not be reached, as no one knew where he was.

After the funeral Mass, Frank found himself standing on the same windy hill, not far from Helen Stephenson's grave. With himself and with Father Kinnely were Fathers Paulino and Stacey. And in the center of the men dressed in black with their white collars was Mrs. Katowski, holding a lone rose.

"I am the resurrection and the life," Father Kinnely said solemnly into the damp, still overcast morning. The sky overhead was dreary and gray, stretching, as Frank remembered, toward a horizon of infinite memories.

"They who believe in me, even if they die, shall live, and whoever lives and believes in me, shall never die," Father Kinnely prayed. He then said to everyone, "Ten years ago, God saved Maria. He delivered her from the jaws of death and handed her precious life back to us. And we failed her." He looked to Mrs. Katowski, who took her vivid red rose and gently tossed it into the hole at her feet. The coffin lay there for only a brief moment before the first shovel of dirt, thrown by the lone cemetery worker, covered it.

Mrs. Katowski howled in grief. Father Paulino took her shoulder and pulled her closer to him. He held the woman's head to his shoulder as she screamed with so much heartache that even the cemetery worker, who had seen a hundred burials, felt embarrassed. He stopped his shoveling and looked at his feet.

Father Kinnely was immobile. Frank wondered if it was Maria or Helen Stephenson he was thinking about as he stared blankly into the open grave. Father Paulino put his arms around Father

Kinnely. He knew Kinnely was devastated seeing Helen Stephenson's "miracle" die a junkie's pitiful death.

Frank slowly walked away from the small group, wanting to leave them all to their private pain. Before he got into his car he had a fleeting but vivid glimpse of the three priests dressed in their long black coats gently consoling the lonely woman, and he thought of Roxanna and her father's funeral. The way the priests must have been there for her mother, standing at the graveside with her. The enormity of the eternal sky and the shortness of a life. The limitless and the infinitesimal.

In the midst of his reverie, Frank noticed a lone teenager standing off a short distance—a teenager from the knife incident in the park. The teen was fragile-looking now. He must have been Jimmy.

"The coroner said it was bad heroin. Where did she get it, Jimmy?" Frank asked bluntly.

Jimmy looked at Frank. The anger in his eyes was gone. "Some guy. Nobody we knew."

"Were you with her? Did you see him?" Frank asked.

"No. It coulda been any dealer. Any guy. She told me she never saw him before. I shoulda been with her."

Frank saw how devastated he was. He watched as Jimmy fought back the tears. Frank put his hand on Jimmy's shoulder. "She loved you. She told me," he said. He then turned and walked back to his car.

Back in his room that night, Frank knelt by the bed and listened to his own voice. He wanted so much to believe that someone was listening. He wasn't praying for himself, he was praying for Roxanna, Kinnely, Maria Katowski, and her mother. He was praying for all the souls who had passed through the schoolyard hoping that the tears of blood were shed for them.

Chapter 12

In the ten years that the tears had fallen, dozens of the faithful had come forward announcing that the Blessed Virgin, through Helen Stephenson's intervention, had cured them of a malady. Father Kinnely had collected the names and now it came time for Frank and Corey to begin their cross-examination of the medical files and their interview of the "cured."

Out of forty-five people who said that they had been cured by the tears of blood, Frank and Corey easily dismissed thirty of them outright, as their medical reports were unclear or they had not been cured of any life-threatening diseases.

After reviewing the cases even further, they found out that several of the people, whose diseases were supposedly cured, had experienced recurrence and died. That left only a small handful remaining, three of whom had left the country and would be nearly impossible to locate. When they totaled up what they had left, they had only six potential candidates.

They knew that Maria Katowski was their ace in the hole and

their best shot at a canonical miracle. Even though she had died since, her personal testimony, to Frank, was powerful, her doctor's reports were compelling, and on top of that, a packed church had witnessed her cure.

Though they were convinced that she would be their first of the three miracles needed, they also knew that they could not approach the tribunal without at least several more miracle cures in their presentation.

The five others they chose to interview all had strong medical reports, eyewitnesses to the "cure," or could give strong personal testimony themselves.

Frank and Corey set up a large table in the auditorium and asked each of the people they needed to see to come at a scheduled appointment.

Ivan Kiev, a Russian emigrant, was the first they saw. He was a wide man with lightning blue eyes. He had a shock of white hair on his head and strong features. Despite being weathered for his seventy-two years, he still looked fierce and vital.

"I'm blind in this eye," he told Frank across the table, gripping a wooden cane in one hand and gesturing with the free one. "Then last year I pray to Helen and—I see again!"

"Do you have medical reports to prove you were blind in your eye to begin with?" Frank asked.

"Huh?" Ivan Kiev muttered.

"You see, sir, we know that you were able to see out of that eye because you have an excellent report here from Mount Sinai. But we realized, before we called you in, that you need to prove that you were blind *before* the miracle," Corey said, trying to explain the bureaucracy they were going to face.

Ivan Kiev was confused, but it didn't take long for Frank and Corey to realize that the man had never visited a doctor before the cure. He thought it beneath him.

Ultimately, they had to dismiss his claim.

Next, they saw a forty-year-old woman named Lydia Sanchez. She was a small woman with dark hair and eyes, overweight but bursting with energy. Her exuberance captivated Frank and Corey.

"The Blessed Virgin appeared to me in a dream. She spoke to me and said—'Helen is a saint!' So, I prayed to the statue and this happened!" She showed them scars on the palms of her hands.

"The stigmata," Frank said. He also read her report and saw that she claimed to have been cured of cancer, TB, and pneumonia. It might have been true, but she was still a lousy witness. His instincts told him that the tribunal would want pious, unobtrusive souls to be the fortunately cured, not extroverts vying for attention.

"God calls me his *Angel del Rio*! I am a river to His people!" she shouted.

They thanked her for her time but, like Ivan Kiev, she could not be added to the list.

When Raymond Forche, a handsome black man in his early thirties walked into the auditorium, Frank saw a glow of light fall around him. The auditorium windows were made of glass with a steel mesh fence individually around each. When light did filter in from outside, it was scattered. But for some reason, when Raymond Forche walked up to Frank, the light seemed to follow him. He sat down in front of the two priests and introduced himself.

Frank knew from his medical records that Raymond had been not only HIV-positive, but had been diagnosed with full-blown AIDS. But after praying to Helen, his white cell count, once under a hundred, had gone up to over a thousand. Diagnosed again, after his "miracle," there was no trace of the illness.

"I had TB, I had tumors in my liver, and a tumor in my right arm. But now—everything's gone," he said in a deep and melodious voice. The only residue of any aliment was a slight cough.

"Have you been taking any medication?" Frank asked.

"Couldn't afford any. Only cough drops, actually," he said.

"What about the cough?" Corey asked.

Forche smiled. "I guess I need to put my prayers to Helen into overtime," he said.

Frank looked to Corey, then circled Forche's name.

Whereas Forche was tall and easygoing, Sean Casey was short, slight, and filled with nervous energy. In his early sixties, he had a deep Irish accent. Hazel eyes flashing, he bellowed out his story to the two priests.

"Had prostate cancer. Thought I was a goner. The doctor told me not even surgery would help. I hadn't been inside a church in thirty years. But Molly, my wife, dragged me to the statue and I prayed to Helen. I was in pain, I couldn't tell you how bad. But the next day I went home and not a twinge! I was cured! The doctors say so in that medical report you got there in front of you. I felt so good I thought I'd become a missionary!"

Frank circled his name.

The last person on the list was Brenda Lopez. She had been diagnosed with leukemia. She was a tiny, soft-spoken twenty-nine-year-old woman. Her large brown eyes took everything in. "I was told I had less than a year to live. My mother took me here to pray to Helen," she informed Frank and Corey.

"You're now one-hundred-percent cured," Frank said, gesturing to the doctor's report in front of him.

"Thanks to the Blessed Virgin and Helen. She is a saint in heaven," Brenda Lopez said.

Frank circled her name.

Later that afternoon, after the interviews had ended, Frank and Corey walked across the yard to the convent.

"Someone had to see Father Kinnely and Helen Stephenson together," Frank said as they reached the building. A young heavyset nun, Sister Mary Elizabeth, answered their knock. She let the two priests make their way to Helen Stephenson's old room. They stood in the doorway a moment checking out the hallway. They then turned to another door.

"Let's try this," Corey said.

Frank knocked and Sister Alice answered. Frank was disappointed that it was her room. He had already talked with her and figured she would have volunteered information if she had had any.

"Sister Alice, we need your help," Frank said slowly. "We want you to think back to the last weekend in summer, Labor Day weekend, 1985. It was only a month before Helen died."

Sister Alice listened carefully.

"Do you remember anything happening here in the hallway that Saturday night?" he continued.

"We know it was a long time ago," Corey added.

Sister Alice gave them a half grin. "Time in the convent moves very swiftly. Ten years ago is like last weekend."

"We wondered if you heard an argument in the hallway between Helen and Father Kinnely?" Frank asked. "He tells us that it happened right outside this door somewhere around one in the morning."

"I couldn't have heard anything that weekend, Father Moore."

"Why not?"

"I was away. Visiting relatives. I'm sorry I can't help you."

Frank watched the nun closely. She seemed in control and she looked at him unblinkingly.

"Are you sure?" Corey asked.

"Yes. I'm sure."

"Well, if you think of anything that could help us, please let us know," Frank said.

"I will," Sister Alice said, then closed her door.

Frank and Corey turned, walked down the stairway, and let themselves out into the courtyard.

"She's lying. She saw it all. She's protecting him," Corey said.

"If she's lying, she's a pretty cool liar," Frank said. Then he corrected himself. "She also had a long time to practice."

After Sam left, Frank felt restless. He got into his car and drove around aimlessly, eventually finding himself parked in front of

Roxanna's apartment. He looked around feeling strange, as though he were hiding something. Wearing his collar, he looked in the mirror self-consciously. As he pulled the collar off, he noticed Roxanna making her way downhill toward her apartment.

Frank got out of the car and waited for her. She was carrying groceries. "Hi!" he called out, even though she hadn't reached him yet. She called "Hi!" back.

"I was hoping you'd be home," he told her.

"I'm home every Saturday," she said.

Frank felt clumsy. "Sam had a seminar tonight and I had some time on my hands," he said, taking the groceries from her. Roxanna let him take them despite his obvious awkwardness. She then unlocked her door and Frank followed her inside.

A half hour later, they were both in the kitchen getting hamburgers ready for the stove. It was a spontaneous dinner party. Frank was doing the cooking.

"I don't want them tasting like the ones we had at Saint Michael's—cardboard with ketchup on it," Roxanna said.

"Trust me. I cook with divinity in my hands," Frank kidded.

"Oh, please," Roxanna responded.

"I think the ad campaign would go like this—'His hamburgers taste heavenly.'"

"Stick to dishing out sacraments." She smiled.

He turned a hamburger over. "I used to go to dances at Saint Michael's. A little before your time."

"Seriously?"

"I would take three buses with a transfer. Your uniform colors were blue and gray."

"They were!" Roxanna smiled.

"I went to the all-boys Monsignor McClancy High School," Frank told her.

"Red and white!"

"That was us," Frank said.

Roxanna walked to the refrigerator. "I dated a boy from there once. A sweet boy. I think he was on the track team or something. My God, it feels like centuries ago," she said pensively. Frank watched as she opened the refrigerator and was about to take out a six-pack of beer when she stopped herself. She took out several cans of soda instead and placed them on the table.

After everything was cooked, Frank and Roxanna took their dinner to the landlord's backyard. They set up a small table, making the atmosphere feel picniclike, although it was too chilly. They sat looking at each other, feeling foolish. "It's October. But it was a nice idea," Frank said. It was already dusk.

Roxanna was moody. "I like eating outdoors. We used to do it when I was a kid. I guess we didn't do it so late in the season."

Frank could see how far away that memory of a warm, comforting family life was for her. "It was a nice idea," he said again. After taking everything inside, Frank stood at the door waiting for Roxanna to open it. "I have to go," he told her.

He then watched her turn away and walk to the sofa. She opened it up; it opened to a bed. She then placed a pillow and a blanket on the couch. Frank continued watching her, feeling awkward again. But the warmth he felt from just being there was worth the embarrassment. His room in the rectory was cold, sterile. Here, he felt he was in a house. Someone's home. Someone female. He didn't want to leave.

Frank then watched Roxanna turn and walk down the long hallway to her room. She closed the door behind her without saying anything. Frank got undressed then sat up in the recliner waiting for Roxanna's bedroom light to go out. When it did, he shut off the living room lamp, closed his eyes, and fell to sleep quickly.

In the middle of the night, Frank woke up, but he didn't move. He heard Roxanna step out of her room and walk into the kitchen. He could see her quietly put the night-light on and pour herself a glass of water. From where she sat at the table, he knew she could see his outline in the darkness of the living room.

Roxanna opened a cabinet. Frank knew there was a half-empty bottle of Scotch sitting there waiting. She looked at it a long moment. He knew she wanted a drink. But she stopped herself. What he didn't know was that she stopped herself for him. She stopped herself for the stranger who had entered her life as if by a miracle.

Frank knew she had no idea what he really wanted from her. He had no idea what he wanted for himself, actually, other than to ease the loneliness that permeated his entire being. He could see her close the cabinet, then put out the light.

She then went back to her bedroom. Frank couldn't see the small smile on her face. She was thinking about the strange man who was sleeping next to her bedroom, and the thought comforted her.

The following afternoon Frank went to the rectory, where he saw a commotion in the schoolyard. He came across Father Stacey. "What's going on?" he asked him.

"It's the Virgin, Father! She's here!" Stacey said, gesturing to the other end of the schoolyard. When Frank turned, he saw a swirl of white mist hovering in midair above the statue.

"I don't see her," Frank said.

"The boy does!" Stacey told him, pointing at a young boy standing at the foot of the statue under the swirl of wind. He pushed past Stacey, making his way through the crowd. Dozens of people were kneeling and praying. Some looked up, transfixed by what they were witnessing; others looked away, afraid of the unknown. None were brave enough to walk over to where the boy was standing.

Frank finally reached the young boy. There was a strange silence at that end of the yard. All routine noises had disappeared. Even the swirling wind was soundless.

The young boy looked no more than six or seven years old. He had a mop of brown hair and was wearing a coat that looked too big for him. Frank stepped up beside him, and when he did, he could see that the young boy was smiling. His large brown eyes beamed with joy. Both Frank and the boy were only a few feet from the swirling cloud.

Light was everywhere. It seemed to blast down from the sky as if all the sun's light shone only on that spot on earth. The closer Frank got to the statue, the more he had to shield his eyes.

"Do you see her?" the boy asked Frank.

"Who?" Frank asked.

"The Virgin Mother," the young boy replied.

"Where is she?"

"In the cloud!" the boy shouted happily.

Frank looked at the mass of light, wind, and cloud. And he saw the image of a face, the outline of a figure in the light.

The young boy knelt and made the sign of the cross. "She loves us, Father. She's praying for us."

Suddenly, it was as if the sun had fallen into the yard. Everything and everyone became a thousand times brighter. People fell to the ground and held their hands up to their eyes. Frank fell to his knees as the wind picked up. He managed to turn to the boy, who was standing and smiling at the statue, unaffected by the wind and light. He then turned to Frank, putting out his hand to him. Frank struggled with the wind and took it.

Just then, the swirl of wind stopped. The orange light lifted, and the natural light of day returned.

A short time later in the school auditorium, Frank and Corey sat across a table from the young boy. His mother and father sat nervously at each side. In her early twenties, the mother had a look of anxiety on her face—the tension of someone trying to juggle a job, motherhood, a marriage. Though she was nervous, Frank noticed a sweetness in her eyes. The husband, looking like a boy himself, was an electrician, Frank learned. Though they clearly didn't have much money, the mother tried dressing up with a clean blouse and a skirt. But the husband didn't seem to care what these priests felt about him. His hazel eyes were filled with suspicion as he watched Frank and Sam's every gesture.

"The Virgin Mother said that we should pray. We won't ever have peace in the world unless we do," the young boy told Sam and Frank. His voice was clear and his eyes still gleamed.

"What else did she tell you, Michael?" Sam Corey asked.

"She said to love one another. That's what she told me. We have to love one another."

Frank noticed how the young mother seemed perplexed by her son's sudden confidence. The boy's father just frowned.

"And Father Sam?" Michael said.

"Yes?" Sam Corey asked.

"Mother Mary loves you. She told me," young Michael smiled. The boy then turned to his parents, who looked worried.

On their way out of the auditorium, the young father seemed to be struggling with something within himself. He stopped Frank at the doorway as his family and Sam Corey made their way up the stairs. "He ain't gonna be—"

Frank was confused. "What?"

"My son. You know. He ain't gonna be weird the rest of his life now, is he?" the young man asked without irony.

Frank looked to the little boy at the top of the stairs. He could see his innocent eyes look enchanted, exalted, saved. "No. He won't be weird," was all Frank could say.

Once out in the fading light, Frank and Sam watched the tiny family walk toward their car. Sam Corey shouted after them. "Thanks, Michael!"

The little boy turned and smiled. "You're welcome," he said as he got into the backseat of the car. His parents drove away.

"'Become as little children, or you shall not enter the kingdom of heaven'" Frank said. "I believe we're ready for the next step," Frank told Corey. "I'm going to see Cahill tomorrow morning."

Chapter 13

Frank faced Cardinal Cahill and John Beliar in Cahill's office. "I want to forward the petition to Rome. We believe we have enough evidence to bring the case before the tribunal," he told them.

Cahill walked silently to his chair behind his desk. It was John Beliar who spoke first. "Frank, do you know enough about the integrity of this woman?"

"She loved. Despite her own insecurities, her fears, and despite God's seeming indifference—she loved. That's all I'm sure of," Frank answered.

"I'm not sure you're right," Cahill said.

"Are you questioning my decision?" Frank asked.

"Yes. I am."

"Then you don't have any confidence in my judgment."

"I'm expecting more from you," Cahill told him.

"More from me? How?"

"You're an intellectual. You're a scholar. How can you say that you believe there is something mystical going on here?"

"You want proof?" Frank asked.

"I want you to act like a postulator!" Cahill said, losing his patience. "Turn your back on Willow Lake, Frank. It was unfortunate that it happened, but now you have to go on. You can't make up for what took place there. It wasn't your fault. You can't redeem yourself now for some mistake you think you might have made then. This process that you're involved in is not going on for your sake. There are many other lives involved. I want you to get tough with yourself and rethink your conclusion."

Frank was silent a long moment. He looked to Beliar and then to Cahill. "I have struggled with my decision, Charles. You underestimate me."

"Perhaps I've overestimated you."

"Then remove me."

Cahill stopped. He took a deep sigh, then sat down at his desk. "You've reached your decision because you've read her diary?"

"Yes."

"Alright, then answer me this—wasn't it through reading Falcone's journals, letters, and diary that you discovered certain things even the police weren't aware of?"

"That's true," Frank answered.

"What did you find out, Frank?" Cahill asked.

"I discovered that he didn't die in an accident. He had gone to the lake that day to kill himself. You know this."

"But before you found this out—miracles were happening there, weren't they? People were going to this Willow Lake, praying to this Father Falcone, and they were actually experiencing miraculous cures. Isn't that true?" Cahill asked.

"What's your point, Charles?" Frank asked.

"Isn't that true, Frank?"

"Yes. I witnessed several miraculous cures myself. It's all in my official report."

"Miracles were happening to people paying homage to a man whose immortal soul had been lost for all eternity. They were praying to a man who had committed the one unforgivable sin—despair." Cahill was face-to-face with Frank.

Frank didn't blink. "The miracle cures stopped when I made my findings public."

"And those already cured?" Cahill asked.

Frank was slow to respond. "They eventually became ill again. Some died immediately after."

"And what do you think would have happened to all those unfortunate souls at Willow Lake if you had never read Falcone's journal? If you had never discovered what his true intentions had been?" Cahill asked sharply. "Can you tell me what is to be gained by judging and exposing this woman any further?"

"But what if she is worthy?" he asked.

"Say she is. What difference will that make to those out there in that schoolyard? They already believe."

"It will confirm for them that God does exist. That God loves them," Frank answered.

Cahill was suddenly animated. "But that's what we're supposed to do—tell them that God loves them. Bless them when they're lonely, absolve them of their sins when they're scared. They don't need a miracle for that. It's what they expect of us, Frank. It's what they demand."

Frank felt a wave of defeat rush over him. It would be so much easier to agree with Cahill. It would be so much easier to let him take control. But Frank knew he had to resist what was so appealing. He had to push on. If he let it drop, he knew Cahill would negate the petition. He had to keep it a personal quest. It was the only way to see it through to the end. "As postulator I am required to inform you that after my extensive investigation I have reached the conclusion that there's sufficient evidence to forward this petition to the Vatican," Frank said.

Cahill shot back. "Whose will are you pursuing—God's, or your own?"

"A person can be human, with all their flaws and insecurities, and still love—despite God's seeming indifference. She had faith, Cardinal. And she may have been blessed."

"Frank, you are aware that sometimes it takes the tribunal the lifetime of a postulator to reach a conclusion?"

"I know it can take a lifetime waiting for an answer," Frank said.

Cahill walked back to his desk and sat down. At his fingertips lay Helen Stephenson's file, along with Frank's typed thirty-page report on the validity of the petition for her canonization. "Frank, you're a priest who has written a book that's been praised in all theological circles! The kind of priest who is obviously prone to publicity and popularity! Can you honestly sit there and tell me that you are willing to spend the next ten years, maybe twenty years of your life, leafing through pages and pages of written testimony, research, photographs, biographies? And all of this done without fanfare and in the privacy and solitude a monk in the Middle Ages might find barely tolerable?" Cahill asked. "The average process usually takes several lifetimes," Cahill added.

"Right now my job is to find out what God wants."

"And you know what God wants?"

Frank searched his mind for a response.

"What are you telling me, Frank? God is your only logic? Is that it?" Cahill asked sharply.

"Helen Stephenson's love may be my only logic," Frank answered.

Cahill tried another tack. "You have never come face-to-face with a 'devil's advocate,' have you?" he asked.

"No."

"The devil's advocate or 'The Protector of the Faith' as he is called now, will not care that you may believe in this woman's sanctity, nor will he be concerned with your years of research and sacrifice. He won't give a damn that a statue cried type O human blood or AB positive! What he will give a damn about is you! If he senses for one moment that you question your faith, he will quickly obliterate you. He will rip open your insides. He will do that without forbearance because he must defend the Church against false notions and passing fads."

"I'm well aware of that," Frank said. "I'm not going to kill this one, Charles. Not until the tribunal hears the case."

"No one is asking you to kill anything. I'm just telling you that you are missing something here. You are missing a great truth and it bewilders me how you don't see it."

"What truth?" Frank asked.

Cahill thought a long moment, then answered him. "Perhaps it's better to wait. Perhaps you should find out this truth yourself, in your own way, in your own time." Cahill was quiet a moment, then spoke again. "Or maybe you know this truth already and you're afraid to admit it to yourself."

Beliar stood up. He turned to Cahill. "I think Frank has made his point quite eloquently," he said.

Cahill hesitated, studied Beliar a moment, then nodded. "I agree. He has." He took out his pen and signed a document on the desk before him. "All right. I'll recommend the case be forwarded to the Vatican."

Frank was relieved.

"The funds you need will be transferred to that bank account. Saint Stanislaus has already transferred all their monies for this woman's canonization to the diocese. It will pay for your transportation, research, and then for the transportation of the witnesses to the tribunal," he continued. "You'll be on your own from here on in. It is an official assignment from this day forward. If you don't live to complete the task, I will name a replacement. And if I die before that time, my successor will. There will be weeks, months, years when it seems that no one in the world cares about your Helen Stephenson. Those days you will wonder why you care," Cahill spoke, looking more through Frank than at him.

Frank said nothing, then nodded a good-bye to Cahill and walked out of his office feeling contrary emotions of fear and exhilaration.

A cold wind blew down from the north that night as Frank and Corey sat in Corey's car parked outside Roxanna's house. Frank decided to tell her that the cardinal had pushed forward the petition and he wanted her to know firsthand from him. But he didn't want to see her alone. He was afraid of himself and his feelings for her. So he had asked Sam to drive him there.

They were only sitting in the car a few minutes when Frank saw Roxanna making her way down the hill. The bus had just let some passengers off on the top and she was one of them. She was walking down into the quickly fading twilight of mid autumn.

Frank got out of the car and met her when she was only a few yards from the house she rented. She saw him the minute he crossed the street. He stopped when she stopped. They were face-to-face. "How are you?" he asked.

Roxanna saw Corey's car parked on the other side of the street. She could see the young, handsome priest trying to look away, trying to mind his own business. "What's the matter, Frank? Why don't you come in?" she asked.

"I can't. Roxanna, on my recommendation, the cause for your mother's canonization is being forwarded to Rome. I wanted you to know," Frank told her.

Roxanna looked down at the pavement a moment. She then looked up at him. "Do you know what I don't get? You don't believe any more than I do."

"I need to see this case all the way through," Frank told her.

"But why?" she asked.

"I have to. For me."

"Let some other priest do their dirty work. Why are you helping them do this to my mother's memory?" she asked.

"It's not only about Helen."

"You can't call her that. You have no right. You didn't know her. None of those people in that damn schoolyard really knew her!"

"But I know her. Through you. Most of all, through you," Frank said softly.

"And you really think that?"

"Yes."

"Is that why you see me?" she asked.

"Of course not," Frank told her.

"Then why do you?"

"You know why," Frank said.

"No, I don't. I don't know why."

Frank felt Corey watching him from the car. He felt the chill in the air and he wanted to hug Roxanna. He wanted to make her pain go away as well as his own. "I want to be here. With you."

Instead of crying, Roxanna smiled. But it was a smile of anguish. "Go back. Go back to your Church, please." Even the smile disappeared.

"Roxanna."

"It's crazy. You and I. It's so crazy," she told him. She then turned and walked up the stoop to the door. Frank stood there, immobilized by a sudden feeling of loss. It was all over between them. The innocence, the warmth he had known with her, it was gone forever. There was nothing he could do. The knowledge cut through him.

He could do nothing but watch her walk into the house.

When her kitchen light went on he could see her standing at the table. He wanted to be there with her.

He walked back to Corey's car and got in.

"It's cold," Sam told him.

"Sorry," Frank replied. "She won't help us," he said, looking up at her door. "I know what she's thinking: we find her mother a saint—then what is she? 'Sometimes the way through the world is more difficult to find than the way beyond it,'" Frank said.

"Wallace Stevens?" Corey asked.

"Yes," Frank said, his eyes still on her door.

"Should we go?" Corey asked.

Frank thought to himself, if only I weren't a priest. If only I could take off the collar for good. That day might yet come.

But not yet.

"We need to do some investigating, Sam. We need to know more about her. I hate to think this way, but perhaps we need to know more about her daughter now. Can you help me?"

"Of course."

"Thanks. Take me back to the rectory," he told Corey. He was quiet on the ride back. He had to forget what he felt about Roxanna. He was still a priest.

Trying to forget Roxanna and put her out of his mind as he waited for a reply from the Vatican, Frank kept himself busy with the sick in the makeshift tent, Kinnely's invention. Corey had his classes but other than minor paperwork, Frank had nothing. He didn't want to go back to the archdiocese, so he spent nearly every day tending to the sick.

Though he continued to bless them, he now did it out of habit and he did it for them, not for himself. It was a meaningless gesture for him, but they seemed to desperately need it. So he carried holy water with him when he visited the tent and blessed them with it.

One cold November morning a few days later he saw Cahill's limo make its way into the schoolyard. The faithful parted like the Red Sea did for Moses. The limo drove as close to the statue as it could, then it stopped and Cahill got out.

Wearing his red cap and his red robes over his black cassock, Cahill blessed the crowd with more authority and exuberance than Frank could ever muster. He took center stage in the yard and watched as the multitude kneeled in awe.

Cahill spotted Frank out of the corner of his eye and called him over. Frank managed to reach Cahill through the crowd and heard him say, "Frank, I'm here to see you. Let's talk in the car."

Frank got into the limo beside the cardinal and saw the crowd watch with curiosity. Every so often, as he spoke, the cardinal would wave his hand up to the crowd, blessing them.

"I've gotten word from the pontiff. Because of the politics involved and all of the publicity we've been receiving, he's decided to send the tribunal here. The process will take place at Saint Patrick's. My jurisdiction will be authentic and it will follow

Vatican policy. You will meet the cardinals involved and the devil's advocate sometime next month." Cahill grinned. "You may not have to wait a lifetime to see the fruits of your labor. A decision could be made in weeks. Most postulators would feel like they just hit the metaphysical lottery with this decision, Frank."

Frank felt a strange sense of foreboding as the cardinal continued to bless the faces in the crowd outside the limo window. "May I quote a pagan philosopher?" Cahill asked, coyly.

"It seems appropriate," Frank said, going along.

"The great Roman poet Pindar says, 'Don't dwell on the immortal but exhaust the limits of the possible.'"

Frank was silent. He saw something in Cahill's eyes he never saw before—the look of the godless: those whose entire being is summed up in what they can achieve through manipulation and coercion with little concern for the consequences.

The two men said their good-byes and Frank got out of the limo. The true test had now begun.

Chapter 14

It was a bright, sunny, chilly Tuesday afternoon when Cardinal Cahill dispatched three limousines to pick up the tribunal when they landed with their entourage at Kennedy airport. With a police escort leading the way, the limos crossed the Queensborough Bridge and then drove crosstown several blocks southwest to Fifth Avenue, finally reaching their destination, Saint Patrick's Cathedral. What would normally take an hour in normal Midtown traffic took only ten minutes.

Cahill greeted the three cardinals of the tribunal in his office. Beliar was at his side when he did. The three cardinals were named Fishetti, Ricci, and Vochez. Fishetti was the sovereign of the tribunal. He was in his early fifties and was thin with strong, angular features. His brown eyes were warm and intelligent. He was even-tempered and actually had an aura of spirituality about him. Cardinal Ricci, on the other hand, was a smaller man with thinning hair and he seemed quite impressed with himself. In his early sixties, he said very little, but analyzed everyone around him. Cardinal Vochez was the only non-Italian with the group, being half Russian and half Polish. He had a shock of strikingly white, wavy hair and blue eyes that were small and penetrating. Nearly seventy, he was a small man with oddly large shoulders.

Each of the cardinals wore a bright red cassock and a red cape, with a white blouse. They each wore a red hat folded three times and all three wore large gold crucifixes around their necks.

"Welcome to Saint Patrick's," Cahill said to them. He then introduced John Beliar and told the tribunal that they each had comfortable rooms waiting for them at a local bishop's private residence on Central Park West. An agenda was agreed upon and the tribunal was set to meet the following morning in a spacious conference room on the fourth floor of Saint Patrick's.

Frank and Sam Corey were told to report to the cathedral an hour after the cardinals' arrival. It was not appropriate for them to meet the cardinals straight away, but an initial meeting with the devil's advocate was imperative.

Wearing their best black suits and white collars, Frank and Corey were welcomed into the cardinal's office and found themselves facing Cahill, Beliar, and the formidable Archbishop Rudolpho Werner. Frank was instantly struck by the archbishop's size. He stood six feet four inches tall with large shoulders and a large belly. He was a Jesuit, an order completely loyal to the Pope. And though he was an archbishop, he preferred the coarse white woolen habit and the sandals of a medieval mendicant monk. New York's chilly weather didn't seem to affect him.

Along with his feet, the other uncovered part of him was his head—and it was a mass of flesh. The neck was beefy, barely distinguishable at a double chin. The cheeks were round and soft, like a newborn baby's, and his entire head was hairless.

Frank had to stop himself from staring at the archbishop's lips, which were thin and bloodless. His tiny blue eyes bulged from beneath his arched forehead. Frank was also struck by how stunning and piercingly blue his eyes were. German, he spoke fluent English. Frank felt as if he were facing the grand inquisitor. Werner also had two young seminarians with him. They were boyish-looking with short blond hair and feminine features. They stood at his side silently.

Several chairs were set up in the office for the private introductions. Everyone sat except for Werner's two assistants, who stood behind him to either side of his chair. Frank made eye contact with the archbishop, knowing that they were adversaries and that their battle was about to begin.

"As Defender of the Faith, it is my duty to persuade the tribunal not to sanctify the soul in question," Werner said slowly, taking his time to direct each sentence to Frank and Corey, then to Cahill and Beliar. His accent was thick, but he made sure each word was pronounced correctly.

"We understand," Frank replied.

"I read your book, Father Moore," Werner said.

"Thank you," Frank responded.

"I was not impressed," Werner told him. He then turned to his assistant at his left and nodded. The young man placed a thin black book in front of Frank. "My book," Werner said. "I recommend you read it before we begin tomorrow. Though I won't be referring to it directly, it will certainly inform you of my views on canonization."

Frank opened Werner's book and glanced at it. It was written in German. He then handed the book to Corey. Corey glanced at it but didn't seem as worried as Frank. He nodded to him, then turned his attention back to the archbishop. Corey was mesmerized by the proceedings. To be so young, and to witness the power of the Church so closely, was fascinating.

"I would like to make it clear to you that the soul up for judgment was married. And in my opinion, that in itself presents too much of an obstacle for her to be judged a saint," Werner said.

Frank was taken aback. He didn't think he would be put on the defensive so early in the debate. But he was prepared, and his quick-wittedness did not let him down. "Is it marriage or women, Archbishop Werner, that you find so offensive?"

Werner grinned. "I believe carnal knowledge perverts the mind and spirit," he said sharply.

"Saint Thomas More was canonized and he was married," Frank rebutted.

"And Saint Teresa had three children," Corey interjected, though he responded more on impulse than anything else. He looked apologetic for speaking out loud in the company of so much authority.

Werner sat back in his chair. "You cite the exceptions," he responded.

Frank looked to Cahill. He judged from the glint in Cahill's eyes that he was enjoying himself, so Frank leaned forward. "The exceptions, Archbishop?"

Werner's clear blue eyes studied Frank a moment. "Yes."

"Aren't all our contemporary laws based on the findings of the Council of Trent, and didn't the Council hold the married state above the state of celibacy?" Frank asked.

Frank could see him grip the chair tighter. Werner knew he'd been trapped. "Fortunately, we no longer burn heretics," Frank joked. Cahill laughed, then stopped immediately. Frank and Corey followed. Frank thanked the cardinal for his hospitality and then turned to Werner. "I look forward to seeing you again," he told the annoyed archbishop. Werner was seething as Frank and Corey left the room.

Beliar brought a tray of tea to the cardinal and the archbishop. "He's one of our best," Cahill said. "His sensibility is contemporary, he's from this area, and he has handled a similar case once before."

"The case of a priest," Werner said. "A personal mentor, actually."

"Yes," Cahill said. "Frank prevented the case from going any further than an initial investigation. He put out the fire before the flames of superstition grew too grand."

"I look forward to seeing what kind of mind he has," Werner said.

"His mind is first-rate and his heart is big," Cahill said. "I hope to see him made bishop someday. His assistant, Sam Corey, is a young star on the rise also. Young, but enthusiastic, as you can see."

"I can see that Frank Moore has a first-rate mind and I can see that his heart is big," Werner said, savoring a cup of tea. "But it's faith that concerns us. A man's faith in his god. Is his faith strong? That is the pertinent question."

Cahill gestured to Beliar. "John, can you bring in those wonderful Italian pastries we bought especially for our guests?"

That night, Frank and Sam Corey worked diligently in Frank's room in the rectory. Laid out on the desk before them was a German dictionary and Werner's book. Frank paced as Corey carefully translated each word of the religious thesis. "He's a virgin," Frank said.

"No doubt. And he doesn't seem to like women much," Corey responded.

"What have you found out about him?" Frank asked.

"First off, being a Jesuit, he's a top-notch scholar. His specialty is Saint Augustine. I bet he tries to hit us over the head with him," Corey said.

Frank went to the several books he had placed on the shelf the first day he decided to stay in the room. He found several books on Augustine, including *City of God*.

"Augustine is your man," Corey smiled. "You drilled him into my brain back at the seminary."

"If he's an Augustine scholar we better reread Thomas Aquinas, too." Frank smiled.

"Should we find some Dante to read over?" Sam asked.

"Dante wouldn't hurt, considering we're facing an inferno ourselves right now," Frank answered.

"I prefer to read *Paradiso*." Corey smiled.

Frank thought a moment. Roxanna might be his Beatrice. Did God send her to him? He didn't know where the thought came from, but he had it and it bothered him that he did. He stopped. He had to get her out of his mind or he wouldn't be able to concentrate. "Thank God you know some German," Frank said.

"*The Chained Soul*! It's so medieval!" Sam replied. He then wrote down the following passage as he translated it. "Reading Joseph, we know that to celebrate—"

"Stop!" Frank said.

"What?" Corey looked up. He was tired and his eyes were getting watery.

"Saint Joseph!" Frank said.

"Huh?"

"What order is Sister Alice with?" Frank asked.

Corey thought a moment. "Black habits mean Sisters of Saint Joseph."

"Exactly," Frank said as he opened his desk drawer, pulling out Helen Stephenson's diary. He went looking for a certain entry on a particular date. "Don't the nuns have to stay in and pray to the founder of their order on their feast day?"

"They used to," Corey replied. "But not anymore."

"But they did ten years ago," Frank said quickly. He then found the entry he was looking for. "Okay, that's the date." Frank turned to the wall, where a religious calendar hung. It marked holidays and feast days. Frank again found what he was looking for. "The Feast of Saint Joseph. They're the same day! Sister Alice was not visiting relatives. She was in her room that night!"

"Holy Shi—Saint Stephen!" Corey beamed.

Frank and Corey made their way quickly across the courtyard. Despite the late hour, they knocked on her door, but were surprised when a young, heavyset woman with a sweet face answered. She was in a long flannel robe and looked a bit mystified as to why these two priests were suddenly at her door. "We're so sorry. Sister Alice, please," Frank said.

"She's not here anymore, Father. Her transfer came through," the nun said.

"And who are you?" Corey asked.

"Sister Veronica," she smiled.

"Where was she transferred to?" Frank asked.

"I don't know, Father," she replied.

Frank and Corey went back to Frank's room in the rectory. "I'll track her down," Corey said.

"Get her back here, Sam. You have to. We need to know what she knows. Maybe Kinnely spent the night with Helen. Maybe he didn't. We need to know the truth," Frank said.

"I have a very good contact in the archdiocese," Corey said.

"And don't get her testimony over the phone. I need to question her in person."

"Don't worry, Frank. I'll find her."

"Thank God for your contacts," Frank said.

"You're thanking God now. As they say, 'Act like you have faith'—"

"'—And you shall have it.'" Frank finished the quote.

"Are you ready for the tribunal tomorrow, Frank?"

"I'm ready," Frank answered quietly.

Part Three

Chapter 15

Frank hardly slept all night. By the time he did drift off, it was nearly four. He woke up immediately when the alarm went off at seven, showered and dressed, then got a ride to Saint Patrick's from Father Paulino.

Wearing his black cassock and white collar, Frank wanted to look priestly. He asked to be dropped off a block away and walked to the side entrance of the beautifully designed gray stone cathedral. He was met at the door by a Swiss Guard. Frank was surprised to see them standing at every entrance to the cathedral. With his briefcase in hand, Frank followed the guard up two flights of stairs and down a long corridor. There they were both met by another Swiss Guard who took Frank to a large double door. The guard did not enter. Frank was then met by another guard inside.

Frank was startled by the size of the conference room. It was set up to look like a courtroom. Frank was early, and the only one there. He was ushered to his table as the guard went silently back to his post. A bottle of water and several glasses were on the table in front of Frank.

Frank sat. He faced a makeshift stage and three empty chairs. To his right was another table, and behind the tables were several chairs. To the right of the makeshift stage was a witness stand. The stage and the witness stand were newly made, and Frank could still smell the fresh wood.

The room was well lit by several lamps and four floor-to-ceiling stained glass windows, which depicted the stations of the cross. Rays of bright light filtered into the room. The windows lit up blue, brown, gold, red, and yellow. It was a beautiful merging of design and art.

Moments later, Werner entered with his two assistants. He barely acknowledged Frank. He sat down, opened his file of notes, and sat in silence until another door opened and the tribunal entered. Cardinals Fishetti, Ricci, and Vochez took their seats on the stage facing Frank and Werner. Right after they were seated, Cardinal Cahill entered from a side door with John Beliar and sat in the chairs behind Frank and Werner.

Fishetti blessed the proceedings with a short prayer, then turned to Frank. "This tribunal will hear the testimony for the cause of Helen Stephenson. Will the postulator begin."

Nervous, Frank stood. He walked several feet forward, facing the stage at an angle so that he could direct everything he said to Werner as well as to the cardinals facing him.

"I don't come here as a pious man waving a flag of faith and righteousness. I have witnessed, with my own eyes, truly remarkable events. I believe that it is God's will at work here for the cause of Helen Stephenson." Frank then sat.

Fishetti turned to Werner. "Will the Defender of the Faith present his opening statement?"

Though Frank found the room cool, Werner was sweating. He stood and did the same thing Frank did from his side.

"It is my responsibility to discourage this tribunal from beatifying Helen Stephenson. I see before me a simple task: to show you that this woman is not worthy of sainthood," he said, then sat. He looked pleased with himself as one of his assistants poured him a glass of water, which he quickly drank.

The rest of the day was spent discussing Helen Stephenson's life. It was an outright old-fashioned debate. Werner would make a point and Frank would rebuke it; Frank would make a point and the archbishop would rebuke it. All of this occurred under the tutelage of the tribunal. Everything was argued, including Helen Stephenson's physical, intellectual, and moral qualities. Her attitude toward her parents, and even her childhood playmates, were open for discussion and scrutiny.

The archbishop had no problem with Helen Stephenson's hope, prudence, justice, fortitude, poverty, and obedience. As promoter of the faith, he allowed Frank to defend Helen's obviously strong show of these virtues. But when it came to Helen's motivations, his attitude changed. "I find your proposal, that Helen Stephenson lived the life of a true servant of God, inaccurate," he said in his rough German accent. The archbishop narrowed his eyes. "The woman was married. That in itself creates an obstacle very few, if any, can overcome in the complete devotion to God and His Church."

Frank saw that he was going to continue to nail that element of his argument no matter what Frank said about it. Frank had to attack it once again. But this time, in the presence of the tribunal. "Are you saying, Archbishop, that because this woman was married it was impossible for her to achieve sanctity?"

The archbishop's thin lips muttered "Yes."

"Archbishop Werner, there have been several married saints—Saint Monica, Saint Margaret of Scotland, Saint Elizabeth of Hungary, and Saint Elizabeth Seton."

"Of course. But the exception does not make the rule!"

"Well, Archbishop, Saint Thomas More was married twice!" Frank said with a smile. "He must have been exceptionally saintly then." Frank heard a muffled laugh from the tribunal.

The archbishop sat back in his chair and shook his head. Frank could see the sunlight on the wall behind the archbishop, glaring as if it were focused on him alone.

"What is the basis of your argument against a servant of God being married and still dedicating her life to God and the Church?" Frank asked.

"Carnal knowledge," the archbishop said quickly. "The perversion of the mind caused by the desire of flesh. This woman had been intimate with a man for over a decade. She knew the temptation of the flesh. Because of it, I imagine her 'affair' with this pastor had to eventually lead to intercourse."

"That is an assumption, Archbishop," Frank said quickly. "There is no proof of an affair! Just because this woman was married, we cannot truthfully state that she was any more prone to temptation of the flesh than someone who is virginal! May I quote Saint Augustine?"

The archbishop's tiny blue eyes turned quickly to Father Corey. "Eh?" he mumbled.

"Saint Augustine, in his treatise, *De Bono Conjugali*, wrote 'What food is to conservation of the individual that sexual intercourse is to the conservation of the race.'"

"Sexual intercourse is not a prerequisite for sainthood," the archbishop said haughtily. "I hope it is safe to assume that you realize that Saint Augustine grew up a pagan before his conversion and that his licentious life as a pagan involved him in Manichaean thinking!"

"I'm of the belief that the Saint Augustine of *The City of God* had his roots in learning the evils of the flesh, which enlightened him to the good of physical love," Frank replied.

"Desire of that sort can only create havoc," the archbishop said strongly.

"Then let me quote Saint Augustine again," Frank said. "'The union of man and wife is the first natural bond of human society.'" He slowly pushed the archbishop's folder to the other side of the table. "Do you know that quote, Archbishop?"

"Are you questioning my knowledge of Augustine?" the archbishop asked.

"Of course not. I'm only questioning your intention in this debate," Frank said confidently.

"Augustine created Church dogma!" the archbishop shouted.

"Yes," Frank replied. "Then please answer me. Do you know the rest of the quote? Because I believe that desire does not create havoc as you have stated. I will finish the quote from memory," Frank said. "'So that when the warmth of youth has passed away, there yet lives in full vigor the odor of charity between husband and wife.'"

The archbishop sat back in his chair.

"The Catholic Church has never ceased to teach that marriage has a spiritual as well as physical foundation," Frank told the room. "And with all respect to your position, Archbishop Werner, let us dispense with intimidation and get on to the business of proving or disproving the sanctity of this woman's life."

The archbishop bit the inside of his mouth.

The next morning the debate began all over again. As Frank debated, Sam Corey made sure all of the witnesses were accounted for and ready to testify when needed. He was, however, having a hard time tracking down Sister Alice.

The weather had changed from sunny to overcast, followed by a typical late-November dampness in the air. Frank was a few minutes late, and when he arrived he found Werner had taken his table, leaving Frank his old side of the room. Frank was perplexed until he figured out it was a ploy of Werner's to throw him off. Frank was going to have none of it. He simply took Werner's table, poured himself some coffee that he found there, and began.

"Do you have a problem with me sitting here?" Werner asked.

"No," Frank said.

"Nowhere is it written that one side of the debate must sit on a particular side of the table for the duration of the debate," Werner explained.

"I see," Frank answered. Frank noticed Cahill and Beliar had already taken their places.

The archbishop began his assault. He unleashed a salvo on Helen's sincere wish to bring a "little bit of God" to her small parish. The thrust of the attack was on her manipulation of Father Kinnely. "Even if this priest raped the servant of God, was she not enticing him with her sexuality by simply being there?" the archbishop asked. "And because of this manipulation, I have come to suspect her true love of neighbor, her chastity, her true love of God and her faith!" Werner said.

"Her faith?" Frank broke in.

"Yes, postulator—her faith," the archbishop said, sharply. "She clearly used this priest for her own aims!"

"What aims?" Frank asked.

"Her goal may have been simple attention," the archbishop answered.

"What if she used this priest, Father Kinnely?" Frank asked. "Is it morally wrong to use someone to achieve a greater end?"

Archbishop Werner smiled. He smiled like the cat that had caught the canary. "If she would manipulate a parish pastor for the supposed love of God, where would that manipulation end? Where is the woman's sincerity?"

"She was devoted—" Frank shot in.

"To what?" the archbishop questioned. "Her will or God's? She left her only daughter—" the archbishop began.

"Her journals clearly state that she was in anguish over that decision," Frank said, thinking of Roxanna and the last time he had seen her. He wondered if she still looked the same, thought the same, felt the same way about him.

"One can easily suggest that she used her daughter, keeping from her a mother's love. One can easily suggest that this daughter, who refused to be a witness, resents this supposed servant of God," the archbishop said.

Frank could still hear Roxanna condemning her mother.

"In my mind, I believe that this woman pursued her own will and not the will of our God," the archbishop said to Frank.

Frank thought about the bottom of the pool.

"Do you agree with me, postulator?" the archbishop asked.

Frank suddenly felt all his energy run from his body. He could barely turn his head to look at the unrelenting steel-blue eyes of the archbishop.

"I didn't say I agreed," Frank said tiredly. Maybe they were right, all of them, Frank thought to himself. Maybe they're right and I'm wrong. It's possible.

"Father Moore?" Cardinal Fishetti said.

Frank heard his name as if it had been whispered under water.

"Is the postulator all right?" Cardinal Ricci asked.

Frank could see Roxanna condemning her mother's memory to the cold, dark grave she lay in. He could see the pathetic body of Maria Katowski, pale and lifeless, in the back of the ambulance. And he could see Helen Stephenson at her husband's funeral—standing at the grave dressed in black, among the men in black—unmoved and unresponsive.

Frank could envision that hot summer night in the convent where a lonely pastor and a lonely widow looked for solace in each other's arms. And above all, Frank could taste Roxanna's lips on his. He could feel her urgency, her desire. He remembered his own desire building up in him as she pushed her body against his. Weakness was mortal, he thought to himself. We are not gods. We are not angels. We are human beings. That is our suffering.

"You must allow for the facts," Frank said, finding his voice.

"The facts? The facts intrigue you, don't they postulator?" the archbishop asked.

"We must follow the facts," Frank answered, "or we will fall into assumptions," Frank answered.

"Assumptions? Is that what they are, postulator?" the archbishop asked Frank. "And can faith be proven by facts?"

Frank was silent. It was his faith being questioned. He looked around the room. He was the bull ready to be killed. But he refused to make it that easy for them. He summoned his energy. He pushed Roxanna out of his mind. "What is your question, Archbishop? You seem to me to be asking if this woman, this servant of God, had the right to use her will to pursue God's will?"

"I see only her will, and not God's will, in her life," the archbishop said.

"You have no facts to support any adultery on her part. In fact, Father Kinnely's own testimony states that the woman denied him sex. I see her courage and compassion making her a martyr to her faith."

The archbishop tried to break in, but Frank stopped him. "Furthermore," he continued, "the question of her will or God's is a moot point! Saint Augustine on Christian doctrine says, and I quote from the Bobbs-Merrill publication, 1958, 'Some things are to be enjoyed, others to be used, and there are others which are to be enjoyed and used. Those things which are to be enjoyed make us blessed. Those things which are to be used help and, as it were, sustain us as we move toward blessedness in order that we may gain and cling to those things which make us blessed.' If Helen Stephenson used Father Kinnely's position as pastor of Saint Stanislaus Church to assure the success of her charitable organizations then, in all logic, dear Archbishop, according to Augustine, the end justifies the means."

The archbishop frowned.

Frank turned to the tribunal, wanting to make sure they heard everything. He looked at Cahill, who was watching him closely.

"I am not convinced," Archbishop Werner said.

"I see that Helen Stephenson may have used her female attractiveness to allure, or better, ensure that her place in the parish was maintained. But I cannot condemn it nor can I condemn her need for attention. Of course she wanted attention! She was doing God's will and God's work, and it required every bit of attention from an indifferent world. And as to the question of her motherhood—and how she abandoned her daughter—I say this, we are *all* God's children and our responsibility is to God, to His Church, and then to our neighbors. Helen Stephenson not only believed that in the abstract—she lived it! Unfortunately, her daughter did not understand it." Frank narrowed his eyes at the archbishop. "And you yourself should know what it means to give up and sacrifice for a calling. One has to try not to hurt those who are closest to us—but we don't always succeed. Helen Stephenson was called by God to bring love to this world. The evidence is obvious to me and one day it will be obvious to you," Frank said. He felt he had managed to dodge the sword, for the moment.

"Postulator," the archbishop said to Frank, "you are impressed with the power of facts, well, as you see, I have presented you with some facts!" Werner had his assistants distribute several files to the members of the tribunal as well as to Frank.

Frank looked them over. He noticed that the articles all had to do with the statue and the following Helen Stephenson had developed since her death.

"It has been made clear that the alleged servant of God had a cult following. I can easily quote over a dozen articles, which you have rightly and naturally supplied me with, which state how hundreds of fanatics have shown up to pray at the statue which stands outside of her window," the archbishop said.

"Saint Bernadette had a following which developed into the pilgrims at Lourdes," Frank replied, calmly.

"Yes, certainly. Yet it specifically states in canon law that a cult following negates the possibility that God is working through the alleged servant of God." The archbishop looked to Frank. "You were witness to these gatherings, postulator?"

"Yes," Frank answered.

"And what did you see as the facts?"

Frank looked to Werner. "There were crowds."

"Were these crowds persuaded to disperse?"

"No," Frank said, remembering the conversation with Father Kinnely.

"Were they persuaded to attend?" Werner asked.

Frank shook his head. "No," he said. "Though Father Kinnely had looked for publicity and press—"

The archbishop placed both his fat hands on the table. "I have to state now, in the course of these latter investigations, that I find evidence that a public cult has been shown to the servant of God and I petition for Helen Stephenson to be denied before we go any further." Werner turned to the tribunal. Frank was stunned. Werner had taken the advantage and gone all-out. The tribunal conferred. Frank glanced at Cahill, who was clearly aware of what could happen in a matter of moments. The entire cause could be dropped.

Frank turned back to the tribunal. He could see that Ricci and Vochez were in agreement. It was over. But then they turned to Fishetti and the sovereign was shaking his head, and had the authority to override their majority vote. He turned to Werner. "The tribunal denies your petition to dismiss this cause. However, your point is a valid one and we will take it into complete consideration." He then turned to Frank. "The postulator will have his witnesses ready for tomorrow's session." Fishetti stood and, with the other cardinals following, left the room.

Werner was clearly rejoicing. He felt that he had won the day. Frank noticed Cahill and Beliar talking in the back of the room and wanted nothing to do with them. He walked to the door and had the Swiss Guard escort him from the cathedral.

Frank could not go back to his room at the rectory. He parked his car down the block from Roxanna's and then walked to her house. Her light was on. He stood out in the cold across the street knowing that he couldn't knock on her door. What would he say? But he wanted to see her, be with her. The thought occurred to him that another man might show up. A man who could comfort her, make a commitment to her, love her the way he was himself unable to.

Frank walked up to the top of the hill, where he knew he could see down into her kitchen window. The light was on and the curtain was drawn. Frank stood on the hill a long few minutes, conjuring up what she might be doing. It didn't take him long to accept how foolish it was for him to be standing there. He went back to his car and drove to the rectory.

Father Stacey was waiting for him in the vestibule. "Father

Kinnely resigned today," a nervous Stacey told him. "Father Cahill assigned me temporary pastor."

"Where is Kinnely?" Frank asked.

"Packing," Stacey said. Frank gave him a nod and looked him directly in the eyes. "You'll make a fine pastor," Frank told him. He then went upstairs and found Kinnely sitting on his bed in his room. Frank slowly opened the door. He walked in. Kinnely was a broken man. He looked up at Frank, his eyes red. He'd been crying.

"It's all I have, this church," Kinnely said.

"You couldn't have expected to go on," Frank told him. "Not after your testimony to me."

"I wanted to see Helen through this. I failed her in life, why couldn't I come through for her now?"

Frank heard the plea in the man's voice. "You did all you could," Frank told him. "Where are they sending you?"

"The retreat home at Sacred Heart," Kinnely told him. "In Bayside. Not too far from here." Kinnely stood up and looked at his half-packed suitcase. "Cahill told me to stay away from Saint Stan's. He doesn't want me influencing those who come to pray," he said.

"It's better that you do stay away," Frank said.

"If I stay away from here, I'm staying away from Helen," he said, his eyes wide open in pain.

"Helen's no longer your responsibility," Frank told him.

"But I loved her," Kinnely said, looking at Frank. "I loved her. I loved her in a way I knew I shouldn't have. Can our God really condemn us for that?" Kinnely asked.

What God? Frank asked himself. What kind of a God would allow His people so much suffering? Frank looked around the room. A parish priest's life left nothing to the imagination. The walls needed painting, the room was cluttered, small, sterile, like his own room down the hall. All the years of sacrifice, all the years of listening to the little people and their little problems, and this was his reward?

Frank felt an inclination to leave the room, to get on with his own life, to pull himself away from the troubles of a parish priest. It wasn't his problem. He was above this kind of disappointment, this kind of small-minded living. He could be a bishop, Cahill had told him. He should be rubbing elbows with dignitaries, not pastors of neighborhood parishes.

"I loved her," Kinnely said again.

Frank thought of Roxanna and left the room. He didn't even say good-bye to Kinnely. He walked down the darkened hallway, passed the small lit lamp on the end table and thought of a life without the woman he loved. He thought of Kinnely and how he would spend the rest of his days in the retreat home with the other priests, many much older than he was, and it saddened him. Sad for those tossed aside, those priests whose loneliness was neither badge nor wound but a perpetual emblem. It was something they brought upon themselves and yet they had no idea how to rid themselves of it.

Frank entered his room and put on the light. He saw no difference between his temporary room and Kinnely's. Kinnely had lived in that room for twenty-five years and it was just as desolate as Frank's.

Frank then sat on the bed, not even bothering to undress. He was too tired, mentally and physically, to care about anything anymore. He had already fallen asleep when the phone rang. It was only ten. He answered.

"Frank! I found her!" Sam Corey's voice said on the other end.

"Sam? Where are you?" Frank asked in a deep, hoarse voice.

"I'm home now, but I'm leaving tomorrow morning."

"You found who?"

"Sister Alice! Man, it was hard. But my friend over at the archdiocese said that she had put in a transfer for overseas and he thought she'd already left, but it seems that she never did. Her trip was temporarily postponed because of some political problems. So, for the moment, she's teaching in a small school not far from here," he said.

"Where?" Frank asked.

"Upstate. In Kingston, near Albany. At a parish called Saint

Matthew's. I'm driving up to see her tomorrow."

"Bring her back, Sam. You have to bring her back."

"I know. How did it go today?"

"I'm presenting the miracles in the morning," Frank said, realizing the strangeness of such a sentence. "The miracles," Frank said again.

Chapter 16

The next morning Frank presented over a dozen witnesses to the tribunal. Each took an oath swearing to the validity of their miracle cures. They were then examined by a medical doctor flown in from Rome especially for the occasion. The doctor checked the status of their current health, weighing it against the medical records Frank had provided.

In some cases, when the witness's personal physician was available, he or she was called in to testify. Their religious faith had nothing to do with their testimony. They were there to explain how their particular patients were cured without medical help.

Brenda Lopez, Raymond Forche, and Sean Casey were each given their opportunity to tell the tribunal how their prayers to Helen were answered. Their cures were the only miracles. The bleeding statue wasn't considered a miracle, nor was the swirling cloud and appearance of the Virgin Mother. A miracle happened only when someone was taken from the grip of death.

The only person who had been cured but was not present to be interviewed, was Maria Katowski. Her mother was there, however, and she was a stunning witness for Frank. She had gone through a tremendous change since her daughter's death. Her whole demeanor was different. She looked rested, at ease, grounded. She had stopped drinking entirely and was working closely with Father Paulino on continuing the drug clinic Saint Stanislaus was running. It was the one Helen Stephenson had started over ten years earlier.

With her hair done up and wearing a new skirt, she took the stand and told the tribunal how she had forgiven herself for ignoring her daughter's need for love all those years ago. She told the cardinals the details of Maria's cure and how she was sure she was going to lose her daughter to lupus. She also told them how she once resented Helen Stephenson but now prayed to her regularly. Her testimony was so complete, and her self-confidence so formidable that Werner didn't even attempt to question her.

However, at the end of the day, when the room was cleared of all bystanders and witnesses, Werner faced the cardinals. "The Defender of the Faith would like to have Maria Katowski's name removed from the list," he told them.

"What?" Frank stood up in outrage.

"The young woman died of a heroin overdose—" Werner began, but Frank cut him off.

"Maria Katowski's tragic death was not Helen Stephenson's fault! And all of these illnesses fit the criteria of being serious: there was objective proof of their existence; prior treatments had failed; and the cures have been rapid. They were not only exceptional—they were also inexplicable," Frank responded.

The tribunal conferred. Frank waited but he was not patient. Fishetti turned to him and Werner. "Maria Katowski's name will not be removed from the list." He then closed the folder in front of him. "We will adjourn for today. Does the postulator have any more witnesses?"

Frank nodded. "One more," he said, hoping.

"And the Defender of the Faith?" Fishetti asked.

Werner looked at Cahill. He then turned to the tribunal. "Just one."

The next day, Sam Corey made his way to Saint Matthew's parish in Kingston, in upstate New York. He traveled winding country roads several miles off the New York Thruway, getting deeper and deeper into rural New York.

He found the church up on a hill. The sky was overcast and it looked like rain. Corey parked, asked a passerby for directions, then found the convent. He didn't want to call ahead and scare Sister Alice off, so he took a chance that she was there. He was directed to the school, which stood a hundred yards away, and walked there. Sister Alice was in the schoolyard playing with the children. When she saw Sam Corey standing on the other side of the school fence watching her, she knew.

A few minutes later they were having tea in the back room at the convent. Sister Alice was tense but open. Sam Corey didn't have time to waste, but he understood the delicacy of the matter at hand. "God forgives, Sister. But He can't forgive what isn't confessed. If there's anything you wish to tell us—please speak up while the tribunal is in session."

Sister Alice put down her tea cup. "I've disgraced my order."

Corey leaned forward. "We need your help, Sister. We need you to return to New York and testify to the truth." Sister Alice understood. Sam Corey could see it in her eyes.

"I will tell everything to Father Moore," she said.

Sam looked out the window. He could see the dark clouds. "We have to leave tonight."

"But my duties here?" she asked.

"A postulator's request takes precedence over all other obligations," Corey told her.

"I'll pack my things," she told him.

It was raining by the time they reached the car and were ready to leave. Sam could see that Sister Alice was nervous. "I'm a terrific driver," he smiled.

"I'm a terrible passenger," she said.

He took the Saint Christopher medal from the rearview mirror and handed it to her. She squeezed it and held it tightly. "Thank you," she smiled.

Corey turned on the engine and then drove into the rain. He hadn't gone very far when the rain was turned into a drizzle and fog began to appear. A half hour later, the rain had stopped and the fog had thickened. "Is there another road we can take?" Corey asked.

Sister Alice shook her head. "None that I know of."

Sam Corey slowed down. He had to strain to see. There were no lights on the road and only one car every few minutes appeared from the other direction on the two-lane highway.

"Maybe we should turn back?" Sister Alice asked.

"I have to get you there by morning," Corey answered. Sam was worried. Not because of the weather, but because he couldn't shake the sound of depression in Frank's voice. It was the same quiet desperation he had heard right after Frank had returned to the city having read Falcone's journal. Sam Corey had helped him on that case, too. It was going very well until Frank made the discovery. Now, Corey wanted to get back to New York to be there for his friend. The last time, after he brought his findings to the archdiocese, Frank had disappeared. Corey didn't want to see that happen again. This time he'd be there.

Suddenly, there was a curve in the road. Sam Corey put on the brakes. He skidded to a stop. The front wheel on his side slid ten yards, almost landing them in a ditch.

"Can't we turn back?" Sister Alice asked again.

Corey was nervous. Feeling the control of your car disappear as you gripped the wheel was a terrible feeling. He threw it into reverse, then backed up and got back on the slippery highway. Fallen leaves had made everything twice as slick. He drove forward, turning briefly to the nun at his side. "We're fine," he said. Then he picked up speed.

That was the last thing he said before he saw a small blast of light ahead exploding up and over the small hill he was driving toward. The fog made the light illuminate everything it touched outside of the dark shadow of night encircling it.

"Look!" Sister Alice shouted.

Corey saw a man standing alongside the road, hiding his eyes from Corey's headlights. Corey put on the brakes and slowed down. He pulled up beside the man.

"He's a priest!" Sister Alice said.

Corey pulled to the side of the road and stopped the car. He looked and saw the man's white collar and black cassock. "What's a priest doing out here?" Sister Alice asked.

"Maybe his car broke down," Corey answered as he got out of the car. He leaned back in before he closed the door. "I'll only be a minute. Maybe he needs a lift." Sam then closed the door and walked in front of his car toward the man.

Corey walked through his own headlights and stopped. The man hadn't moved.

"Father Corey?" the man said with a pleasant voice.

Corey stopped. He couldn't see the priest's face because the light was blinding him. He stepped closer. "Do I know you?"

"Yes. You do," the priest answered.

"Who are you?" Corey asked. He was right in front of the man by now. He was staring at him but his face was still hidden by the darkness caused by the light.

"I'm Frank's mentor," he answered.

"Frank Moore's mentor?" Corey asked. "But that was Father Falcone," Corey said. "Father Falcone is dead," Corey said when he saw the priest reach out his hand.

"I've come for you now, Sam."

Corey felt a shiver of steel race into his spine. *"I've come to swallow your soul,"* the priest said to him.

Immediately a second blast of light enveloped everything. Sam was blinded. He felt as if he was in a dream, trying to wake up: he wanted to move but he couldn't. He heard the loud screech of metal and tires. He thought he saw a lone tree racing toward him. He could see himself standing above his own body as it was crushed by the tree from one side and the seat of his car from the other. He saw blood exploding from his mouth, eyes and ears. He could see his entire chest crushed by the hood of his car after his head crashed through the windshield.

He saw and heard all these awful things but he didn't feel any pain at all. None. In fact, he was very tired. So very tired that he could barely stay awake to see what happened next. What did happen next was that a woman appeared to him. He was paralyzed, unable to move, with his face at a ninety-degree angle on the hood of the car, when he saw a woman standing in the light. She was standing only a few feet from him. He didn't recognize her at all, but he suddenly felt good about things. He knew that something awful had just happened to him, but this woman somehow made him feel relieved.

She didn't say anything to him, but he could feel her smiling; not see her smile, but feel it. He wanted to ask her if Sister Alice was all right but Sam Corey was slowly losing all consciousness. In fact, in a few short seconds, he could see nothing of the road, or the tree, or the bright light. But the woman stayed. She stayed with him and he felt comforted. *"Thank you so much,"* he told her. And then he died.

Monroe County Sheriff Bill Miller told Frank over the phone that when the state troopers found Corey's car at the first light of dawn, Trooper Jaystone had gestured to the heavyset, fifty-two-year-old sheriff and said, "It must have been the fog. I doubt he knew what hit him." In the gully, alongside the road, Sam Corey's beautiful new car was a wreck. He had skidded off the road and hit a tree head-on. His body was thrown through the windshield and he was killed instantly, whatever "instantly" means to an intelligent mind as it is erased from existence.

A medical report would state that he died of internal injuries including a broken spine and a crushed skull. But for a young man who had died so violently, Sheriff Miller told Frank, he could not forget the look of serenity on the blood-soaked face. The eyes were closed and the lips together.

The nun in the passenger seat was still alive, Miller continued to tell Frank over the phone. She was barely conscious and in pain when they found her. Her eyes were swollen shut where she had bumped her head, but outside of bad bruises, she was all right. As the ambulance crew removed her from the car, Miller told Frank, he saw her gripping something in her hand. It was a Saint Christopher medal.

Over a week later, Frank, still reeling from the shock, went to the Saint John's University campus and found one Father Heany, Sam Corey's immediate superior. Father Heany was chairman of the theology department and he led Frank to Sam's office. It was a small cubicle in a modern building, but Sam Corey had filled it with his personality.

Father Heany, of retirement age, was a big man with straight gray hair and sad blue eyes. Wearing his black cassock, he stood in front of Corey's desk feeling as much grief as Frank. "What does God have in mind when such awful things happen to such wonderful souls?" Heany asked, looking down at Corey's books and files. He didn't wait for an answer as he stepped away from Corey's desk. "If there's anything you need, just let me know. Oh, and Frank, if there's anything you'd like to have, you can take it. His family told me that they were going to donate his books and lectures to the school library, but they weren't sure what they wanted to do with his personal things. Some photographs and things like that are yours if you want them. I'll be right outside." He then walked away.

Frank slowly sat down at Sam's desk and looked it over. Corey's books were neatly aligned on the small bookshelf above the desk and there was a row of files on his lectures. There were also several photographs on the wall. One was a photograph of his graduation from the seminary. Frank had his arm around him. Hanging on the photograph was a pair of black rosary beads with a gold crucifix. Inscribed on it was "For Sam Corey on the anniversary of his vows. April 3."

"I feel like I was reborn this morning," Corey had told Frank the day he took his vows. Frank remembered that day clearly. He remembered the bright sunshine, the happy smiles, the splendid light of intelligence in Corey's eyes. He remembered putting his arm around him for the photograph. Frank took Corey's rosary beads and held them.

Just as he was leaving, he saw a small motto on the desk in front of him. It read: "The only tragedy in life is not becoming a saint." It was a quote from Léon Bloy.

"He was a saint," Frank told Father Heany. "If anybody ever was."

That night, Frank went to the college swimming pool. He had decided that, in the morning, he was going to see Cahill and ask to be relieved of his duties as postulator. He had done all he could. He had failed. Without Sam Corey in his life, he felt alone, defeated. Without Roxanna, he felt lost.

Frank found the pool to be Olympic-sized and aged. Though he moved slowly and painfully, he swam intensely. He felt each muscle in his body react as he took each stroke. It felt good and refreshing.

Frank always took his goggles with him everywhere he went and wore them as he swam. He liked the old ceiling above the pool and he liked the archways to the large room.

The entire room was painted an aquamarine; so was the bottom of the pool. There were white and blue paintings on the wall which Frank paid very little attention to.

He took each stroke trying to forget, endure, survive. But as he swam, the water around him began to insulate him so that he soon felt that there was some world existing other than the one he was in.

Frank reached one arm up, then the other. He was unable to see the bottom of the pool but it was there; its peace and serenity called to him.

Frank swam, trying to push thoughts of Father Falcone from his head. He could see the priest floating before him. He knew it was a mirage; an image created by the mind lost in the floating sensation of the pool.

Frank wanted to hold his breath. He wanted to peer into the darkness knowing that he could immerse himself in it for eternity. Above all, Frank wanted to lose himself in the darkness.

Frank then thought he heard a voice. He heard it from the bottom of the pool. Looking down, Frank could see his own face looking back at him.

"Frank!" he heard again. This time he drew his face out of the water. He heard his name again and looked around. He tore off his goggles.

Helen Stephenson was standing there, at the side of the pool. She was looking right at him.

Frank stopped swimming. He had to tread water to stay afloat. He could see Helen's eyes; they were clear and blue and unblinking. She wore a black sweater over a blue skirt.

"Pray to me, Frank," she said to him. Her voice was as clear as her eyes. She sounded as Frank thought she would sound.

Frank grabbed the side of the pool. He turned to look again and she was still there. Quiet, unassuming, just like she looked in her photos. He pulled himself up. "Helen," he said. But in an instant she was gone. He looked around. She had disappeared.

Frank felt the water drip from his face. He felt the sting of chlorine. He walked to his towel and dried his face with it.

He then put the towel down. He could hear the slight splash of water as it pushed against the side of the pool. There were no windows lighting the room, only the glow of the overhead lamps.

"She was here," he said out loud, to no one but himself.

Chapter 17

Frank sat at his table as the Swiss Guard escorted Sister Alice into the room. She was walking with a cane and her right arm was in a sling. Though many of her fellow sisters in her order no longer wore their habits, she continued to wear hers. She was given the choice and had resisted the change. Reaching the witness stand, Frank could see how well she disguised the sling on her arm. She was sworn in by Cardinal Ricci and then faced Frank. She looked right at him, clearly prepared for whatever he was going to ask.

Frank started off by asking her how long she had known Helen Stephenson and then pointedly asked how she felt about the woman.

"I was jealous of Helen," Sister Alice said without reservation. "Philip, Father Kinnely, always took her advice on matters that I thought were my duties."

Frank's tone was direct but soft. "Sister, did she stay in her room all night, the night that is in question?"

"Helen stayed with me that night," she answered. "I lied to

you when you originally asked me because I wanted to see Philip punished for caring about her so much."

"Thank you, Sister," Frank said, completing his examination.

"I just want to say how ashamed I am for my sins. I've gone to confession and I know God has forgiven me. I hope you do, Father." Sister Alice looked clearly at Frank when she spoke.

Fishetti turned to Werner. "Does the Defender of the Faith wish to question the witness?"

Werner stood up. "Sister, do you believe Helen Stephenson was a holy woman?"

Sister Alice looked ahead but did not respond.

"Did you hear the question?" Werner asked.

"I did," Sister Alice answered. "She was a very aggressive woman. When she wanted something done, she didn't allow anyone to get in her way."

Cardinal Ricci suddenly jumped in, using his prerogative. "But did you believe she was saintly?"

"I'm not the one to judge that," she answered.

"You are under oath," Fishetti told her. "Please answer the question and answer it truthfully."

"In my definition, a saintly person is someone pious and humble. Helen was outspoken, she believed women should be priests, you know. And she was defiant. Sometimes actually belligerent. I'm not sure if she was a saint."

Fishetti nodded. "Thank you for your testimony."

Frank stood up again. "One last question?" he said and Fishetti gave him permission. "Before, you asked me to forgive you. I'd like to ask you this one last question—do you think Helen, if she were alive today, would forgive you?"

"I have no doubt that she would," Sister Alice answered quickly.

"And why is that?" Fishetti asked.

"She was a kind woman. More than kind, actually. She was quite understanding concerning the flaws of others."

"Thank you, Sister," Fishetti said. Sister Alice stood and left the room.

That night Frank dreamed he was at a picnic with Sam Corey and Roxanna. There was chicken and fruit and wine on the blanket and a great big basket of bread. "I love the mystery of life," Sam said. He was dressed in jeans and a pullover sweater. "I love to look up at the blue sky and just watch the clouds drift!"

Roxanna, dressed in a simple blue skirt, poured wine. "It's all a dream," she said to Frank as he watched her looking at him. "It's all a dream—the hills, the grassy fields, the moon at night, and all the stars. They aren't really there. That's why pain and loss don't matter," she said.

Frank saw Father Falcone standing down at the bottom of the hill. He was wearing his black cassock and white collar, looking pale and tired in the bright sunlight. "Frank?" he said loudly, his voice drifting in the wind as he walked up the hill toward the picnic blanket.

Frank tried frantically to wave him off but the priest ignored him. Frank turned to Sam and Roxanna but they were deep in conversation and didn't see the priest.

Falcone reached Frank and put his hand on Frank's shoulder. Frank shuddered when he did. "Frank, I know the truth: You are alone in the world. There is no God. There is no one. When you die, your greatest fear will become a reality—you will stop existing forever," the priest said, with a deep voice sounding so real, so close.

Frank wanted to run, but he couldn't. He wanted to wake up, but he felt fastened to the bed as if someone had placed giant arms on his shoulders and legs. "Don't deny yourself anything. Take what you want from whom you want. You're wasting your life on this stupid thing. There are women out there who want you. There are so many pleasures in the world, Frank. Take them!" Falcone then gestured toward someone walking up the hill. Frank saw a dark figure approaching. "I want you to meet my friend. A brilliant man. He will show you the way. He will open the world up for you. He is the living truth. His presence on earth is everywhere. He won't let you down. Follow him and you'll learn why you're here on this planet. You'll learn how to stop your suffering. Get to know him well."

Frank watched the man walking up the hill. The sky was bright blue and the grassy hills rose high and low behind him. However, when he was only a few feet away, Frank realized something was terribly wrong. The man's face was gone. What was left was purple and bloated. He had no eyes, no ears, no mouth. What was once a face was now a mass of flesh.

"I am Satan," a voice said.

Frank screamed and sat up. He saw an apparition sitting at the edge of his bed. It was the corpse of Father Falcone staring silently at him.

Frank reached over and turned on the light. Falcone was gone. Frank got up and looked around the room. He was alone. It had all been a nightmare.

He walked to the sink and washed his face. The nightmare was still vivid in his mind. He closed his eyes and pushed out of his brain the ancient fear of demons. Falcone was dead. His ghost lives only in my memory, Frank thought to himself.

Frank knew he wouldn't be able to go back to sleep. He walked downstairs and into the den, where he saw a light on. He found Father Stacey reading a book. Stacey looked up. "Are you all right, Father?"

Frank's voice was deep and harsh, but he answered, "Yes."

"There was someone here to see you," Stacey said.

"Who?" Frank asked.

"A priest. He didn't leave his name."

"What time is it?" Frank asked.

"Nearly midnight. I thought it odd that he wanted to see you so late, but he rang the bell and I was sitting here and I answered the door. He said he saw the light on. I told him that you were sleeping and he said he'd be back," Father Stacey said.

"Did you ever see him before?" Frank asked.

"He did look familiar, but I couldn't place the face."

Frank walked outside. It was damp, but the temperature was moderate. He walked around to the schoolyard and stepped over to the statue. The spotlight Kinnely had put up for it was on. There were several people praying. Frank noticed one man standing facing the statue. Frank couldn't see his face because of the light's glare, so he moved closer to him. Something about the man looked familiar. Frank stopped several feet away. The man didn't move. He was wearing a long black coat and a dark wool cap on his head. He was broad-shouldered but thin.

Frank stepped over to him. He looked at the man's profile. Since the man was standing between Frank and the spotlight, it was hard for Frank to make out his face. What Frank did see was a thick dark beard and a prominent nose. Frank walked over to him and then the man turned. "John?" Frank said.

It was John Beliar. He acknowledged Frank with his eyes.

"Why are you here?" Frank asked.

Beliar's voice was soft but resolute. "Don't give in to Charles."

"Give in?"

"Don't let him bully you. Don't let him sway you from your intent."

"Why did you come here to tell me this?" Frank asked.

"Because it's your soul they are about to question. It's your faith and your belief they are going to put on display."

"I see."

"Are you up to it, Frank?"

"I don't know."

"Sam meant a lot to you," he said.

"He did."

"And so does the daughter, doesn't she?"

"She does."

"Be careful with her."

"What do you mean?"

"She's going to testify. For Werner."

"How did he get her to testify?" Frank asked.

"It was Charles. He actually came out here to see her. He questioned her in his limo. Before he went out there he said to me, 'If the mountain won't come to you, then you must go to the mountain.'"

Frank couldn't believe what he was hearing.

"She's Charles's trump card. Be prepared." With that, Beliar turned and walked away.

Frank was sitting at his table when Roxanna walked into the room. She was wearing a long, pleated skirt and a dark blue blouse that matched her eyes. Instead of pulling her hair back, she let it fall carelessly to her shoulders. It made Frank think that she wanted to show the cardinals that she wasn't afraid of her sexuality, that she wasn't intimidated by their authority. She wanted to make it clear they had no authority over her.

Frank hadn't seen her for weeks, and when he did, the rush of memories warmed him. He missed her. He wanted to see her and was almost glad when she walked into the room. Yet she didn't look at him at all. Not even a glance.

She took the stand and Frank gripped Corey's rosary beads. He wanted to run out of the room and avoid at all costs what was about to happen. But he couldn't. All he could do was listen to the greeting the tribunal gave her and then wait patiently as Werner questioned her.

Werner's early questions had all to do with Roxanna's childhood memories of Helen. Roxanna painted a picture of a loving family as seen through the eyes of an only child. She was spoiled, loved, cared for. Roxanna's memory of her parents was that they were always there for her, always ready to give her what she needed. But then her father fell ill with cancer. He suffered for three years. Helen, a nurse, cared for him until he died. And when he did, everything changed for Roxanna.

"Did your mother love your father?" Werner asked Roxanna.

"I don't know. Like I said, she was a nurse. My father was ill with cancer for a long time. I could never tell when she was just caring for him—or when she was truly loving him," Roxanna answered.

"Did your mother love you?" Werner asked.

"No," Roxanna said quickly. She was hurt by the answer.

"Why do you say that?" Werner asked.

"Because she left me to live with her priests."

"Did your mother believe in God as far as you could tell?" Werner asked.

"She believed in priests," Roxanna answered. "I don't know anything about her feelings about your God."

"Did she have sex with Father Kinnely, her beloved pastor, that you know of?" Werner asked.

"I wouldn't put it past them," Roxanna answered.

"Thank you," Werner said, then walked away.

It was now Frank's turn. In front of him was Helen's diary. He brought it with him during the entire process, but today would be the first time he would use it. He was officially told Roxanna would be a witness for the devil's advocate just that morning and had had little time to prepare. Frank could have asked for a postponement, but he didn't want one. He wanted it over now.

He walked up to Roxanna as she continued to avoid his eyes. He could see the tension in her body. She sat straight up and kept her back erect. She was there to bear witness, with the intention of destroying her mother and the man she grew to care for.

Frank opened the book and read from it. "'I love Roxanna but I love my God more. This is so hard for a mother to admit. So hard for a daughter to understand.'"

"Stop," Roxanna said. She looked at Frank directly for the first time.

"You've read this, haven't you?" Frank asked.

Roxanna answered slowly. "You know I did."

"And still you say that she didn't love you?"

Roxanna didn't answer. Frank read from another page. "'She is my joy but He is my life. I hope one day she forgives me for abandoning her—for without her forgiveness I can never be in peace.' Your mother wrote that particular passage on April 3, on her birthday. She died that summer of a massive heart attack. Do you remember the day she died, Roxanna?"

Roxanna slowly relaxed her body. "Yes."

"She was in the convent. She was alone. A nun found her on the floor. An ambulance took her to Queens General. She died in the emergency room," Frank said. "When did you see her that day?"

"I never did."

"Why not?" Frank asked.

"I was unable to get there. I was sick," Roxanna said softly.

"Did you go to the funeral?"

"Yes."

"Did you make the arrangements?" Frank asked.

"Father Kinnely did," Roxanna told him.

Frank walked around to her right so that he could face the tribunal and Werner. "'She is my joy.' She was talking about you. Will you ever give her that peace?"

Roxanna didn't answer Frank, who steadied himself, knowing what he had to do.

"You were married for four months several years ago to a man named Robert Woods. Is that true?"

"Yes," she answered slowly.

"He sued you for divorce, didn't he?"

"So?"

Frank walked away from her, then turned. "On what grounds did he sue for divorce?"

"That's nobody's business—"

"He sued on grounds of adultery. It's in the public record," Frank told her. "You worked as a paralegal for a year but you were let go because you had a drinking problem. Is that true?" Frank asked her. He could see her grow tense again and she didn't answer. She just looked at him. "Do you drink occasionally? Are you drunk once a week? Or are you drunk every night?"

Werner stood up. "I beg the tribunal to stop the postulator."

Ignoring his protests, Frank pushed on. "Do you consider yourself promiscuous? Are you the type of person who goes to a bar, gets drunk, and picks someone up to have sex with?"

Fishetti called to Frank, "Postulator."

Frank ignored him, too. He pressed Roxanna. He stood face-to-face with her. She glared back at him.

"Did your mother drink, Roxanna? Did she sleep around like you do, did she steal from her employers, did she cheat on your father?" Frank asked sharply.

Roxanna stood and screamed at Frank. She released her demons in front of them all. "No, she didn't! She was perfect! She was a damn saint! She was beyond feeling what I feel! Is that what you want to hear? God damn you, Frank Moore! God damn you!"

Frank understood the pain he had caused. He wanted to reach out and hold her, but he knew he couldn't. Roxanna then turned to the tribunal. "How dare you people judge me! You're all hypocrites! You hide behind your collars and your crosses . . ." She stopped herself. Overwhelmed, she walked off the stand. Tears running down her cheeks, she walked to the door. She didn't want them to see her cry. She wanted to hold on to at least a fragment of her dignity.

Frank could do nothing but stand there and watch her leave.

Later that afternoon, Cahill was sitting behind the desk in his office with Werner, Fishetti, Ricci, Vochez, and John Beliar when Frank entered the room. After his cross-examination of Roxanna, a recess had been called, and Frank was told to join the others.

Cahill directed Frank to a chair beside the desk. He sat, then heard Werner speak. "How well do you know this daughter?"

"What has that got to do with anything?" Frank asked.

"Were you intimate?" Ricci asked.

Frank didn't answer.

"Do you love her?" Werner asked.

"Yes," Frank answered.

There was a silence in the room.

"Do you believe in your vows?" Werner asked.

"Yes. And my weakness does not give me the right to mock them. I believe in them. I always will. I just hope I have the courage to continue honoring them," Frank answered.

Frank looked around the room. Dressed in their red and black, the powerful cardinals and the lone archbishop eyed him with all the potency of their offices.

"Do you believe in your God?" Werner asked.

"I'm not sure."

"You are the first postulator I have come across in over twenty years who has had the effrontery to pursue canonization for a servant of God and yet you yourself do not believe in that very God. For such an outrageous act, you can be punished by the vestry!"

"It has taken me all of my life to realize that I don't know if I believe in the God of my Church, or in any god at all," Frank told him. "I say this to you now—I want to believe. I search for evidence. I pray for proof. I hope against hope that God hears my prayers, but I'm troubled with self-doubt."

Vochez spoke. "We all suffer from doubt. The key is to control it."

"Have you pursued this cause for some glory you think you'll find?" Ricci asked.

Frank shook his head. "What glory?"

Fishetti spoke up. "Then why have you pursued the cause for this woman?"

Frank remembered the light in Maria Katowski's eyes when she spoke about Helen. He saw the glow of emotion in Father Kinnely's face when he did, and all the faces in the rain in the schoolyard. "The woman loved. She loved beyond the small capabilities of her own fragile existence. I don't believe she was born with it. I believe it took her a whole lifetime to learn it, but she loved and I believe her love was so great that others recognized it as something special." There was compassion in his voice as he spoke.

Fishetti nodded to Frank. "Thank you. You can go now."

Frank turned and left the room.

The following morning Frank listened as Werner completed his closing arguments. "As devil's advocate it has been my duty to bring to light what God sees and we cannot. I believe I've accomplished that task." Werner then sat. Fishetti turned to Frank and gestured for him to begin.

Frank stood. He took his time and looked into the eyes of each member of the tribunal as he spoke. "I am but a messenger and that is all. I hope the tribunal understands that. I hope you accept that my failures and my unworthiness have nothing to do with Helen Stephenson. She didn't choose her messenger. If she could have, I know she would have chosen someone else. Someone with courage and true spiritual strength. I don't know if God lives in the heart of Man but I'm sure that Helen Stephenson believed it." Frank then turned to Werner. "I refute everything the devil's advocate has done in this hearing. I refute his trying to paint a picture of an unscrupulous woman in Helen Stephenson. Helen was torn. She had to struggle between the love of her daughter and that of her God. Who of us here has not had to make that kind of choice? And if the choice was easy, where is the virtue? There has never been a soul canonized who did not have to suffer. And it's clear that Helen suffered deeply. I believe Helen was in a state of grace when she died, which is more than most of us can ever hope for."

Frank was done. He took his seat at the table and then was excused as the tribunal conferred.

He went down to the steps of Saint Patrick's, watching believers enter and leave the church. The late November air was cool. Frank watched those walking by making the sign of the cross and saw how many just looked up at the cathedral, alone with their private prayers. How much of our soul is lost in time? Frank thought. We lose bits and pieces of ourselves as we go through our daily routine, unobservant of life's mysteries. Frank wanted to believe in something other than himself. It was just too difficult to have faith, to love, to survive with the burden; because loving was a weight. And if God did love us all, Frank thought to himself, He too had to bear such a tremendous responsibility.

A Swiss Guard found Frank and brought him back to the room where the tribunal was to render its decision.

Frank and Werner stood and faced Cardinal Fishetti. Cardinals Ricci and Vochez were seated. Fishetti looked at Frank, then at Werner, and then at Cardinal Cahill and John Beliar in the back of the room. "We have reached a decision. We have determined that two of the miracles are canonical—that of Maria Katowski and that of Brenda Lopez. We have decided that the ordinary process of canonization for Helen Stephenson will halt its investigation and will not move forward until we are compelled to do so; that is, until we are compelled by a sign from God. We cannot go any further until we are sure of a third miracle. Hopefully, it will occur *nostra aetate*: in our lifetime." Fishetti then turned to Frank. "The tribunal wishes to express its gratitude to the postulator and may God go with him." Fishetti then led the way from the room, with Ricci and Vochez following. Werner and his entourage followed right behind them. Frank was unable to move. He heard the shuffle of feet behind him and figured that it was Cahill and Beliar leaving the room. Suddenly, Cahill's voice boomed behind him. Frank turned. Beliar was already gone but Cahill remained.

"Frank, there are two Gods: Our God, and theirs. Our God understands dominion, consequence, expectation. He hasn't time for their frivolous problems—'Dear God, help me find a job, help my child survive this illness . . .' So, in His brilliant scheme of things, He's constructed another God for them: Us. It's an enormous responsibility and one day you'll truly understand it," Cahill told him. "This is the truth I had hoped you would learn. On your own. Perhaps now, you have."

Frank said nothing. He watched Cahill walk away. He then sat down at the table facing the empty stage where the tribunal had sat. Soon, there was complete silence. It was oddly similar to the silence he often heard when he prayed: the silence of no response. He thought of Sam Corey, Maria Katowski, Helen, and most of all, he thought of Roxanna. Their faces flew through his mind. There was no going back. They found only two miracles. They needed three. They needed a sign from God to show them the way. Frank had been looking for a sign from God his whole life.

He saw the clouds parting outside through the window and the bright rays of sunshine filtering into the room. He was drenched in the light, and he was alone. "I believe because it is impossible," he said to no one but himself. He tried to make them sound like something other than words, but that's all they were. That's all they could be.

As he walked out of the room and down the hallway, he saw Beliar standing there waiting for him. Frank stopped.

"John?"

"I envy you," Beliar said.

"Envy me?"

"I envy your gift," was all he said. Then he walked away.

The next morning Frank emptied everything out of his room at the rectory. He said good-bye to Father Stacey and Father Paulino. Father Paulino had become ill. He had contracted the flu but hadn't taken care of himself and it had rapidly developed into pneumonia. He stayed in his room with a high fever and a local doctor came to visit him. Father Stacey scolded him: "I told you to get rest, Alfred! Now look what you've done to yourself!" Father Paulino, his lung congested and in pain, nodded in agreement, then closed his eyes.

Though not allowed into Father Paulino's room, Frank did sneak in to wish him well, telling him that he would pray for him.

"Pray to Helen," Paulino said. "I do," he coughed. His round face was getting thinner.

"He's not doing well," Father Stacey told Frank as they stood outside the room. "I'm worried for him. Like Father Kinnely, he put so much of his energies into the statue. And now that the people have heard the news about the tribunal's decision," Father Stacey told him, "they're not showing up like they used to."

"I'm sorry," Frank told the thin man standing before him. Frank then realized that Father Stacey, somewhat cool and detached, had as much commitment as Kinnely and Paulino. He just didn't show it. His cool demeanor hid how much he truly cared.

Frank wanted to take one last walk through the yard but then stopped himself. It was too much for him to face. He had done it again. He had become the miracle-killer. Willow Lake, Saint Stanislaus, it was an absurd joke: a priest killing hope.

He got into his car and drove past Roxanna's house. He took the chance that he would see her standing outside. He wanted to see her face one more time. But what would that accomplish? He knew he loved her, but he was a priest and unless he was going to take off the collar for good, he had nothing to offer her. He couldn't be a man and a priest at the same time. He had tried, and neither of them felt it was enough. And he wasn't yet ready to forsake his vows. Not after another failure.

So, he drove away. He went back to his room at the archdiocese and sat up at night wondering if he would run away again. He wondered if he was going back to where he had been when they found him—alone, writing furiously, dodging his demons, trying to put the inadequacy behind him.

An impulse compelled him to go into the chapel and pray. In Saint Luke's chapel he prayed for guidance: he wanted someone to tell him what steps to take, what direction to go in, what path to follow. He knew it was ludicrous for him to pray, but he wanted to try. And then the thought hit him. He would call Father Heany and ask if he could take Sam Corey's place on the faculty. He would lecture on theology. With his reputation and his book, *The God Within*, he should have no problem securing a teaching position.

Frank felt good, if ambivalent, about his plan. For him to teach theology and to be unsure about his belief in the God on which he would lecture seemed, at the very least, insincere. But then, as Sam had said, act as if you have faith and you will have faith. Lecturing offered him a purpose. It gave him an opportunity to work out what was inside him; to find out what he really cared about in life and what genuinely mattered to him above all else.

Several days later, Frank had secured a position to lecture on theology at Saint John's University. He was to begin his first semester that spring term, which would begin after the holidays. Along with the teaching position came an apartment near the campus. It was modest but comfortable, and it was near Corey's old place. Frank found comfort in that.

Packed and ready to leave, Frank spent his last night at the archdiocese packing his most prized possessions: his books. He packed them neatly in a box, and then came across Helen Stephenson's diary. He picked it up and placed it in a separate smaller box. He then picked up Sam Corey's rosary and placed it beside the diary. As he did, he found a small plastic bag. Inside it was the white cloth he had first collected the statue's blood with. He placed the plastic bag and cloth inside the box and sealed it.

The phone rang. It was James, the novitiate. "The cardinal wants you to come down to his office. He said it was urgent."

Moments later, Frank was standing in Cahill's office. Charles Cahill looked distraught.

"Are you okay?" Frank asked.

Cahill nodded slowly. "I'm going to miss him. He was devoted."

"Who?"

"John. He's gone," Cahill said quietly.

Frank looked around the room. The majesty of the office was evident even in the semidarkness. Only a desk lamp was lit.

"Where did he go?"

"I don't know. He left a note. He said he was leaving. But that's all. He didn't say where. I found the note this morning. He left it on my desk."

"Maybe he needs time alone."

"He said he was leaving the priesthood."

Frank was shocked. John Beliar seemed the type of man born to be a priest. His intellect seemed matched only by his devotion.

"Did he say anything to you about this, Frank?"

Frank thought a moment. "He didn't say anything, didn't give me any indication that he was dissatisfied with anything."

"Are you sure? Please think," Cahill said. He sounded lost.

"Actually, he did say something to me, but it wasn't about his wanting to leave. In fact, what he said to me was peculiar."

"What was it that he said?" Cahill asked quickly.

"He said something about being jealous of my gift."

"Your gift?"

"Yes," Frank answered. "What gift did he mean?"

"I believe he meant God's grace."

"What?" Frank said.

"God's grace. You have it, you know. It's there. He was envious of it. I suppose he wished he was you," Cahill said.

Frank excused himself and went back to his room and noticed, just as he was putting out the lights, that it was beginning to snow. He looked at the calendar—it was December 1 already. It was snowing early in the season, he thought to himself.

That night he had a long, deep sleep.

Chapter 18

That Spring

Frank was living on campus at Saint John's University when he heard from Father Stacey that a small pilgrimage had been started by those who believed. They left flowers as tokens of love. Though they no longer visited the schoolyard, they began to visit Helen's grave. Father Stacey also told him that Father Paulino's health was worse. The antibiotics no longer worked. Frank went to visit him several times in Saint John's Hospital on Queens Boulevard. He was on a respirator, fading in and out of consciousness.

Though the winter was cold, by the end of March everything had turned sunny and warm. Frank enjoyed his days on campus. Some of his students were inquisitive, others just wanted a passing grade and to graduate. A few worked very hard and seemed to like school, while others seemed distracted by their troubles and worries.

Frank began visiting the chapel on campus several afternoons a week. He didn't pray. He sat there thinking. He thought about how his life seemed more and more like a journey, but without much direction. A quote from Goethe struck him on occasion as he sat in silence. Goethe once said that humanity's plight reminded him of a drunken man on a horse passing through the woods at night. "The man has no idea where he is, but the horse is going somewhere." Frank smiled to himself, but never for long. I hope it's about more than that, he thought to himself.

Frank spent his nights reading. He was planning to write another book, but the world seemed too cluttered with movies and television and fashion models and sports stars. It didn't seem as if there was any room for a book about a priest struggling with his doubts about God's existence; about the honesty of God's love. So, Frank studied and thought about Roxanna. He couldn't walk through campus seeing the young women students without thinking of her. In the rain or the bright light of a sunny day, she was always in his thoughts. He wrote her several letters but they all came back with NO FORWARDING ADDRESS stamped on them. He even tried the phone book but figured out that she had either moved out of the city or she didn't have a phone anymore, not even an unlisted one.

Frank heard from Father Stacey that Roxanna had begun to drink again. She started by sitting in the kitchen alone with a bottle of whisky. By midnight, she'd be drunk and unconscious sleeping with her head on the table. The lights would burn all night and when she awoke at dawn, she'd go to bed and stay in it all day.

Father Stacey heard from her neighbors that she lost her job and had to move. She had found a basement apartment on 64th Street, only a few blocks away. It was half the price of her old place and half the size. It had only one window and was always damp.

Occasionally, after Sunday Mass, a few parishioners would come over to Father Stacey, telling him what they had heard about Roxanna. The biggest news was that she had found a new job—as bartender three nights a week at a bar called O'Neal's. Father Stacey also heard that when she wasn't working there, she was drinking there. She would occasionally bring a man home, usually another drunk. They would fondle on the bed, sometimes even make love, but she always told him to leave the next morning. She didn't want anyone close. She didn't want anyone to know who she was or where she had been; and more than that—she compared them all to Frank. She knew what the strangers she picked up wanted from her, but she was still mystified by what Frank wanted from her. In the long run she had concluded that he either used her to try to make her mother a saint, or he truly loved her. She knew that last thought sounded absurd, but she wondered if it were true. He may have loved her in his own awkward, abstract way. The only way he knew how.

The more she thought that he loved her, the more she wanted to bury herself in a hole. A deep dark hole where she could hide until death found her. If life was only a dream, she thought, then she could wake up and it'd all be over.

Hearing all this about her, Frank thought that the winter must have been brutally lonely for Roxanna, and he was right. Her drinking made her put on weight, she stopped taking care of herself, and soon she didn't leave the basement apartment unless she had to be at the bar. And the only reason she went to work was because she could drink there. She stole from her boss and he knew it, but he felt sorry for her. She was famous, even around the barflies at O'Neal's, as the woman whose mother was almost deemed a saint. "For a drunk, she must have some divine genes," someone would say just loud enough for Roxanna to hear. But she stayed and took the punishment. She heard the insults and swallowed her pride because she knew what Frank made her see: her mother had been a virtuous woman: she, on the other hand, was not.

When she looked in the mirror in the bathroom in the bar, feeling a buzz from the booze, the face that looked back at her was never hers. Roxanna swore to herself that it was someone else.

The person in the mirror was someone doomed and lost forever. Not someone alive and breathing. When she looked into the mirror, Roxanna saw a ghost of someone long dead. More accurately, she didn't see a ghost at all. She saw a member of the living dead. "A member of my club," Roxanna would say to herself, thinking of Frank.

She didn't want to think about him, though she desperately wanted to see him. She wanted to see him because he seemed to know her. She was sure that he knew who she was; he was the only man she could say that about. And perhaps that was why she tried leaving him behind. He was a man who knew too much, and that made her feel even less than what she was. When the end of March arrived, Roxanna was nearly exhausted from a winter of isolation and drink.

One night on the television, she saw the TV newscaster Dotty West doing a live report from Saint Stanislaus. As the camera panned over the schoolyard, Dotty West faced the camera, telling the viewers that the pilgrimage to the statue had just about come to a dead stop. Since the ruling by the tribunal, only a handful of believers came to pray. The blood, which only flowed in October, had stopped altogether, and with it ended the excitement and intrigue. "Since the Vatican announced that it didn't have enough evidence to warrant beatification of Helen Stephenson, very few people have come here to pray. The archdiocese has issued a statement that its investigation has been completed."

Roxanna shut off the TV. She didn't want to see any more. That night, on her way to work at the bar, she took the long way, walking across the overpass. She had been avoiding it ever since the night she kissed Frank there and wanted to block him from her memory. But this night, she decided to walk across her favorite place on earth. She reached the tall cyclone fence and looked out at the glimmering lights of the Manhattan skyline. She leaned against the fence and felt the strain of her own existence. Her life had been a bitter journey and yet she felt that she had traveled so short a distance. There was something missing, something left out of the equation.

She pulled up her collar as the spring breeze grew cold. A life without joy is a life of toil, she thought. The toil to survive all the loss and disillusionment. She turned her back on her favorite place in the world, making a promise to herself that she would never return to it.

That night, as she was lying in bed trying to sleep, she remembered that Thursday was her mother's birthday. April 3. She didn't know why she remembered, but when she did, she started to cry, because her mother was gone and now she was alone. Her mother had been dead for over a decade, but she felt the loss acutely for the very first time. She cried all night and didn't leave her basement apartment until it was already dark. And then she walked the streets that night and cried some more. All her tears were gone the following morning, on Thursday, the day of Helen Stephenson's birth.

"It's great to have you here, Frank," Father Heany told Frank as the two men walked through Saint John's campus. They made their way to Saint John's Hall, where they had a faculty meeting on the fourth floor. Frank sat in the room with the eleven other faculty members. Only half were priests, the other were lay men and women.

"And, as a reminder, today, April 3, is the new date the university has marked for your midterm grades to be delivered to the registrar's office. I'm sorry you have so little notice, but if anyone needs any extra time, I'll make a call for you," Father Heany told the faculty.

Frank stopped taking notes. He suddenly felt as if someone was trying to get his attention, as though he needed to remember something terribly important but what it was exactly was lost in his memory.

After the meeting, he went immediately back to his room. He found Sam's rosary and read the date inscribed—April 3. He put the rosary in his pocket and left. He got into his car unsure of why he was heading where he was. He only wanted to get there.

He parked across from Saint Stanislaus and walked into the schoolyard. It had all changed. The makeshift hospital was gone and the spotlight had been removed. Frank, wearing his long black coat and white collar, walked toward the statue at the far end of the yard. He walked past the brick wall, glancing at the rectory and then the convent. He looked up at Helen's closed window. And then he looked into the courtyard. A woman was sweeping. Her hair was gray and she wore a housecoat. She turned to him and smiled. For a moment Frank thought he was looking at Helen. But it wasn't Helen, it was Mrs. Katowski.

"Father!" she said, smiling when she turned and saw him. She walked over to her side of the brick wall and stopped, still holding the broom.

"How are you?" Frank asked her.

"I'm living here now. In a spare room in the convent. On the second floor. I'm kind of like the janitor for the ladies. I call them that. The nuns. They're great," she said. The lines of grief were gone from her face. Her eyes were wide and alive.

"Everything's changed," Frank said.

Mrs. Katowski didn't answer. She had reached a place inside herself far away from where the memories she'd rather not have dwelled.

"It's good to see you," Frank told her. She nodded and went back to sweeping, not even asking him why he was there. It didn't matter to her. She had found her peace.

Frank slowly made his way to the statue. Before him he saw an elderly woman kneeling and praying. She was dressed in black and had unruly gray hair. Frank looked and saw another elderly woman kneeling a few yards back. She was tall and well dressed. Only the sick and old remember how to pray, Frank said to himself.

He had no idea why he was at the statue other than that it was the anniversary of the day Sam Corey took his vows. It felt right to be there, for Sam. Frank took a few more steps forward and that's when he saw a woman who looked deep in prayer kneeling at the foot of the statue. He hadn't noticed her before. She was wearing a dark jacket and jeans and was directly under the statue, her head tilted up and her hands folded in prayer.

Frank noticed how she was kneeling on the hard pavement, motionless, concentrating totally on the Virgin above her. With her back to him, she continued to pray, seeming oblivious to her surroundings.

Frank walked over to her and knelt. He turned and glanced at her profile as he did. He felt as if the air was forced from his lungs. "Roxanna?" he said.

She slowly turned to him, tears running down her cheeks. Frank could see the blue eyes almost red with sadness.

"She was born on this day," she told him. Frank leaned closer and took her hand in his. "How will she ever know how much I loved her?" she asked.

"She knows," Frank told her. He could see a small bouquet of flowers in her right hand.

"Will she ever forgive me?" she asked him, needing to know.

"She already has," he said to her.

Frank saw in her eyes that a horrible sense of guilt had been lifted. It was an extraordinary moment, all the years of resentment suddenly cleansed; and it happened to Roxanna. If one believed in a soul or not, it was in that moment that Roxanna's being was made whole again. Everything in her life up to that moment was allowed to drift and disappear. She was suddenly and quietly faultless and new.

Frank helped her to her feet and then hugged her. He held her close, smelling the remnants of her perfume and the scent of her hair. He then looked at her and the two were face-to-face. She looked into his deep oval-shaped brown eyes, and then looked at his collar. He was still wearing it. She gave him a look of recognition. She then lovingly touched his face and then hugged him again.

As they stepped back, Frank felt the need to say a thousand things to her. He wanted to tell her how much she had meant to him, and how it would have been impossible for him to have gone as far as he did without her in his life for those brief few months. He couldn't love her the way she needed to be loved, but he did love her. And he always would.

He wanted to say all that to her, but he realized that she already knew. She knew because the way he held her now was so different from the way he had held her before. She could tell by the way he took her hand and then touched her face, as she had just touched his, that what they felt for one another was special, unique, a wonder.

He gestured for her to leave with him, but she wasn't ready. "I'm going to stay awhile," she said. He understood. "My priest, Frank Moore," she said to him, touching his cheek one last time.

"I'll always be here for you," he said.

"I know you will."

"If you ever need me, if you ever feel lonely or lost. My life is your life," he said to her.

She took his hand and held it tightly; and then let it go.

He looked up at the blue sky. "Do you feel that?" he asked.

"What?" she asked him.

"It's going to rain," he told her, echoing Sam Corey's mystic connection with God's world. He then took one long, final look at the woman he loved and turned. He walked away from the statue and crossed the schoolyard. As he walked away he realized that he had just been party to a miracle. They were both brought together for a moment of forgiveness which transcended time and space and became Grace. There was no need for a marvel cure, no need for swirling clouds of dust and light, no apparitions dancing across the sky. What had just happened to them, Frank thought, was monumental to an ordinary life, but far from supernatural. Their moment at the statue would not need to be deciphered by ancient prophets studying the heavens for messages from beyond. It was also not a coincidence made refutable by a cynical mathematician. It was something else. It was the unexplainable. Its source was the same benevolence that cured Maria Katowski of lupus and delivered Brenda Lopez from certain death; and Frank was a witness to it.

As he walked away from the schoolyard, he realized that he was a participant in the third miracle. And the third miracle was not just one event, but many. It was there for those who believed. Its source was a foundation of love surpassing Helen's natural death. A saint can do the unthinkable. A saint can force a change of destiny with an influx of love guided by the hand of God.

These were Frank's thoughts as he left Saint Stanislaus, leaving Roxanna to nourish herself in her mother's company. He swore to himself that he would resist ever forgetting them, allowing age and the tarnished sphere of memory to dilute them.

For Roxanna's part, she waited and watched as Frank walked slowly away from her. She watched until he reached the other end of the yard, until she couldn't see him anymore. She watched until he disappeared into the bright sunlight.

She turned to the statue, knelt down, and placed her bouquet of flowers at its feet . . . and she prayed.

Epilogue

Two weeks later, Father Paulino, close to death from his persistent pneumonia, asked to be taken back to the rectory where he could die in familiar surroundings. One night, as he lay suffering with a terrible fever, Father Stacey covered him with a blanket. The blanket was a gift Helen had given him many years earlier.

"Now, I'll pray to Helen so that she will help guide my soul," Father Paulino said as Father Stacey covered him with it.

Father Stacey kept the bedside vigil, fighting sleep all through the night. Drifting off some time after four, he woke at dawn. Prepared to find his beloved friend having passed away, Father Stacey was amazed to see that Father Paulino was no longer in his bed. Stacey frantically looked around until he went outside and there, kneeling at the statue, was Father Paulino.

Stacey, realizing what had happened, gripped Paulino's shoulder. Paulino then stood, leaned forward, and kissed the stone. His fever was gone. The color was brought back to his face, his cough was now only a painful memory. "It was Helen," he said.

Father Paulino was examined by several doctors, whose findings were unanimous and conclusive: he had cured himself. But Father Paulino knew otherwise. He immediately sent the news of his miracle cure to Rome. Cardinal Fishetti gathered the tribunal together; they conferred and then they made an announcement: God had given them a sign—there was now a third miracle. Helen Stephenson was immediately beatified.

Frank got the news after he left the chapel at the campus early one afternoon. There was a fax waiting for him from Cardinal Fishetti's office. Fishetti wanted Helen's postulator to know that Frank had been, in the eyes of the Church, pursuing God's will.

Frank read the fax, then sat down. "I believe because it is impossible," he said to himself in an untroubled voice. He wanted it to be a miracle, and it was. He reached into his desk drawer and took out a plastic bag containing a white cloth. The stains were still there from the tears of blood. Looking closely, Frank could see, they created the image of the Virgin's face.

The End